REIGN

TARA LEE
DL GALLIE

TRIGGER WARNING

This book mentions a sexual assault and there is a scene dealing with the aftermath of an assault, not sexual. These scenes are not graphic but they do allude to what did occur. If these scenarios are triggering, we suggest proceeding with caution.

The Lords rule supreme. They're cruel, reckless, and
crave the power their status brings.
Their world is corrupt—filled with lies and secrets.
They rule Crestwood Prep like their fathers before them, but
nothing lasts forever.
Secrets are about to spill free, lies uncovered.
The Lords aren't as invincible as they once thought.
Let The Games Begin.

This is our school, our kingdom. My brothers and I rule, we are The Lords.

My secrets have always been just that, mine, but my biggest secret is about to be exposed.

I'm in love with two people—Alani Thomas and Hudson Finley.

They love me, and I love them.

I thought it was game over now that my secrets were out, but it wasn't.

Nothing is as it seems, and the endgame isn't as clear as I thought.

REIGN

"DID YOU HEAR?" Saint asks, dropping into the seat across from me while I'm trying to study in the library. Looking up at my brother, I wait for him to continue, but if he tells me about the chick he nailed last night in graphic detail, again, I will stab him in the face with the pencil in my hand. I love my brother, but I do not need to know *that* about him and his antics. "Arlen Hearst committed suicide last night."

"What?" I screech, earning myself a scowl from the librarian as I sit up straight and repeat Saint's words over and over in my head. My heart races at the news, and a part of me doesn't believe what my brother is telling me.

"Arlen took a dive off the cliffs last night."

"Bullshit, he … what? How? Why?" My chest tightens as it sinks in that Arlen is no longer here.

"I'm just telling you what Rian overheard when he was in admin just now."

"Well, why isn't the school swarming with cops?"

"Because we're the elite of the elite, we do as we please. But what do we care? He's a fucking Hearst. One less Hearst cunt to deal with."

"What are we talking about?" Thatcher asks, dropping into the seat next to me.

"Arlen Hearst committed suicide," Saint informs Thatch with just as much joy as when he told me.

"Ohh well, one less Hearst cunt around."

"That's what I just said." He offers Thatch his fist and they fist bump.

"You two really are fucking assholes at times," I snap at them. While they're both excited over his death, I'm processing and hoping I'm hiding how I really feel, because they don't know what I know about Arlen. They don't know anything about him. He's not like the other Hearsts, at least with me he isn't, well, wasn't I guess now.

"Says the asshole," Saint throws back at me. "And what do you care anyway? He's the enemy, Reign, and a dead Hearst is the best kind of Hearst."

Shaking my head, I stand up, grab my things, and walk away from them. I can't be around them right now because there's a chance my secret will slip out, and with my emotions all over the place, I can't let that happen.

Pushing the library doors open, I step outside into the late afternoon drizzle. "Fucking great," I mumble.

Pulling the hood of my hoodie up, I head toward the cliffs. I need to see for myself, but the pathway up is blocked off, and sure enough, an officer is stationed there. "This area is locked off, son."

Nodding at him, I stare at the cliffs above and mumble, "What did you do, Arl?" Spinning on my heel, I begin walking back down the path, but I come to a stop when a memory assaults me ...

... "How amazing would it be to jump from here?" Arlen says, his face lit up with joy as he looks down at the waves crashing into the rocks below. Twiddling his precious medallion he's always playing with between his fingers.

"Dude, you're fucking crazy," I tell him, shaking my head and joining him at the cliffs' edge. "You can't jump from here, you'd fucking die. If you wanna cliff dive, I'll take you around to Crestwood Cove, and we can jump there."

"Pussy," he throws back at me.

"I thought you preferred dick?"

"I do ... especially yours." He steps into me and cups my dick through my jeans, it immediately comes to life under his touch. He leans into me closer. I can feel his breath on my skin and it tingles. He bites my earlobe and sucks. "I especially love your dick when you're shoving it down my throat."

"Mmmhmpf," I groan loudly when he squeezes my dick again, but then I realize where we are and shove at him. "Not here, Arl. Anyone could see."

"I hate we have to hide this. I'm not ashamed of you."

"I'm not ashamed either, I just ..."

"Aren't ready to come out yet."

Nodding, I reach up and cup his cheek. "There's that, but there's also the fact I like pussy too. I don't know who I am. I feel like such a fraud living a secret life."

"No," he growls, "you are amazing." His voice is commanding, and I almost believe him. He steps into me again, reaches up, and cups my cheek in his palm. Closing my eyes, I lean into his touch. Opening them again, I stare at the one person who knows my secrets. "You are amazing, Reign Vanderbelt, fucking amaz-

ing. That's all you need to know. I'll wait, but I won't wait forever ..."

"Looks like we'll never get our forever," I sadly murmur and continue down the path as the rain gets heavier. I walk past the school and just keep walking.

"Hey," a soft voice from behind says. Looking over my shoulder, I see Alani Thomas standing there. Books in her arms and a pink umbrella in her hands. She looks so fucking cute right now. "How are you?"

"Don't know," I tell her. My shoulders slump because after seeing what I just saw, I believe Saint's words. *He's gone and we won't get a chance at forever.*

"Are you okay?" she asks me. I don't know what to tell her, so I just shrug my shoulders. She places her hand on my back, and it's oddly comforting. Tilting my head, I look over at her. She's staring at me with nothing but concern reflecting in her eyes. "I ... why do you care?" I snap like the asshole I am.

"Because I do," she states, her words strong. "There's something about you, Reign Vanderbelt, that I'm drawn to. You come across all tough and asshole-like, just like the rest of your family, but underneath all that, there's something good. You're different. You're ... you."

We start to chat about mindless shit, and I find myself interested in her answers. It's almost as if Arl sent this redheaded angel to me. A shiver racks through her when a gust of wind blasts around us. "Come here," I demand, opening my arms to her. My tone is harsh and I expect her to tell me to fuck off, but she surprises me when she steps closer, inadvertently poking me in the head with her umbrella. "Ouch," I hiss, snatching the umbrella from her to hold it above the two of us, without taking out an eye.

"Sorry, joys of being a shortie, I seem to poke people lots."

She slides her arm around my waist and snuggles into my side. Even though she's much shorter than me, she fits into my side perfectly.

"You poke people, huh? Didn't realize you were hiding a dick underneath that sexy as fuck school skirt of yours."

"With my umbrella, you dick. And thank you for the sexy comment. You rock those school trousers too. I've always been a fan of your ass. Eleven out of ten, bet I could bounce a quarter off your tight gluteus maximus." She looks up at me and surprises me when she slides her hand into mine and laces our fingers together. Hand in hand, we silently walk and eventually find ourselves at the pond near the front entrance to the school. We come to a stop and stare into the dark, murky water. After a while, she asks me again how I am, but truthfully, I don't know how to answer her. Offering her a shrug in reply, silence envelops us once more.

"Why are you out here in the rain?"

"I was walking back from a study session and I saw you at the cliffs. Something compelled me to see if you were okay. Are you okay?"

"Is anyone okay?"

"That's very philosophical of you, never would have picked that."

"There's a lot you don't know about me."

"Ohh, I bet there is, and you know what?"

"What?"

"I bet you don't give yourself enough credit for just how amazing you are."

Looking over at her, I see nothing but truthfulness in her eyes. She believes what she's saying. This chick doesn't know me, she just knows the rumors about me, but from only being with her for a few moments, she can see what Arlen saw in me. Once again, giving me the feeling he sent her to me. "You are something else, Alani Thomas."

"You have no idea, Reign Vanderbelt, no one does." Color

me intrigued with that reply. "Now I think you need to buy me a coffee."

"I do now, do I?"

"Yep." She lets the 'p' pop. She tugs on my arm, and we begin to walk away from the lake. "I think you and I are going to become fabulous friends."

ALANI

… earlier that day

I'M on my way to English when I meet up with Hudson. He throws his arm around my shoulder and pulls me to his side. I snuggle in and fit as if I'm meant to be beside him. "Hey, Bitsy."

A shudder runs through me at the nickname he's given me, but whenever I bring up my distaste for it, he turns it all around and makes me realize it's in an affectionate way, and I don't hate it as much as I should. Just like I don't really mind Reign calling me Red.

Craning my neck up, I take him in. Hudson is gorgeous and tall. Yes, I'm aware everyone is taller than me, but Hudson is like this sexy giant teddy bear, well, with me he's a teddy bear. He's all tanned and muscular, with sultry eyes that are like diamonds when they land on me, they pull me in and everything else around me fades into oblivion.

My heart begins to pitter-patter when his thumb grazes my collarbone, and then he does that lip thing that's sexy on all guys where he licks his lip. Then his teeth catch it and slowly he releases it. H O double T hot.

He leads me to our seats and casually lays his arm across the back of my chair.

Reign enters in all his swagger, looking like hell, but he holds his head high as he makes his way to the back of the classroom. As he saunters past me, I fantasize about him kissing me, and more, right here in the middle of the classroom. Quickly, I shake that thought away because I can't be thinking of him when I'm sitting next to Hudson, the guy whom I'm currently hooking up with. I'm not a slut. Yes, we aren't exclusive and we've had conversations about threesomes—hello, who wouldn't want to be sandwiched between two hot as fuck guys?—but that's never going to happen, this isn't a porno ... or LA.

His cousin Rian fist bumps him as he sits down, teasing him, "You look like shit, man." He just groans and the sound behind me makes me shift in my seat. Hudson notices and smirks at me.

Hudson is well aware of my crush on Reign Vanderbelt. In all honesty, I'm pretty sure he has a thing for him too, I mean, it's Reign-fucking-Vanderbelt. He's ... well, he's a god, so of course Hudson's noticed him, a blind person would. I'd be lying if I said I haven't pictured the two of them having their way with me, even though it's not ladylike. That's what my mother would say, I have to be proper. And polished. And perfect. One must always act like a lady, Alani ... but sometimes 'Mother' a lady just wants to fantasize about being taken by two sexy as fuck men at the same time, just not in English would be ideal.

"Shit," Reign curses behind me. That one word, four letters, ripples through me. What the hell is wrong with me, that the word 'shit' causes such a visceral reaction.

Both Hudson and I turn around and look back at him, he's searching in his bag, biting his lip as he does.

"You good?" Rian asks him.

"I don't have a pen." He continues to search his bag, getting more annoyed and frantic as time goes on.

Opening my pencil case, I reach in and grab a blue and black pen. Turning back around, I hold them out for him.

"Here, you can borrow mine."

Rian chuckles slightly, Reign drops his bag and reaches for the pens. He grabs them and a spark ignites between us when his fingers brush mine. I must be the only one to notice because he didn't bat an eyelid.

"Thanks," he growls. Giving him a brief nod, I turn back around and face the board, waiting for Mrs. Plunkett to start the class.

"Thank you ," Rian singsongs.

"Shut up, Ri," Reign snaps, annoyance clear in his tone.

Fifty minutes later, the bell rings, ending class. Hudson shoves his things into his bag and stands, waiting for me while I do the same.

I'm particular about how I do things, it's something my father drilled into me from a young age. Perfection is key, he always says. But, of course, I like to live on the wild side and push the boundaries with my parents. Don't they know the more they try to control me, the more I will rebel against them?

My father was never accepted as a Lord back in the day, but he's determined to make the Thomas name shine. To be honest, who gives a flying fuck? It's not as if outside of this fucked-up town being a Lord means anything. It's just a pretentious title created by a pretentious bunch of old fuckers years ago.

"Come on, babe, it's burger day and I'm fucking starving," Hudson says, grabbing my hand to pull me up.

"I'm coming," I softly reply.

He chuckles and kisses the side of my head. "Not yet." He winks. Hudson and I have yet to take that final step in our, whatever it is, but when that happens, I can't wait. It's going to be explosive; I feel it in my clit.

Shaking my head, I try to cover my smile because Hudson's head doesn't need to get any bigger. I've learned to deal with his dirty talk, it's one of the things I love about him. He's happy to be the joker, the guy who delivers a good punch line but he's crazy smart. He's basically a genius and the things he can do with his tongue and fingers are magical.

Hudson threads his fingers through mine and leads us out of the classroom. Everyone here knows we fool around so I don't mind the PDA.

"Thanks, Red," Reign says from behind, halting me. Turning around, I see my pens sitting in his outstretched palm.

"Keep them, for next class." He nods and slips them into his bag. Hudson leads me through the door and toward our lockers. By the time we get to the cafeteria, it's packed with students, and of course, the Lords are sitting high and mighty at their table.

The Lords consist of the Vanderbelt brothers; triplets Thatcher, Saint, and Hendrix, and the youngest brother, Reign. Their father and grandfather were both Lords, so of course the legacy lives on through them. Then there's Theon, Hendrix's best friend; a Lord by association. And of course, we can't forget Rian Vanderbelt, their cousin. Rounding out the group are Lennon, Hart, and Conroy. Not sure how they fit into the hierarchy but nonetheless, this school is ruled over by nine guys with superior God complexes.

Hendrix throws some fries at Theon, he just picks them up and eats them, chuckling as he does. Sometimes they can just be normal teenage boys, like now with the fries, but other times, they become pretentious doucheholes flinging their dicks around as if they own the joint. Do I fall in line? Yes, because I was raised to follow the rules. But do I love breaking them from time to time? Also yes. This princess likes to rattle her cage and be a normal teenager occasionally.

Hudson places his hand on my lower back, guiding me to the food line. By the time we have food, the only spot free is with the Lords and Quinn Ellis. She's Hendrix's on-again, off-again girlfriend. They must be 'on' at the moment because she's sitting on his lap, practically eating his face. Those two have more arguments than is required for teenagers but for some reason, Quinn always takes him back.

Reign notices us standing there and he nods to the vacant spots and like a moth to a flame, I find myself obliging and taking a seat with the Lords.

Hudson digs into his burger, moaning around it like it's the best thing he's eaten all day and with his mouth full, he asks, "How's your dad?"

The question makes me freeze. My father expects so much from me, I'm beginning to think he doesn't actually love me, not like a father should. I'm just a person to carry on the Thomas family name and much to his disgust, I'm a girl. I just shrug in response, not wanting to have this conversation right now and to reiterate my unease with the question, I dig into my burger.

Later that day, I'm out for a walk when I notice a lone figure in the distance. They look so sad standing on the path to the cliffs. They lift their head and I see that it's Reign. I know I should stay away, he's a Vanderbelt and my parents despise that family, but it's weird, I can feel his hurt and like at lunch earlier today, I find myself walking toward the cliffs and him without a second thought. It's as if he was silently calling out to me. I need to stay away, but I can't stop myself.

"Hey, how are you?" I ask when I reach him.

He shrugs at me but doesn't answer. Lifting my hand, I place it on his back, offering silent support.

The waves below crash into the rocks ,only for the current to be sucked back out and for it to do it again. It's an endless cycle of waves building, crashing, retreating. Repeat.

"I … why do you care?"

"Because I do. There's something about you, Reign Vanderbelt, you come across all tough and asshole-like, just like the rest of your family, but you're different."

He nods at my assessment but doesn't say anything further. A shiver washes over me, the temperature dropping as the wind picks up.

"Come here," he demands and like a lap dog, I sidle up close to him and slide my arm around his and in the process, I accidentally poke him with my umbrella. He teases me about being short and as we snuggle in together, we begin to chat mindlessly. I ask him again if he's okay and he throws the question back at me. Inadvertently alluding to the fact that he is NOT okay.

"I'll take that as a no, you're not okay." Silence envelops us again but it's not awkward. The urge to touch him fills me so I slide my hand down his arm. I lace our fingers together and squeeze. I don't know why I do that, but I just felt like I needed to. He squeezes my hand back and we go back to silently staring out to sea.

"Do you like brownies?" he asks out of nowhere.

"I don't mind a good brownie, but I'm a sucker for red velvet cupcakes. How about you?"

"Cookies, I'm all for the cookie." I get the impression he's not referring to food right now, and my thought is confirmed when he winks and then smiles. When Reign Vanderbelt really smiles, the whole world smiles with him. "I remember when my brothers and I were little, before Mom, well, that doesn't matter. Anyway, I remember baking cookies in the kitchen with my brothers, Mom, and our housekeeper, Lisette. Life was so much simpler back then."

"If only life was all about red velvet cupcakes, cookies, and sexy asses."

"You are something else, Alani Thomas."

"You have no idea, Reign Vanderbelt."

And he doesn't.

To the outside world, I'm a doting daughter. A straight A student. Model citizen but no one really knows me. No one knows the real Alani Thomas, hell, I don't even really know who I am. But I'm eighteen, who knows who they are at this age? Isn't being a teenager about trying new things? Making mistakes. Learning from those mistakes. With that train of thought running in my mind, I feel like now is a perfect time to explore.

"I think you need to buy me a coffee," I throw out there.

"I do now, do I?"

"Yep." I let the 'p' pop and before he can refuse my coffee request, I pull on his arm and we head back toward school for our coffee date. "I think you and I are going to become fabulous friends."

"I think we might be too," he agrees, and my chest puffs out at that.

He once again surprises me and we make our way to his car. I just meant we'd grab one from the school cafeteria, but I get the sense he needs to get away from here, so I blindly follow him, and I realize I'd follow him anywhere. I have no fucking clue why I feel like that. I don't know the guy on a personal level, but there's something drawing me to him. I'm powerless to stop it, and I'm okay with that.

The car ride is silent as Reign drives. I open my mouth, ready to speak a few times, but for some reason, nothing comes out.

I catch myself watching Reign, his knuckles have turned white, gripping the steering wheel tightly. His jaw ticks like he's fighting an internal battle. His blond hair falls just the right way, giving him that sexy bad-boy look. His eyes are a gorgeous blue that remind me of the Caribbean Ocean but there's a sadness hiding behind them.

I shouldn't like a guy like Reign Vanderbelt. I definitely shouldn't want a guy like him either, but I can't help it, he has this pull about him that I can't ignore. No matter how much my father would disapprove of it, for some inexplicable reason, I want him. I suddenly feel the need to be around him, to touch him.

Gerald Thomas is not a fan of the Vanderbelts, in fact, not many people in this place are. If you ask me, I think they're harshly judged. People are jealous of their wealth and status. Money and power always corrupt people and jealousy over money and power is the wickedest evil of them all.

We arrive at the diner in town and Reign parks the car, but he doesn't make a move to get out, so I wait. Waiting for him to make the first move. Finally, he murmurs, "I can't believe he's gone."

He leans over and rests his muscular forearms on the steering wheel and blankly stares out the window.

Who's he referring to? "Reign," I whisper. I've never seen him like this, so … so broken. "Reign," I utter his name again and this time he turns his head, swallowing deeply before lifting his gaze toward me.

His eyes travel over me. Starting at my legs, he travels over my stomach, past my tits—I notice a swallow as he passes them—before finally landing on my face. He groans, throwing his head back against the headrest. Chuckling, he shakes his head with a grin on his face before he turns to look at me again.

"Reign, I want to help. Please let me help you," I tell him as I unbuckle my seat belt.

"You want to help?" I nod softly. "Come here," he demands, patting his lap. He moves his seat back, making room for me.

Nodding, I slide across the leather and climb onto his lap. My legs straddle his thighs. His hands immediately go to my hips, his fingers slowly edging the material of my skirt up.

My breath hitches when his fingers touch my warm skin. Then I start to wonder what they'd feel like inside me. What they'd feel like caressing my breasts, tugging on my nipples.

"Fuck, Alani," he hisses, leaning forward, his nose strokes over mine. He makes me shiver when he places a soft kiss on my jaw and then his lips brush mine. I almost don't believe it.

Reign Vanderbelt

is

kissing

me.

His tongue darts out, wetting my lips. A wanton moan slips past my throat and then it happens, Reign's lips crash to mine. One hand grips my cheek forcing my body to his, while the fingers on the other dig into my hip. Holding me in place over him.

His tongue pushes its way into my mouth, and I suck on it before pressing mine into his. Back and forth our tongues dance around one another, falling into sync the longer we kiss.

Pulling back and breaking our lip-lock, Reign stares at me. His eyes are filled with lust, pain, and something that looks a little like regret and seeing the regret reflecting back at me, it's that emotion that cuts me.

"Reign," I whisper.

"I'm sorry," he interrupts me, "I shouldn't have done that ... I ..." He slides me from his lap, but I don't miss the obvious bulge in his pants as he does. The bulge I felt digging into me only a moment ago. The bulge I wouldn't mind seeing in the flesh and taking in my mouth. My hand. My pussy, even my ass.

Adjusting himself, Reign climbs out of the car and walks to the front before he leans against the hood.

Sitting in the car, I watch him through the front windshield and give him a couple of moments to himself before I exit and join him.

Resting my ass against the hood, I lean my head on his shoulder.

"I shouldn't have used you like that, Alani," he says, breaking the now awkward silence that's developed. "It was wrong of me."

"I-I don't mind that you used me, Reign. That kiss was hot."

"You should," he snaps. "You deserve better than that." He looks over at me. "You should stay away from me. No good comes from being my friend." Then he quietly mutters, "I'm no good."

Before I can reply, he pushes off the car and heads inside the diner. Leaving me staring after the boy who's so confused with himself.

If only he could see what I can.

If only he could see just how beautiful he is.

HUDSON

I'D HEARD about Arlen Hearst, hell, the entire school, no country, had heard the news. It spread like wildfire, gossip always did here but generally, there was very little truth to the gossip—not this time. It's one-hundred-percent true. Arlen Hearst killed himself on school property, but his family has somehow brushed it under the rug, and the fact a student killed themselves is nothing.

Ohh, to be filthy rich like that.

I didn't know Arlen, not personally anyway, but I have a feeling he'll be missed by some.

Needing a book for my assignment, I head to the library,

but I don't get to my schoolwork because instead, I find Reign Vanderbelt with a bottle of vodka in his hands, sitting alone in the back of the stacks. His glassy gaze is staring into the bottle like it has all the answers.

Reign is the proverbial tough guy. The girls want him and the guys, they want to be friends with him. And then there's me, I want him but not like the other guys do, I want him in the way the girls do, but Reign is straight, therefore, my fantasy will remain that, a fantasy. I mean, I'm not a complete fucking idiot; I'm not going to throw myself at someone who will not return the want, no one wants to be rejected like that.

Sure, I'm open about who I am, and everyone knows that I enjoy the company of both guys and girls. Why only have chocolate when you can have vanilla too? And right now, there's only one girl who makes me feel things I shouldn't, not at eighteen anyway, but seeing her get into his car earlier had me thinking maybe she wasn't just mine after all. And then I started picturing the three of us together. Her and me. Her and him. Me and him. Her, me, AND him. The possibilities were endless but there's one problem in that scenario, he's not bi and therefore, my fantasy will remain that, a thought in my head only.

Shaking away that fantasy, I take a moment to appreciate the man before me. My eyes skim up and down his body, he's ditched the school uniform but his shirt, fuck, that shirt should be illegal. It clings to his forearms and chest, show-casing his muscles in that sexy-as-hell kind of way. Ridge after sexy ridge dips down to his jeans and now I'm wondering what his dick looks like. Is it long but thin? Long and girthy? Short and stubby, that thought has me chuckling and my chuckle garners his attention.

He lifts his gaze to mine, and he looks so lost it breaks my heart to see him like this.

"What's choo wants?" he slurs.

"You okay, man?" I ask him, walking over and squatting down in front of him.

"Depenshs onds zee defsnicin ofds oskays."

"And according to your defsnicin, you're …" I mock him, using the drunk way he said definition but he's that wasted he doesn't notice my tease.

"Drunksd. Sads. Confused."

Here I thought he was unbreakable, but right now, Reign Vanderbelt is at breaking point, and I want to be the person to put him back together again.

"Well, how about we start by getting you back to your room? The Dean is on the warpath tonight." Ever since the news of Arlen's suicide broke, the faculty has been on edge. I cannot tell you how many teachers have asked 'are you okay?' today. Some of the teachers I have never even seen before. Guess the school is in damage-control mode. Can't be good for Crestwood Prep's reputation to have a student commit suicide on school grounds.

He just stares at me, I'm not even sure he heard me. He brings the bottle to his lips and finishes the remaining vodka. "Osdkayd." He nods. "Eisd bed nowd."

A chuckle slips out as I watch him try to stand up. It's like watching a newborn calf stand for the very first time. "Would you like some help?"

"Pleased," he says, looking over at me. He drunkenly smiles and never has he looked so fucking beautiful. He's an Adonis at the best of times but right now, fuck me, there are no words to describe him. He offers me his hand and when I place mine in his, a spark jolts between us. He feels it too because he quickly pulls his hand back, shaking it rapidly to throw away the spark.

Silently we stare at one another, but something passes between us. Even though he's drunk off his ass and I'd love nothing more than to kiss and fuck him, I will not take advantage of a drunk person, no matter how sexy they are.

"Come on," I say again and offer my hand. He hesitantly takes it and this time there's no spark, but I do notice our hands fit together perfectly. It's as if our hands were formed in the same mold. "Let's get you to bed."

"I betsd youd saysd dhat toods allds da girlsd."

"And boys," I add, earning myself a sexy as fuck smirk from him.

"Ands da boyds," he slurs as I pull him up into a standing position. He stares at me for a few beats before he stumbles and falls into me, but I was waiting for it to happen, so I just hold on to him tighter so he doesn't drop. "I got you," I reaffirm, and then we begin our stagger to his room.

Reaching his room, Reign just stares at the door. It's almost as if he's telepathically willing it to open. "Keys?" I ask.

"Pocksdet," he tells me, but he makes no move to grab his keys.

Shaking my head, I slide my hand into the pocket of his jeans, trying ever so hard not to brush his dick but it's hard—pun intended—not to. Having my hand in his pocket confirms my thoughts from earlier, he's long and girthy.

"Dats snotsd myd keysd," he slurs.

With my hand still in his pocket, I lift my gaze to his, and I see him hungrily staring at me. He licks his lips and then he shocks the ever-loving shit out of me when he grips my cheeks and presses his lips to mine.

My eyes widen and I freeze.

Reign Vanderbelt

is

kissing

me.

Holy-fucking-shit.

Before I have a chance to kiss him back, his body goes lax, and I realize he passed out.

"Fuck," I mumble.

Pulling his keys from his pocket, I unlock his door and drag him into his room. Kicking it closed behind me, I get Reign onto the bed. Staring down at him, I smile. He looks so peaceful right now. He's content and all his worries have disappeared. However, when he wakes in the morning, they'll all come crashing back to him and they'll be laced with a vodka hangover and, no doubt, regret over kissing me.

Turning around, I make my way to the door, and with my hand on the handle, I'm about to open it and leave when he mumbles, "Thanksd youd, whaatch's yourd namesded."

"Good night, Reign," I whisper back before slipping out and heading to my room.

Lying in bed, I stare at the ceiling and play the kiss over and over. Was that just a drunken thing? Or is there more to Reign Vanderbelt than I thought?

REIGN

"UGH," I groan as I crack open my eyes. Morning light is shining brightly through the open blinds. Clearly in my fucked-up state last night, I forgot to close them. My head is pounding and when I push up into a sitting position, the world spins and my stomach rolls. Diving off my bed, I race into the adjoining bathroom—perks of being a Vanderbelt—and I make it to the toilet just in time to throw up.

Vodka is just as gross coming back up as it is going down. Why I continue to drink that shit I will never know, but I also want to know, how did I end up back here? The last thing I remember is sitting in the library with my bottle of vodka and drinking to Arlen and his memory. I could really do with my brothers right now, but this is my secret and even though he's gone, I'll keep it. I'm not ready to share that part of me with anyone yet.

This is what I get for loving someone in secret.

Resting my arms on the toilet seat, I lower my head and begin to mourn Arl all over again. I can't believe he's gone. Why didn't he tell me he was struggling? I could have helped him. I would have been there for him.

As Mom used to say, "A problem shared is a problem halved."

"Rise and shine, fuckface," Saint sings from within my room, and the sound of his voice grates through my vodka-addled brain.

"Fuck off," I groan as I vomit again.

"Rough night?" my brother asks from the doorway.

Not having the energy to face him, I flip the bird over my shoulder and throw up again.

The faucet runs and then a glass of water appears. "Thanks," I tell him as I grab the glass from him and take a sip. Rinsing my mouth, I spit it out and then drink the rest. Holding up the empty glass, Saint takes it and refills it. Giving it back to me, he also pops two white pills into my hand. "Thanks," I mumble again as I swallow the pills.

Pushing myself up, I spin around to lean against the vanity.

"Wanna explain why your vodka hungover on a Wednesday?" he asks me, leaning against the doorframe, looking at me. Worry is etched on his face.

"Not really," I reply with a shrug.

"Do I need to be worried about you too? You're not going to go all Arlen on us, are you?"

"Don't fucking say his name," I hiss. Pushing myself up, I walk over to him and grab ahold of his shirt and pull him to me. "Never say his fucking name again."

"Ease up, asshole," he snaps, "what's got your panties in a twist? Alani a dud fuck? I saw the two of you drive off yesterday."

Sighing, I ignore his question and push past him. Throwing myself onto my bed, I stuff my face into my pillow and sigh. I turn my head to him. "You can see yourself out," I mumble into my pillow.

"Well tough shit, I'm not going anywhere until I know you're okay."

"I'm fine, Saint," I growl. Looking over at my brother, I shrug. "I just … I just needed to let loose. You of all people know what that's like."

"Fair enough but, dude, I'm here if you need to talk."

"I know, but right now, I just want to sleep away this vodka fog and then chow down on a Double Quarter Pounder and a Diet Coke." Flipping onto my back, I lace my fingers on my chest and close my eyes.

"You and your fucking disgusting hangover cure," he spits back at me, and no doubt his face will be scrunched in disgust. Everyone has that one magical hangover cure, and a greasy feed from McDonald's is mine. A chuckle escapes me when I crack open an eyelid and I see him scowling and shaking his head.

"I'll bring you back that shit later, but if you need me in the meantime, just holler."

Lifting my hand in acknowledgment, I roll over and let the vodka fog engulf me where I dream of X-rated things that will never happen between Hudson Finley, Alani Thomas, and me.

HUDSON

I KEEP SEEKING REIGN OUT, hoping to bump into him again. It's been days and there's no sign of a wallowing Reign in need of rescue … or another kiss. Actually, there's been no sign of him at all. It's like he's disappeared into thin air. I keep playing our kiss over and over in my head. That kiss knocked me for a loop and it's a kiss that I want to do again, but I'm beginning to think, it was just a one-off. A drunken mistake. I know I sound like a girl, but that kiss was everything a first kiss should be, even if the instigator was blind rotten drunk. But don't they say your true inhibitions come out when you drink?

Fuck, I'm an idiot, of course it was a one-off. It was just a drunken fucking mistake, on his part. But why do I wish it was so fucking real? That there could be more?

No good can come from lusting over Reign, I need to forget and move on. I need to just focus on someone else and as if the universe is giving me a sign, I see her; Alani Thomas, my Bitsy.

She may be tiny, but fuck, she could bring a man to his knees. A man like me is what I mean. Maybe I need to take it to the next level with her so I can move on from my Reign fascination.

She and I have been dancing around each other for a few weeks now. A kiss here, a fondle there. Maybe it's time to take her to bed. By fucking her I will fuck him out of my system.

"What's up, Buttercup?" the girl in question greets as she drops into the seat next to me. We're in the library studying, well, I have my books open but not much studying is getting done. Unless recounting the kiss with Reign is classified as studying? I mean, I'm remembering and memorizing the feel of his lips on mine. The way his tongue slid into my mouth. The little moan he made when I nipped his lip. "Earth to Hudson," she says, snapping me away from my memories, "you were off in la-la land. You thinking dirty sexy nasty things?"

"Maybe," I reply with a shrug.

"Wanna share with the class?"

"Nah, cause then I'd have to kill you and, Bitsy, that's the last thing I want to do because I have plans for you."

"Is that so?" She leans into me, and I can smell the coconut of her body wash. "And what plans do you have?"

"For starters, we wouldn't be in a library, we'd be in your room, lying on that soft rug of yours because your bed is teeny tiny …"

"Go on." She places her hand on my thigh and steps her fingers up toward my dick.

"There'd be less clothes."

"I'm liking where this is going." She places her hand over my crotch and gently presses down.

"I'm liking where your hand is right now."

"Keep telling your story and maybe we can make this fantasy of yours come true." She looks up at me and bats her eyelashes. "So, we're in my room, on my rug, naked."

"I didn't say naked, I said with less clothes."

"Same. Same. Now, continue?"

"Maybe I want to leave you hanging. Keep what I have in store for you as a surprise."

"Ooooooor, we can pack this shit up, head to my room to start the show, and reach the finale."

"You drive a hard bargain but it's one I'm happy to oblige you on, let's go."

We quickly pack up our things and head up to her room. This isn't what I had planned for right now, but I'm not going to turn Alani down, not when we clearly want one another, and no, I'm not doing this to forget about him. Well, maybe a little but I'm mostly doing this because Alani and I have been dancing around this for long enough. I like her. She likes me. Sleeping together is the next logical step in our, whatever this is.

Walking hand in hand up to the girls' floor, of all the people in this entire school to run into, it had to be *him* and his brothers who we pass on the stairs. His gaze drops from my face to our joined hands, to Alani, down to our hands and then back to me. A look flashes over his face and I can't read it. Is it jealousy? Or is that just wishful thinking?

"Boom-chicca-wow-wow," Hendrix singsongs, thrusting his hips back and forth. He continues to sing and his brothers join in too. But not Reign, he just keeps marching down the stairs, seemingly pissed off now.

"Shut up," Alani hisses, flipping them the bird before she turns the corner.

"Are you sure you still want to do this after that?" I ask her. I don't want to pressure her into anything that she doesn't want to do.

"Yes." She nods her head rapidly. "Those dickheads are just jealous that you're about to get laid and all they have is Mrs. Palmer and her five daughters." We stop at her door and she unlocks it. "Now, you coming? Or am I going to have to dig out Buzz and do this myself?"

"Ohh, you'll be coming, Bitsy, and it won't be because of a battery-operated piece of vibrating rubber. It'll be because of my dick hitting you in spots that no one has ever hit before."

She turns to face me. "Prove it."

"Ohh, I will. I. Fucking. Will."

ALANI

HOLY SHIT, *did he just say that to me?*

I had a suspicion Hudson Finley was a dirty talker, but he's never been that crass or descriptive before, and I cannot freakin' wait to see if he can back his words up.

Stepping into my room, I lock the door behind us. I don't want Quinn, or anyone for that matter, barging in here and seeing this. Hudson Finley and his dick are mine and mine alone.

"Sooo," I say, "how are we going to play this, Huddy Boy?"

"Huddy Boy, really?"

Shrugging my shoulders, I keep my eyes locked on him. Dropping my school bag to the floor, I lift my hands and pop open the top button on my blouse. I continue down my chest until they're all undone and I've untucked my shirt from my skirt. Sliding my hands over my breasts, I give them a squeeze before I grip the material of my blouse and slide it off my shoulders. It flutters to the floor, leaving me in my lace demi cup bra, school skirt, knee-high socks, and my Mary Jane shoes.

"This is so much better than I imagined," Hudson tells me. He grabs his shirt by the back of the neck, pulls it up and over his head, and drops it onto my bed. Why is it so sexy when a guy does that?

"That was hot."

"What was?"

"That." I swirl my finger around at his discarded shirt.

"Removing my shirt was hot?"

"Mmmhmpf." I nod. "Hot. As. Fuck."

"Duly noted." He nods and beckons me forward with his index finger. Playing coy, I lift my hand and call him over to me. "Uhhh-uh, Bitsy, I'm running this show. You need to get your sexy ass over here now or I'm going to spank that sexy ass of yours."

Biting my lip, my cheeks darken and my pussy throbs at the thought of him spanking. "Huh," he says, "you like the sound of that, don't you?" I nod. "You want me to turn your lily-white ass cheeks pink with my hand?" I nod again.

"Only there's one thing wrong with that statement."

"And what might I have wrong?"

"My ass isn't lily white." To prove my point, I spin around and lift up my school skirt, exposing my beautifully tanned G-string clad ass.

"Why are your cheeks golden brown?"

Lowering my skirt, I turn to face him. "I like to sunbathe naked in my backyard. Much to the disgust of my mother," I tell him. "She found me nude sunbathing once, and boy oh boy, did she go off at me, sneering, 'A lady does not prance around naked in her backyard. What if a drone flew overhead? You are lucky it was me who came home early and not your father. He'd have a heart attack at seeing his daughter like that. What have you got to say for yourself, young lady?'" I drift off thinking of that day and how I told her I was sorry and promised it wouldn't happen again. Just another day where I'd disappoint one of my parents.

"Hey," Hudson says, cupping my cheek. "Where did you go just now?"

"Nowhere." I shake my head and cover his hand with mine. Lifting it off my cheek, I step closer to him and place it on another cheek. A cheek that he was just admiring and picturing pink. "I'd much rather you cup this cheek," I tell him as I slide our joined hands to my skirt.

He squeezes my ass cheek and even though my skirt is in the way, my skin heats at his touch. "I think I need to make an adjustment to my plan, I really need to see your ass pink."

"That's an adjustment I'd be happy to allow." Leaning over, I rest my palms on my bed and thrust my ass into the air. "Have at it, Huddy Boy."

"You'll pay for that." He walks over to me, lifts my skirt up, and begins to caress my ass cheeks. A moan slips from my lips as he continues to massage me and then there's a crack, followed by a burning sensation on my ass. Holy fuck, he actually spanked me. He spanks me three more times and then drops to his knees, kissing and caressing my glowing cheeks. My ass cheeks are burning right now and my pussy is throbbing. I have never been so turned on in my life.

"Fuck, Hudson," I whisper-hiss, "I need you to fuck me, and I need you to fuck me now. I'm so turned on."

He chuckles against my ass. "How turned on?"

Before I can reply, he moves his hand between my thighs and cups my mound, rubbing my clit through the soaked material of my G-string. "You're so wet, Bitsy, I'm gonna need to taste you before I fuck you."

"Yes," I pant like the wanton hussy I am right now. Who knew a spanking could be so sexy?

Removing his hand from between my thighs, he grabs my hips and spins me around to face him. With his eyes locked on mine, he lowers the zipper on my skirt and it falls to the carpet below. Stepping out of it, I kick it to the side. Swallowing deeply, he hooks his fingers into my G-string and tugs it down my legs. Tapping my foot, I lift and he pulls it off. He does the same with the other foot and then he scrunches them into a ball and brings them up to his face. He inhales deeply and breathes in my scent. "You smell delicious, I wonder if you taste as fine?"

"Only one way to find out," I tell him. Lifting one leg up, I rest my foot on the edge of my bed, baring myself to him. Raising my eyebrows at him, I egg him on to hurry up. I have no clue where this brazenness is coming from, but I like her.

He doesn't leave me hanging for long. Reaching up, he grips my hips and presses his face into me. His tongue circles my clit and then he licks down to my opening. Spearing his tongue into me, I drop my head back and cry out.

Holy fuck, his tongue is like heaven.

Like a starved man, he goes to town on my cunt. Licking, sucking, and biting. When he slips a finger into the mix, it's game over. My legs tremble as the most intense orgasm of my life ripples through me. Every nerve ending in my body is buzzing, I'm thankful that my bed is behind me because I collapse back onto it.

Lying here, I stare at the ceiling, breathing deeply as I come back to Earth.

Lifting up to my elbows, I stare down at Hudson, who is still on his knees between my legs. "So, how did I taste?" I ask him.

"So fucking delicious. Have you ever tasted yourself

before?" Shaking my head, I watch as he lifts to his knees, swipes his finger through my folds, and brings it to my mouth. Parting my lips, he slips his finger inside and I suck. It's tarter than I expected, but sucking on his finger has my body coming to life again. What is up with that? "Thoughts on your exquisite taste?"

"Well, I don't have anything to compare it to—"

"Bitsy, you can't say shit like that to me, now I'm picturing you going down on a chick."

"Not going to happen." I shake my head. "I'm all about the sausage."

"Taco. Sausage. I'm a man of many tastes."

Staring at him, I think about that statement and now I'm picturing him with Reign. *What the fuck?* Why am I thinking about the two of them going down on one another? Shaking my head, that scene morphs into the two of them pleasuring me. A moan slips free causing Hudson to raise his eyebrows.

"What are you imagining over there?"

"Nothing," I quickly refute.

"I call bullshit but I'm going to let it pass because I need to fuck you now. This is a little different than what I was imagining earlier in the library, but I think this scenario is much better."

"I'm sure we can try your library scene at another time, but for now, reach into the top drawer there. Suit up and then fuck me."

"Yes, ma'am."

Quicker than I have ever seen someone slide a condom on, Hudson is sheathed and ready to fuck. He shuffles me around on the bed, climbs on, and situates himself between my thighs. He grips the base of his shaft and with his eyes locked on mine, he pushes inside.

A hiss escapes me. He's larger than anyone I've been with before, but he takes it slow, allowing me to get used to his size. Once he's all the way in, he begins to move. Moving his hips back and forth, he fucks me sensually and slowly. I was expecting hard and fast but this, this is exactly what I wanted our first time together to be like.

Leaning down, he covers my mouth with his, his tongue moving in and out of my mouth in sync with his dick and my vagina. This is perfect in every way, and it's something I will remember forever.

Out of nowhere, I explode, crying out into his mouth. He continues to kiss and fuck me until he too explodes. Emptying himself into the condom.

Collapsing on top of me, he breathes heavily in my ear. Lifting his head, he stares down at me. "You are perfect, Alani Thomas, absolutely fucking perfect."

After that first time together, Hudson helped me learn a lot about my body, and since we played the 'what's your ultimate fantasy' game, I cannot stop thinking about a threesome. When he put me on the spot as to with whom, I froze, but I know without a doubt who I want in my threesome; me, Hudson, and Reign. That would be H O double T hot.

We split up to shower and freshen up and then we meet in the cafeteria for dinner.

"You looking forward to Ready or Not?" Hudson asks, taking another huge bite of his burger. That boy is obsessed with burgers. He'd eat them for breakfast, lunch, and dinner.

"Yeah, it'll be fun, just like always."

'Ready or Not' is basically a huge game of hide-and-seek. It's been a tradition here for as long as I can remember. It's a fun way to blow off steam, or sexual tension in most people's cases, and give in to the desires that you normally wouldn't. The addition of neon masks gives the players a sense of anonymity, allowing the contenders to really let loose, but there are rules and apart from that one time, everyone abides by them.

"He's watching you," Hudson says out of nowhere.

"What? Who?" Of course, the moment I look up, Reign is

in my line of sight. His gaze collides with mine, his eyes are firmly locked on me. My heart begins to race. Is there a reason he's looking this way? Maybe … no, it can't be, there's no way, my mind is playing tricks on me.

The side of his lip lifts and he graces me with the sexiest lopsided smirk.

Reign Vanderbelt IS noticing me and even though I just had sex, amazing out of this world sex with Hudson, my body zings to life again.

From the corner of my eye, I notice Hudson is watching Reign, whose gaze flicks from me to Hudson. Something passes over Reign's face but in the blink of an eye, it's gone. He glances away before I can even ask Hudson what it is about.

Interesting, I think to myself. Seems I'm not the only one who's caught Reign's eye, the only problem is, what happens when everything falls apart? I'll be left to pick up the pieces if I go there. No good ever comes of liking two guys at the same time, this isn't a Sara Cate novel.

Besides, nothing good ever comes from getting involved with a Lord.

REIGN

LATER THAT WEEK, we are at the house for dinner and as usual, it's a fucked-up family affair. Dad delivers some news that makes Thatcher angrier than I've ever seen him before. Remington-fucking-Hearst, the baby princess of the Hearst clan, is transferring here. Thatcher hates the Hearsts with a fiery passion. I hate some of them but not all of them. Up until a few weeks ago, I was secretly dating one of them. Arlen isn't, wasn't, like the rest of them and for all we know, this Remy bitch is a nice Hearst as well. Maybe she's like her older brother, caring and beautiful with the biggest heart. He loved unconditionally but he was obviously struggling. I just wish he would have opened up to me, but I guess if he was still here, I wouldn't be messing around with Alani and focused on Hudson.

Those two bring me to life in a way I've never felt before. I like them both equally and I know that I can't get too serious with one without hurting the other, I know they are hooking up too, and why wouldn't they? Each of them is amazing in their own right. In a perfect world the three of us would become a throuple and live happily ever after. But this isn't a fairy tale, I don't think I'm destined to be loved unconditionally. To have the white picket fence, two point-five kids, and a dog named Boof. I must have done some messed-up shit in a past life to be punished in this one. Maybe I'm better off alone, hell, Arlen killed himself. Clearly, I'm a horrible person if the man I was in love with chose death over me. Needing to feel wanted, I seek out Hudson when we get back to school.

Flipping off my brothers, I enter through the backdoors of the dormitory wing and head toward the stairs, taking the steps two at a time. Reaching the seniors' floor, I head for his room, careful not to be seen. I'm like Tom Cruise in *Mission Impossible*. In my head I start to sing 'den-den-den-den-den' from the theme song over and over as I stealthily sneak toward his room.

Raising my fist, I knock quickly, practically banging on the door and holding my breath as I wait for it to open. After what feels like an eternity but was in fact only a few seconds, Hudson opens it. His shirt is open, and his pants hang low on his hips. Fucking hell.

In one swift motion, I'm through his door, slamming it shut behind me, and flipping the lock into place before I tug him to me. His breathing has quickened slightly. My fingers fist the bottom of his shirt and I pull him even closer. His lips brush mine ever so lightly.

Hudson silently stares at me, piercing lust reflects back at me. After a few breaths, his fingers grip my shirt, tugging it free from my trousers.

"Want me naked, do you?" I tease, my lips brushing over his again.

"If you get to touch me, I get to touch you. Fair's fair," he says.

Nodding at his assessment, I don't wait a second longer. My lips crash to his in a searing kiss. Hudson moans around my tongue pressing into his mouth. Somehow, I manage to keep kissing him while pushing him back toward his bed.

He falls down onto the mattress and stares up at me. The way he looks right now will forever be seared in my mind.

He's mine, all fucking mine.

Leaning over him, my arms cage him in as my lips find his again. I bite down hard before pushing my tongue back into his mouth. Our tongues tangle in a war of heat and passion.

Fighting the urge to take him right now, we don't have time and a quick fuck is not what I want for our first time. I'm still shocked that this is happening. The last time I was with him, I was drunk out of my head. Vaguely I remember kissing him but this, this is so much better without the vodka haze.

"Fuck, Reign," Hudson groans into my mouth, gasping for breath. Kissing along his jaw to his neck, I sink my teeth into his pulse, sucking and tasting every inch I can.

My cock is rock fucking hard right now, so fucking hard.

Hudson whimpers under me when my hand brushes his cock. Licking up his neck, I kiss him hard again, pushing my tongue inside his mouth. My fingers quickly work his pants open and slipping my hand into his boxers, I free his cock.

My hand wraps around him, squeezing tightly, I earn a groan from him. "Fuck," he growls.

His head flops back, his eyes roll into the back of his head.

Taking my own cock out, I hold us together in my fist.

Stroking us all while he rubs against me in the most delicious fucking way.

His cock leaks, precum drizzles down his shaft into my hand. I work us faster, gripping us tighter in my palm. Fuck, he feels so good.

Hudson screws up his face and I know he's close. Because I'm ready to let go.

My hand is slick between us. Deciding to test him, I suck my free fingers into my mouth to get them slick. I know it's nowhere near enough, but I'll work with what I have. Slowly, I move my hand behind him and sliding my hand into his briefs, I place two fingers at his puckered hole.

"Oh, fuck," Hudson groans. "Please."

He rolls into me, giving me more access. Slowly, I push one finger inside him. I'm surprised at how easily he takes me without any lube. Hudson groans. Pulling out, I thrust two fingers in this time, his ass tightens around my digits. His dick in my hand twitches and I know he's about to make a mess.

With my hand stroking us faster and my fingers pumping into his ass, Hudson's body stiffens. He moans and whimpers loudly as his cum shoots across his stomach.

"Oh my God," I hiss. Seeing him shatter beneath me sets me off and I follow behind him, mixing our cum together.

Hudson winces slightly when I remove my fingers from his ass. He rolls over, lying still under me, his focus is on the ceiling above him. His breathing is hurried as he continues to stare into space.

I fix myself while Hudson just lies there covered in the aftermath we just left.

"I've got to go," I say and before he gets a word in, I exit his room.

The guilt of what we just did sinks in but why the fuck do I feel guilty? Is it because of Alani? My brothers? Our father?

My family wouldn't understand, it's why I kept Arlen and me a secret.

My mind flits back to Alani and I realize I want them both. I want her here with us. But how the fuck would that even work? I can't choose between them and this is one time being a Lord won't help me.

HUDSON

"OH MY GOD," Alani moans, the sound very similar to one she made when we fucked the other day. It's also similar to how Reign sounds just before he comes. "This chocolate pudding is to die for."

"Bitsy, you need to stop moaning like that. My cock is going to burst through my zipper if you keep that up, and I'm seconds away from lifting you from that chair, throwing you down on the table, and fucking you senseless."

"I'd be okay with that," she playfully teases me.

"I don't want anyone to see what's mine ... unless there's

a third person in the room with us." My mind drifts to a vision of Reign joining us. As always, he's the only other person I would allow to see Alani in all her naked glory.

Clicking of fingers in front of my face snaps me away from my threesome fantasy. "Hey, where did you go? And, are you blushing?"

"No," I quickly refute but my rash reply is enough to arouse suspicion and with the 'I'm not a fool' look on her face, I need to come up with something and I need to come up with something quickly. "I … I was just thinking about when we, you know …"

"So why were you blushing just now? Were you thinking of us doing some super kinky things?" She raises her eyebrows at me, and I decide to use that to my advantage.

"Maybe," I reply with a shoulder shrug. Leaning into her, I nibble her earlobe and then whisper, "Tell me your ultimate fantasy?"

Bitsy turns her head toward me and bites her bottom lip in that sexy as fuck way she does. Her tongue darts out, gliding over the teeth indents in her bottom lip. "I've always wanted …"

"Wanted what?" I push her.

"I've always wanted to be in a threesome."

"And who might be in this threesome?"

"Well, there'd be me and you and … another guy."

"And how would me, you, and this guy work?"

"Every way possible."

"You dirty dirty girl," I playfully tease her.

"And what's yours?"

"You'll never guess …"

"I like games, let me see." She taps her chin. "You want to be hog-tied to a tree and be blown by someone in a bondage mask before they fuck you raw. The bark digging into you causes you to bleed and the feel of the blood dripping down your body turns you on like never before."

"Ummm, no, and that was very detailed. Making me think that you might like that?" She shrugs her shoulders at me. "You are something else, Alani Thomas."

"You haven't seen anything yet, baby. Now, tell me your fantasy. How can I make it come true if you don't tell me."

"Well, it's pretty simple, really. I have the exact same fantasy as you."

"You want a threesome?"

"Mmmhmpf." I nod in agreement, tracing my finger in a circle on her thigh. "The thought of you, me, and another is the hottest thing I can think of."

"And who might you want to join us in this fantasy of yours?"

Do I dare tell her who I want? Or should I throw the question back at her? And that's what I decide to do, taking the chicken way out. "And who might you want to join us in this fantasy of ours?"

Without batting an eyelid, she says the one name I never expected. "Reign Vanderbelt."

"Come again?"

"You heard me. That man is fine as fuck, and I think the three of us together would set the room on fire. You know what the ultimate threesome fantasy of mine would be?"

"What?"

"Reign fucking me doggy style while you fuck him in the ass."

My eyes widen. "You are fucking perfect," I tell her before I grip her cheeks in my hands and cover her mouth with mine. Pushing my chair back, I maneuver her onto my lap and intensify the kiss. Running my hands up her back and into her hair, I gently tug on her fiery red locks, causing her to moan into my mouth and grind herself on my rock-hard dick.

The sound of wolf whistles and people singing 'boom-chicca-wow-wow' pulls us apart. She lowers her head to my shoulder in embarrassment, but I'm not ashamed to be making out with the hottest girl at Crestwood while also thinking about the hottest guy at Crestwood joining us. I just need to figure out a way to make our fantasy come true.

REIGN

"WHAT THE FUCK is up with you, man?" Saint asks me, slapping my thigh to get my attention.

"Huh?" I reply, not sure what I've missed.

"Take a walk with me, bro." He jumps up and waits for me to join him.

Without a word, the two of us leave the cemetery and head along the path and up toward the cliffs. Walking to the edge, Saint slides his hands into his pockets and rocks back and forth on his heels. Silently I join him, I cross my arms and the two of us stare out to sea.

"What's up, man? You've been off for ages now."

"I'm fine," I snap at him.

"Yeah, and so's Mom," he throws back at me, his tone pissed off, and at the mention of Mom, my heart aches and I become even more pissed off.

Mom used to be so happy. She was the best mom and then one day, something happened between her and Dad and now we're left with this shell of a woman. If she's having a good day, she gets out of bed, but she floats around in a drug and booze-infested fog. Thatcher is convinced Dad cheated on her and I think he might be right. Nothing would surprise me when it comes to Thornton Vanderbelt. He's the definition of a cunt, like in the dictionary his smarmy smiling face would be sitting next to the definition of the word.

The sound of Saint's voice brings me back to the present. "Talk to me, man, we're all worried about you."

"I'm fin—" He gives me a look that says, 'you finish that word and I'll throw you over the edge of this cliff.' "Okay, I'm not fine but I … I'm not ready to talk about it. It's my burden to bear."

"You know we're here for you."

"I know that, but I need to deal before I can share."

He nods and throws his arm around me, pulling me in for a side hug and giving me silent support. "Thanks, man," I whisper.

"Anytime, asshole, anytime."

"I think I'm gonna head off, I need to be alone."

"Yeah, so you can jack off," he teases.

"Please, I don't need my hand, not when I have—" I cut myself off before I spill a secret I'm not ready to share with anyone.

"I knew you were fucking her." He nudges my shoulder and I see him grinning from ear to ear. "Just remember, wrap it before you tap it. I'm too young to be a cool uncle."

"Yes, Dad," I deadpan but then I get an image of Alani and Hudson playing with a lil' redheaded kid and me watching over them. What the actual fuck? Why am I thinking about a happy family with the two of them? Needing to get away from him, I playfully punch him in the side and walk away.

"FYI, I'm gonna give your kid red candy and send him home to you. I'll do the same with Thatch's kids too."

"Whatever," I reply, flipping him the bird.

Saint and I head back to the dorms together. I thought he would have gone back to the party, so him coming with me, surprises me.

We reach our floor, and he goes to his room while I make my way to mine. I unlock the door and step in. My foot crunches on a piece of paper on the floor. Scrunching my eyebrows, I bend down and pick it up. Reading over it, my heart drops when I process the printed words before me.

I know your secret
Your dirty dirty secret

Which secret? Of all of my secrets, there's one I'm not ready to have come to light yet. One day I'll be ready but today is not that day. I was already on edge and now, now I'm teetering. I don't know how much longer I can go on like this, I need to talk to someone. Someone who won't judge. Someone who will just listen, and I know the one person I need to speak to … I just hope she's having a good day.

The next morning, I pull into the circular driveway at my childhood home and a sense of dread washes over me. On the outside, the Vanderbelt mansion is regal, it looks like we have it all together, but behind the walls of this house lies so many secrets it could sink the *Titanic* three times over.

Parking my car in the driveway, I walk up the front steps and enter. As usual, I'm greeted by Lisette. "Reign, this is a pleasant surprise."

"Hi, Lisette, you are looking younger than the last time I saw you."

"Stop," she scoffs, slapping my arm playfully. "She's in the sunroom having tea. She's good today."

Nodding, I smile at the woman who helped raise my brothers and me. Mom had four under one, she needed all the help she could get, especially since Father was an absentee non hands-on dad. It was like, once he'd gotten her pregnant, twice in the one year, he could walk away. His job was done. I came barreling into the world, seven weeks early, making me the same age as my brothers, just born at opposite ends of the year.

"We're lucky to have you, Lisette."

"It's my pleasure, Reign. I just wish you boys would visit her more often."

"You know why we don't, plus, she has you."

"She does, but she also needs her sons." And with that, she taps my cheek and walks away humming to herself, which means Dad isn't here. When he's here, the house is quieter than a morgue.

Heading out to the sunroom, I find Mom sitting in her chair. She's smiling and I take a moment to look at her. She's still beautiful, even with all the shit Dad and that whore have put her through. Turns out Thatch's suspicion was right, Dad cheated on mom with none other than Rochelle Hearst. Why she stays with him, I will never know.

"Reign," she says with a beaming smile when she finally sees me. "This is a pleasant surprise." She taps the seat next to her. "Come, sit with me."

Walking over to her, I bend down and place a kiss on her cheek before taking the armchair across from her. "Hi, Mom."

"You look like you have the weight of the world on your shoulders, Reign. What's up, baby?"

"I …" But I don't know what to say. I've always been able to talk to Mom, even with what's happened recently, she's always been there for me. It's like the universe knew I needed her today and that's why she's having a good day. And for once, it actually looks like tea in her cup.

Before I can share my woes with Mom, Lisette returns with a coffee for me and a plate of cookies too. She places them on the glass table between us and slinks back out again. She's like a ninja at times, slinking in and out of rooms.

"You know you can tell me anything, Reign."

"I know, Mom, it's just …"

"Sometimes you feel like you don't know what you want, and you try to do the best for everyone else and in the process, it makes you sad or angry."

"Pretty much. I … I have a secret."

"Don't we all," Mom nonchalantly says with a shrug and then shakes her head. "You don't need to share the specifics but give me what you can."

Nodding, I pick up my mug and take a sip. "Okay, so, I like someone, well two someones. One will be acceptable, the other not so much, but …"

"But what?"

"But I don't know what I actually want. If I listen to ev—"

"Reign," Mom interrupts me, "don't listen to other people when it comes to matters of the heart and love. You need to follow your heart, not your head. Love can be precious when it's between the right people." When she says people and not person, it's like she understands and accepts exactly where my heart is and, Mom being Mom, I know she won't pry. She'll wait until I'm ready to share everything. "Deep down, I think you already know what's right, but, Reign, love is scary and you're letting that overrule you. Sometimes you need to listen to the fear but most of the time, it's wrong. Follow your heart, Reign. Open it up and be happy, no matter what you choose."

Feeling lighter than when I came but still confused as to what I want to do about Alani and Hudson, I say goodbye to Mom and as I'm walking out, I run into Father.

"Son," he says by way of greeting.

"Father."

We silently stare at one another and as I look at him, I realize I feel nothing for him. He could drop dead tomorrow and I wouldn't shed one fucking tear. Not wanting to let him affect my mood any more than it already is, I step around him and walk away without so much as a goodbye.

It's amazing how one person can alter your mood. Then again, I know firsthand how two people can brighten up your life during the darkest of moments and I begin to imagine how bright my life would be if I had them both, but is it possible?

ALANI

I'M RUNNING LATE, and that doesn't sit well with me. I pick up my pace and as I race down the corridor, I can hear my father's voice, scolding me. "Tardiness is a sign of weakness, Alani," he'd say, disappointment lacing his voice. "I didn't raise you to keep people waiting," he'd add just to rub it in further.

With his voice still echoing through my head, I start running through the halls, my Mary Janes clicking with every step. I can't get a late slip, my father will kill me. I check the time on my Fitbit and just as I round the corner, I knock into something hard, and it sends me to the ground. Landing on my ass with a thud, I stare as my shit scatters everywhere, and I mean everywhere.

"Ow," I screech.

Not looking up at the figure looming over me, I quickly reach out and begin to pick up my books and pens as fast as I can. Internally singsonging, "I'm late. I'm late. I'm late for a very important date," and I'm picturing the rabbit from *Alice in Wonderland* jumping up and down like a bunny on speed.

"Are you late, Red?"

"My name's not Red." I snap my head up, staring into the gorgeous eyes of Reign. He raises an eyebrow, smirking down at me like he finds me funny. Like he finds me on my knees before him amusing. My jaw practically drops, I swear my brain melts into a puddle whenever Reign is around. His bag hangs off his shoulder while he eyes me with a stupid grin on his stupid, beautiful face. You'd think after my 'I want a threesome with you and Reign' chat with Hudson that I'd be salivating over the man before me but for some reason, he's annoying me right now and my stomach dips with nerves, or is it unease that I might miss out on my fantasy?

"Red?" Reign murmurs my name again, gaining my attention. The deep rumble of his voice causes my insides to quiver, and for butterflies to flit about in my stomach at the thought of more with him. These are the feelings that I should be focusing on, but there's still an ounce of lingering irritation. Probably over him using *that* nickname and for the fact I am late, really late now.

"It's Alani, not Red," I snap, annoyed with the stupid nickname he's given me.

"Nah, I like Red better," he says with a wink.

"Unbelievable," I hiss, shaking my head. Standing up, I ignore him and turn, ready to head to class, but he grips my arm, halting me in my tracks. My skin tingles where his hand is gripping me.

"What?" he growls. Once again the sound of his voice vibrates over me, the annoyance I feel starts to dissipate, and that hunger and desire for him takes over.

"Never mind."

Rolling my shoulder, I try to shrug him off but his hold is tight. Reign looks around the empty corridor like he's double-checking we're alone. He tugs on my arm and pulls me aside, hiding us in one of the many random alcoves around the school.

Leaning toward me, he crowds me in. Tingles explode over my skin from his touch, slowly he leans in farther until our lips are inches apart. His breath fans over my face.

"You know you want to say it, Red." He emphasizes the nickname he's given me, doing it to piss me off further.

"You have no clue who I am. Not the real me, underneath. Even If you knew my name, you won't remember it because you don't care, and why would you? You are a Lord after all," I snap. I have no idea where this hostility toward him is coming from. Especially considering all last night I was concocting different ways to get him AND Hudson to take me at the same time.

Reign's eyes rest cool on mine, sending shivers down my spine. For the sake of my pride, I hold his stare but I shudder —in a good way—when his lips brush my left cheek, his vanilla-scented aftershave wrapping around me.

His stare burns into me, he narrows his eyes and then I feel his fingertip brushing down the side of my cheek.

"I know exactly who you are, Alani Thomas," he murmurs, and the way he draws out my name causes my heart to stutter. I begin to realize that he DOES know me. He tilts his head and the corner of his mouth lifts before he steps back, putting space between us. "Lead the way, Red," he says.

The low rumble of his voice is enough to send me light-headed but it's his hand resting on my hip urging me forward, that has my skin scattering with goosebumps.

Caught in his web, I follow him out of our hiding place and toward class.

When we enter the classroom, all eyes are on us as Reign and I walk into the room, late, but because I'm with *him* it will be fine. I don't miss the whispers and I definitely don't miss the glares from some of the girls as I take my seat, I don't care if they talk because I was with Reign. Imagine the talk when I'm with him AND Hudson, that will set tongues wagging. A smile appears when I think of my father, I know he won't approve. And I'm not just referring to the threesome, he has never liked the Vanderbelts. I'd go as far as to say my father loathes them, most people in this town do but his hatred for them runs deeper, even if I don't know the specifics.

Reign sits behind me with his brother, Saint. I can almost feel Reign's breath on my neck. I lift my arm, moving my hair to one shoulder. Reign's chair shuffles behind me and then I feel the softest touch of his fingers on the back of my neck.

My skin erupts in goosebumps, the teacher stops talking for a moment, and Reign's hand drops. I almost groan at the loss of contact. I want his hands on me, I want him so badly to touch me.

Turning my head slightly, I eye him over my shoulder.

"Eyes front, Red," his husky voice murmurs.

My lip catches between my teeth and I can't help but smile when he continues to touch the back of my neck, his finger-tips ever so slightly skimming my skin, turning me into a wanton, needy woman.

Finally, class ends and when the bell rings, Reign's fingers wrap around the back of my neck, squeezing slightly, keeping me rooted to my chair, unable to move.

"I'll catch you later, Brother," Saint informs his brother and exits the room with more swagger than an eighteen-year-old should have.

Reign stands, pulling me with him and as if I'm being led

to the slaughter, I follow behind him as he drags me toward the library.

Heading to the back where no one can see, Reign spins me so his chest hits my back. I moan unabashedly into the room when his lips brush against my neck.

Reign untucks my blouse, slowly undoing the bottom buttons. His fingers slide over my exposed stomach and then upward until his thumb brushes against the bottom of my breasts. I can feel his erection digging into my ass. He pushes against me, making me groan slightly.

"Fuck, Red. I want you so fucking bad." His teeth bite into my pulse at the same time as he pushes his hardened cock into me again.

God, I'm going to come and he's not even inside me.

"On your knees." He hisses.

Turning around to face him, I gaze into his eyes as he presses down on my shoulders, forcing me to my knees. My eyes never leave his as his fingers slide his zipper down. Once he's able to, he removes his cock and begins to stroke himself.

"Suck it, baby," he demands before brushing the head of his shaft against my lips, his precum coating them as he does.

Licking my lips, I open my mouth, ready to take him but his phone rings, stopping me from sucking him. I pout at the interruption.

Sliding his phone out of this pocket, he hisses when he glances at the screen. "Fuck," he sneers. Tucking himself back in, he answers the call and listens.

"Yeah, yeah. I'll be right there."

Without saying a word to me, Reign leaves me on my knees. Desperate, needy, and so goddamn wet for him. I'm also pissed off that he just left like that. "Asshole," I mutter as I get to my feet.

Picking up my bag, I follow the path he took and begin to question if I really want to get involved with him. What kind of asshole leaves mid-blow job? I don't have time for shit like that, but when it comes to Reign Vanderbelt, I'm positive I'd walk over broken glass for him. There's something about him that's calling to me, and I intend to find out what that something is.

REIGN

LEAVING Alani on her knees like that was fucking hard—pun intended—but in all honesty, I'm not surprised my fucking brothers interrupted me only moments before Alani's lips were going to wrap around my dick. *Fucking cockblockers.*

Entering Thatcher's room, my look of annoyance is clearly written over my face as I slam the door closed behind me.

"What's got your panties in a twist?" Hendrix asks.

Saint smirks, the bastard. "If looks could kill," he teases and to add to the teasing the fucker laughs in my face.

"What?" Thatcher asks, confusion marring his face.

"Nothing, what's going on?"

"We have a problem," Thatcher states but it doesn't enlighten us to anything. There's always a problem lately, it feels like someone is out to get us.

"What problem?" I murmur.

"Dad's called us to dinner tomorrow night."

"Fuck," I hiss. Our father only calls us to dinner when he wants to make an example out of one of us. Our father is vindictive and an asshole. He only cares about his reputation and the perfect family he portrays.

We fucking loathe him, but for our mother, we keep the peace.

"Any ideas as to what he wants?" I ask, but all three of them shake their heads. "Well, this is gonna be fun. Not!"

They all nod in agreement and then we all fall silent. Each of us no doubt going over our recent activities to see if they're the reason for the summons.

"So," Hendrix says, breaking the silence that fell over us, each of us no doubt wondering if it was them who will be the bearer of Dad's wrath at dinner. "What's up with you and that Thomas girl?" From the look on his face, I know he's just being a smart-ass.

Flipping my brother off, I push away from the wall I was leaning against. "I'm out." With my brother's laughter following behind me, I head toward the library, hoping Alani is still there studying and we can pick up where we left off.

Searching for her red hair, I come up empty. Honestly, why I thought she'd be waiting for me is stupid, I do however, find something that does intrigue me. Hudson is reaching for a book, his shirt rides up giving me a glimpse of his tanned skin and toned abs.

My tongue darts out, wetting my lips while I watch him.

Fuck, what is it about him that I'm drawn to? I hardly know the guy on a personal level, but there's something between us that is too strong to ignore, just like with Alani but after I ditched her earlier, that boat may have sailed.

It wasn't like this with him. He had to push and push me, for me to admit anything. And then he got to know me in a way no one ever has before and before I knew it, he'd wormed his way into my heart.

By the time I realized I was in love with Arlen, it was too late. He died without ever knowing exactly how I felt, and I made a vow to never again make that mistake. Life's too short and I intend to live it to its fullest. It's the least I can do to honor the guy who opened my eyes and heart to love.

Striding toward Hudson, I reach above him and grip the book he was reaching for. My chest presses up against his back and I hear his breath hitch. He stills beneath me. The side of my hand slides down his arm, his skin heating beneath my touch, it has my cock twitching and pressing into his ass.

My breath fans over his neck, I don't miss the way his body goes slack, leaning into mine as if we are two puzzle pieces connecting together.

"Here," I utter, handing him the book but keeping him practically pinned beneath me.

His gaze finds mine over his shoulder, "Thanks."

He holds his hand out for the book, but instead I pull it back slightly making him reach for it. Spinning around to face me, his lips are inches from mine. I've remembered the feel of his lips against mine a hundred times recently. The taste. The softness. I want to feel them again. Our breaths mingle together. The air around us simmers with unbridled passion.

Hudson swallows deeply, his eyes fall to my lips and that's all it takes for me to make my move. I drop the book to the floor, grip the side of his face, and crash my lips to his. My tongue tangles with his until he moans around me.

His fingers move up, fisting my shirt.

Feeling how hard he is, how hard I make him, I grind my

cock into his, causing him to groan loud enough for the entire library to hear, but I don't care.

A sound breaks me from my trance and I reluctantly pull away. Both of us are panting. He stares at me, his fingers touching his lips. That kiss was amazing and I need more. Gripping his neck, I yank him toward me again.

The hiss that leaves him has my cock twitching between us.

My fingers brush over his neck, his Adam's apple bobbing under my thumb and I wrap my hand around his neck. Leaning toward him, my lips suck on his skin. My teeth bite down, indenting his beautiful skin.

His legs shake slightly, causing him to grip onto me to keep himself upright. I want to mark him, no, I need to mark him as mine. Why the need, I have no fucking clue, but I bite down harder. He hisses and it's music to my ears.

Removing my mouth from his skin, my gaze slides to the redness already forming, and I smile at the mark I've left. Later, when he's all alone in his room, he'll know I've been there. He'll know he's mine.

"I like this on you," I murmur, running the tip of my finger around the edge of my bite.

Hudson blinks but voices approaching pull us apart. No sooner have I stepped back than Quinn fucking Ellis rounds the corner with her groupies.

Fuck.

Hudson bends to grab the book I dropped and then moves past me and the girls before grabbing his bag off the table and leaving, the girls staring at me like I've grown a second head.

Fuck, Quinn is the last person I want to know what Hudson and I just did.

I glare at her, it's enough of a warning for her to scramble, not saying a word, but I know her, the need to spread this gossip around school will be sitting on the tip of her tongue. I need to be more fucking careful.

But with Hudson Finley firmly planted front and center in my mind, alongside a certain redhead, I don't like my fucking odds. Mom's words of wisdom keep floating around in my head, follow my heart? Or do I keep hiding who I truly am from the world? That's the million-dollar question.

HUDSON

WHAT THE FUCK JUST HAPPENED?

And why do I want it to happen again and again?

Lifting my hand to my neck, I trace around the bite mark on my skin as I slam the door to my room behind me. Walking over to the mirror, I tilt my head and stare at my brand, and that's effectively what it is. Reign Vanderbelt just branded me as his, and fuck, if I don't want that but what I want more than that, I also want Alani to join in.

How can I want two people so much? Two people who I have no chance in fucking hell of getting together with. That's a fantasy that will never come to fruition ... but it's a fantasy that I'm about to pleasure myself to.

Grabbing my shower shit, I head to the showers. Thankfully, they're empty but they won't be for long. Entering one of the stalls, I flip the lock, turn the faucet on for the water to heat—takes forever in this place—and while I wait, I undress. My cock is already hard, harder than it's ever been before because thoughts of both Alani AND Reign is the best kind of porn.

Images of them, us, float through my mind as I wait for the water to heat up. Gripping my dick, I begin to stroke myself. Instead of my hand, I'm imagining that it's Reign's hand on me. Resting my forearm on the wall, I lean my head on it and focus on my dick. Up and down my hand slides, my grip getting tighter and tighter with each stroke. I'm wishing Alani was here so I could slide back inside her sweet, sweet pussy. The other night with her was not planned, but fuck, I'd love a repeat. Then I think about the library earlier, but this time, we weren't interrupted. This time, I spun Reign around and I fucked him. My dick pressing into his ass, the muscles choking my cock as I thrust in and out of his tight hole.

The main door opens, and I vaguely hear chatter as other students enter, but I'm lost in my head to images of Alani and Reign, the two of them lost in pleasure as Reign fucks her. His cock slamming in and out of her cunt. With a low growl, I come. White ribbons spray the wall, dripping down and swirling with the water that's finally hot.

Feeling sated, I step under the spray and wash away the remnants of my release and then I wash myself.

Drying off, I get dressed and head back to my room.

Returning to my room, I open the door and there's a sheet of paper on the floor. Bending down, I pick it up and kick the door closed. I place the mysterious piece of paper on my bed and go about hanging my towel up and putting my shower caddy away. I sort out some laundry and grab what books I need for the next morning.

Flicking on the television, I drop onto my bed and the paper crushing beneath me reminds me of what I found when I got back. Pulling it out from under me, I flip it over and read.

He's lying to you. Don't fall for his tricks.
Just fuck her and forget about him.
Heed this warning and no one gets hurt.

"What the fuck?" I mumble.

Scrunching up the note, I throw it onto the dresser. I don't have time for weird riddles, I have enough confusion in my life at the moment.

Lying back on the bed, I click the television on and begin to flick through the channels. Finding *Fast and Furious* playing, I lose myself in car chases and Paul Walker for a couple of hours.

As soon as the movie finishes, my mind drifts back to earlier this evening. Seeing Reign so goddamn possessive was H O double T hot. I hope that maybe now, he'll finally own up to this. To us, but I guess only time will tell.

The memory of him and me in the library plays in my mind as I lie on my bed. My cock is once again hard and I begin to stroke myself, unleashing the pent-up frustration over Reign and what may or may not be. Sooner than is acceptable for an eighteen-year-old, I come all over myself, but the release doesn't leave me satisfied, I'm still just as confused and pent-up as before I started.

Stripping my cum-soaked shirt from my body, I throw it at the laundry basket and then remove the rest of my clothes. Wrapping a towel around my waist, I head into the bathrooms for another shower.

On my way past the sinks, I catch sight of my neck in the mirror and internally groan. Fuck, it looks like I was attacked by a vampire, there's no fucking hiding this.

Reign Vanderbelt marked me. Left his claim on me and then left before he even told me I was his. I guess Alani is right, he's an asshole. A blond fucking Viking Adonis of an asshole.

Spending more time in the shower than necessary, I finally emerge. Nothing I do is going to cover up the mark on my neck so I say, fuck it. I'll own it. Show him I'm unaffected by his macho bullshit.

Brushing my teeth, I stare at my reflection and sigh, today has been a shit show. I just want it to be done.

I'm okay with my sexuality, everyone knows I'm open about who I hook up with, they all know that I like boys and girls and those I've hooked up with in the past have accepted that. If only my dad was so accepting. When I told him I was bi, I'd never seen him so angry. Apparently, me being with a guy is the devil's work and will bring shame on the Finley family. Mom stood up for me and told Dad to pull his head in, because HE was the one who tarnished the family name. Dear old Dad couldn't keep it in his pants and eventually, that was why Mom left. It feels like he's taking his failure as a husband out on me. Sure, he and Mom had been having issues but fucking her best friend probably wasn't the best idea, even if apparently he was with her before he and Mom got together. It's no excuse, he should have figured out what he wanted before he got married.

It's not my problem, I know what I want in life and I'm not going to hide who I am for the sake of a name, but the same cannot be said for Reign. He clearly still has a lot to figure out and I'm not sure I want to be his test subject, but if I get another session like that with him, I might just forget about him being an asshole and he can test away. He sure knows how to bring a guy to his knees. *Why are the hot ones always fucking assholes?*

Heading back to my room, I flop down onto my bed. My thoughts turn to Reign and why he ran. Is he worried about how his brothers will react if they find out about he and I being together? What would they do? Would they disown him? Beat him up? And that then brings me to my next dilemma, am I the first guy Reign's showed interest in?

Maybe we need to talk, but will he even want to talk to me tomorrow after running out of here so damn fast?

All these thoughts plague my mind until the early hours of the morning, then it all turns to anger and I become pissed. I'm pissed because Reign is taking up my entire mind. I bet he hasn't even thought about me once since walking out.

My last thought before I drift off to sleep, finally, is that he's a fucking Greek god asshole, and I want more of what he gave me yesterday.

"Whoa, what happened to your neck?" Alani asks, reaching for my shirt collar as we walk to class the next morning. I'd pulled it up as high as I could but clearly, it wasn't high enough if Bitsy noticed.

Swatting her hand away, I snap, "Nothing," and tug the collar up higher.

"Yeah, okay, sure. Whatevs." Her tone lets me know she's pissed off I just lied to her. I don't know why I don't just tell her the truth, hell, she might even have advice for me.

"Wow, Finlay, you get attacked by a piranha or something?" Theon taunts, smacking my neck as he walks past.

"Nah, I think it was a vampire," Rian says, laughing as they all pass me. Reign is last and I don't miss the way his gaze lands on my neck. His eyes widen slightly, then drop to the ground. He's clearly embarrassed and his reaction confirms my suspicion. His brothers and friends don't know, and that means I'm most likely his first guy and this will turn into nothing more than an experiment for him.

"Oh, my God," Alani screeches, her gaze flickering back and forth between Reign and me. She opens her mouth to say something, but I quickly slap my hand over her lips, stopping her from saying any more.

"Don't say another word," I hiss.

She nods and crosses her fingers across her chest, her eyes practically bugging out of her head. She licks my palm and I quickly remove it and then she swats my arm. "Why didn't you tell me?"

"Tell you what?" I nonchalantly reply. She eyes me and then drags me into an empty classroom.

"Why didn't you tell me that, that"—she traces her finger of the mark on my neck—"was from Reign?" The look on her face is one of devastation and hurt.

"I don't know, I didn't think it mattered, besides you've got the guy," she scoffs at that, "and you ..." Then I stop because suddenly her reaction all makes sense now. "Is ..."

"Yep," she says.

"Fuck," I sneer, running my hands through my hair. Lacing my fingers together, I lean my head back into my palms. "Bitsy, if I'd known he was ..." Alani stops me with a finger to my lips.

"You're an idiot, Hudson Finley. I'm not upset it's with him, I'm upset I didn't get to see it go down." She pauses and bites her lip. "Lately, I've, umm, done nothing but picture us together. All three of us together."

"Would it sound weird if I said I've pictured that too?"

"Not at all," she replies, grinning in a dirty mischievous way. "So ... he did that?" She runs her fingertip over the bite mark and my body comes alive at her touch.

Nodding, I step back and lean against the wall. "He marked me and didn't even make me come this time, and then he left. Without saying anything, he threw me aside and left me. He regrets it, I know he does."

Sliding down the wall, I lower my gaze and stare at my lap. Alani steps over to me, crouches down, and straddles my thighs. She puts her finger under my chin and lifts her gaze to mine. "I don't think so, I think he's confused. About a lot of things and maybe it will take him some time to figure them out, but you know what?"

"What?"

"You've got me while he figures his shit out. I don't have a dick, but I do have an amazing dildo that we could have some fun with."

That causes me to laugh. She reaches up and cups my face in her hands and then her lips meet mine. Her kiss is soft but it's just what I need. It's perfect. She's perfect. I kiss her back, her taste is an intoxicating combination of arousal and fucking need. The longer we kiss, I realize I need her as much as I need him. I just need to be patient, but in the meantime, she and I can have some fun with her amazing dildo while I, well we, wait for Reign to sort his shit out.

One hand wraps around her throat, the other her waist, and I bring her in closer to me. Sliding my hand up her side, I drag my thumb over her nipple, circling it. She makes a sound so fucking sexy that it should be illegal. She grinds down on me, my cock loving the feel of her heat against him.

Alani's hand works its way under my shirt. Her nails scraping across my abs sends the sensation straight to my dick. I moan into the kiss, my tongue diving deeper into her mouth, until the sound of the bell ringing pulls us apart.

"Fuck," I growl when she pulls back. Alani smiles at me as she climbs off my lap.

"Rain check?" she says, adjusting her skirt and shirt.

"You fucking bet we have a rain check, but one problem …"

"What?" she asks, scrunching her face up in confusion.

"How the fuck am I going to walk around with this all day?" I say, pointing at my cock.

"Just think about this?"

"About what?" I ask her as she opens the door. Before she leaves, she looks over her shoulder. "I'll be walking around in wet panties all day." She blows me a kiss and leaves me sitting here with a rock-hard dick, thinking about her wet pussy.

"Fucking hell," I groan, trying to ease the pressure in my cock before it explodes and leaves a mess. Standing up, I readjust my dick, it's going to be a hard—pun intended—day.

And it was a hard day and my dick only got harder—no pun intended—when I kept playing that make-out session over and over in my head.

ALANI

"YOU ARE AN ASSHOLE, REIGN VANDERBELT," I hiss at him when I see him after school. It's the first time I've seen him since I overheard him talking to his cousins and the things he said about me, they hurt. He's walking around all high and mighty as if his shit doesn't stink and here I am, falling for the asshole. He just wants me, and Hudson, for sex. Hudson and I are better than that so fuck him. "A real fucking asshole."

"Why, thank you," he says with a bow.

He doesn't even realize that he's messing with people's emotions and his nonchalance is the final straw and I snap.

"You Vanderbelts think your shit doesn't stink, well let me tell you, you are the stinkiest of the stinkiest." *Nice barb, Alani, NOT!* I berate myself internally but right now, I'm pissed off and not thinking clearly. "Leave us the fuck alone." Wiping at the tears on my face, I walk away from the guy who I thought I meant something to and to add salt to the wound, he doesn't chase after me. It's clear, I mean nothing to him.

Racing back to my room, I enter and throw myself onto my bed. Crying into my pillow, I let all my frustrations out. A knock on my door startles me. "Go away," I shout into my pillow, but the person ignores my request, opens the door, and steps in.

Without lifting my head, I know it's Hudson. He has this presence when he's in a room and I just know it's him. "Go away, Hudson."

"No," he states, "are you okay?"

"Do I look okay?" I hiss as I sit up and face him.

"Not really, you look like shit."

"Just what a girl wants to hear. Why are you here?"

"I saw you were upset and I wanted to make sure you were okay."

"Yes. No. I don't fucking know."

"Wanna talk about it?"

"Yes. No. I don't fucking know," I repeat again.

"I'm a good listener," he says, walking farther into my room and dropping down next to me.

"He ... he hurt me."

"Who touched you?" he growls, anger swimming in his beautiful eyes.

"Verbally he hurt me, not physically." Not really wanting to talk about him, I change the subject. "How's Lauren doing?" Lauren is Hudson's sister who moved to New York to attend Stepz Academy. She's an amazing dancer and one day I cannot wait to see her on the big stage being the star she was born to be.

"Nice subject change there but she's doing great. Practicing for some big thing coming up in the fall."

"That's awesome. And what about you? What are you up to?"

"Laundry, I'm a few days behind."

"Want some help?" I offer, maybe focusing on that will ease the hurt from Reign blowing me off to his cousins.

"Only if you tell me why you're so sad."

"Dammit, I walked into that one, didn't I?"

"Kinda."

He stares at me, imploring me with his eyes. "I just thought someone I care about cared about me too, but I was wrong, so very wrong."

"I'm sorry," he says, "want me to beat him up for you?"

"Thanks, but he's not worth it." Swallowing, I look at him. "You aren't mad I was with *him*?" It's funny, Hudson and I now both know we're hooking up with Reign, but we can't say his name to each other.

"We aren't exclusive and, as you know, I'm kinda sorta seeing *him* too."

"How do you kinda sorta see someone?"

"It's complicated."

"When isn't love complicated?"

"So, you love this other person?" he asks and I hear hurt in his voice.

"I don't know if it's love but I feel, felt, for him what I feel for you. But hearing that I was nothing more than 'a place to stick it' it hurt."

"Fucker needs a lesson in how to treat a lady." Hearing him come to my defense causes my heart to flutter.

"Orrrr, I could just forget about him and focus on you since I kinda sorta like you."

"I do like that option," he says. "And guess what?"

"What?" I tearfully ask.

"I kinda sorta like you too." He pulls me onto his lap so

I'm straddling him. Draping my arms over his shoulders, I stare into his eyes and get lost. Absentmindedly, I begin to swivel my hips.

"I very much like this option," Hudson whispers, "but can we take a rain check? I have to get to the library, I have a paper due ..."

"And you left it to the last minute ... again."

"You know me too well, Alani."

"That I do, Hudson. How about we have dinner later? Meet you in the cafeteria around seven?"

"It's a date." He kisses me on the tip of the nose, removes me from his lap, and exits my room.

Flopping to my back, I stare up at the ceiling. I'm glad I have Hudson 'cause it makes the hurt of not having *him* not sting as bad.

I still have a few hours till I meet Hudson and when you're upset over a douchehole who hurt you, candy and ice cream is needed. Grabbing my car keys, I decide to head into town for said candy, ice cream, and some retail therapy but of course, fate is a whorebag—thanks, bitch—and as I'm walking to my car, I run into Reign.

"Where are you racing off to?" he asks me.

"Away from you," I spit at him. I quicken my pace, but my little legs and steps are nothing compared to his and he quickly catches up to me. Gripping my arm, he halts me and spins me to face him.

"Hey, what's going on?"

"You have some nerve." I slap him in the chest. "Why don't you go find some other 'place to stick it' as you so eloquently put it earlier."

"That's why you're pissed? Because you heard the tail end of a conversation? Where you missed the part about me saying that in reference to my manwhore of a cousin?"

"Do I look like a fool to you? Just leave me alone, Reign."

Stepping around him, I make it to my car and climb in.

Turning the engine over, I reverse out of my spot and gun it out of the parking lot. Glancing in the rearview mirror, he just stands there and watches me drive away. The farther away I get from him, I begin to wonder if what he said was true. Rian is a manwhore so it is plausible that I only got half the conversation, and if that's true, what if I made a mistake by pushing him away? But if it is true, why didn't he defend himself earlier?

Shaking my head, I turn up the tunes and focus on the road ahead. I can worry about my man troubles at a later date.

REIGN

ALANI CALLED me out on my shit.

She actually called me out.

Not many people ever do that and live to tell the tale but when she did it, it made me take notice. I've been snappy ever since our encounter and dinner with the rents is the last fucking thing I want to do, but it's not worth the wrath if I don't attend so begrudgingly, I walk over to my car and make my way there.

Coming to a stop next to Thatcher's car in my parents' driveway, I turn off the engine and climb out just as Saint gets out of his car grumbling. "I don't understand why we can't just carpool, we're all going to the same fucking place coming from the same fucking place."

Thatch and I watch as he storms up the front stairs. It seems I'm not the only one in a mood tonight.

Saint knocks and then our parents' longtime butler opens the door welcoming us. "Welcome home, boys." I see the moment the word 'home' hits my brothers' ears because it isn't our home, it hasn't been a home for a long time, this is more of a prison. And I thank the Lords—pun intended—for allowing us to stay at school.

As soon as we cross the threshold, I can feel the air shift. Something is wrong and the moment we walk into the dining room and our mother stands and singsongs, "My babies are home," I don't need to know anymore.

"Are you taking your meds, Mom?" Saint asks as he pulls away from her hug.

Mom waves him off, I know she hates it when we baby her. "Oh hush, Saint. I'm perfectly fine and I do not need my child telling me what I should be doing." She grips his cheek lovingly and smiles at him. Her smile used to light up the room, now it's dull and lifeless.

"Mom," Thatcher says just as Father walks in, killing any chance of us finding out what the fuck is going on with her. She scurries away from us, kissing our father on the cheek before she sits, letting him push her chair in.

Fuck, it's going to be a long night.

Hendrix leans toward Thatcher and they both whisper between themselves.

"Is Crestwood still tip-top?" Father's voice booms breaking them apart. Even all these years later, his voice still holds power over us. We give each other a wide-eyed look waiting for him to berate us for whispering at the table, but nothing comes. *What the fuck?*

"Yes, Dad, everything is fine. The Lords still rule."

Looking at Thatch, I eye him in that 'you need to tell him'

kind of way but the fucker just picks at his plate, not meeting Dad's gaze after saying everything is fine, and apart from the Remy issue and my issues, plural, everything at school is fine.

"Is there something you want to tell me?" Dad murmurs. His tone is low and even, scaring the shit out of me. He leans his elbows on the table and steeples his fingers, his expression severe. His gaze filters across us all. Saint keeps his head down, his gaze lifting slowly toward Hendrix. Sharing a look, Saint goes back to playing with the food on his plate.

When no one says anything, Dad ominously says, "You know exactly what I'm talking about, Thatcher. Care to share?"

Clearly, he does know, I don't know why he doesn't just come out with it. It's always a performance with him.

Thatcher clears his throat and answers with two words. "Remington Hearst."

We wait for a response, but he just glares at Thatch and then shocks us when he throws his head back and laughs, he actually chuckles. "I can't believe she actually thinks she can fuck with me." His amused tone and cackle confuses the four of us. "First her son and now this." My ears prick at the mention of Arlen but then again, he could also be referring to Grayson. "After that lil' shit killed himself," okay, he's referring to Arlen, "Rochelle became desperate. That bitch would do just about anything, and I mean anything to make sure her children have it all. Manipulation is a running trait in the Hearst family. Remington is a whore just like her mother, and no doubt a cunt like her brothers and father." He pauses and steeples his fingers once again, sitting there like the pompous jackass he is, but we all straighten and focus because Dad suddenly hates Rochelle? What are the Hearsts up to now? "It'd be in your best interest to keep your distance from that girl. I wouldn't want anything to happen to her ... or you for that matter."

Our eyes all widen, did he just threaten us? His own sons? And what's he alluding to?

Throwing his napkin on the table, he stands abruptly. "I think I've had enough for one night." He turns to leave, but Thatcher finally finds his voice.

"Do you know what this is?" He holds out his phone to show the picture he took of a medallion we found. Dad stalks over and looks at the screen, his eyes widen and his face turns red with anger the longer he stares at the image. The veins on his neck protrude, pulsing rapidly.

"Where did you get that?" he demands.

"Found it," Thatcher snarls, angering him further. I don't know why he doesn't just say we found it at the cliffs, but if I know my brother, he'll have a plan and will only reveal what he thinks is necessary.

"If I were you, Son, I'd forget ever finding that medallion. It'll only lead to bad things."

Shaking his head, he storms out of the room and like a programmed robot, Mother stands, comes around the table, and kisses each of us on the top of our heads before she walks from the dining room, following Father.

"We need to find out the significance of that fucking medallion," Hendrix hisses, munching on a bean. "It might hold some answers." I hate lying to my brothers, but I can't tell them I think it's Arlen's because I'm not one hundred percent sure. Yes, I've seen one on him, but I swear I've seen one somewhere else too. I can't say anything because it will lead to questions and it's questions I don't want to answer just yet.

Saint shrugs, throwing his napkin on top of his empty plate. "Or leave us with more questions."

"I say we do some digging, and in the meantime, we keep our eyes on Remington," Thatcher murmurs.

Swallowing deeply, I bite my lip. "I ... I think I have some answers regarding what Father was talking about."

"What?" Thatcher snaps.

Grabbing my phone, I swipe at the screen and stare at it, lifting my gaze to my brothers, I tell them what just came in. "I just got sent a link."

"A link to what?" Hendrix asks.

Fuck this, I can't be here anymore. With dinner over, I push back from the table and walk away, heading for the exit. Silently, my brothers follow and once we're outside and standing on the front porch, Thatcher reaches out and grabs my arm. "What the fuck are you hiding?"

"Just look." I hold my phone out toward them and watch them and one by one, they react.

"Fuck," Hendrix curses beside me.

Remington is here for us and now that it's been confirmed, Thatcher is going to lose his shit, but if I know my brother, he'll have a plan. He always has a plan, but all our plans are thwarted when a few weeks later, Dad is murdered. Someone shot him. The killer is still out there, and we are no closer to finding out who it was and to be honest, none of us give a shit. Thornton Vanderbelt was a cunt and the world is better off without him.

Maybe without him breathing down our necks, we can be who we want to be but the question remains, who am I and what do I want?

ALANI

RACING TO ENGLISH, I have a little pep in my step. That make-out session with Hudson just now was on fire, I'm ready to combust and even though I want to junk punch Reign right now, I still want him too. *What's wrong with me?* Being the meat in a Hudson and Reign sandwich would be ah-may-zing and I HAVE, just have to make that happen.

"What's got you grinning like a creepy clown?" Remy asks, dropping into the seat next to me. Remington Hearst, or Remy as she likes to be called, is the new girl at Crestwood Prep. She and I connected immediately when Quinn ditched her. Quinn was appointed to show her around, but Quinn is being weird at the moment. Her and Hendrix are clearly off-again cause bitchy Quinn is in the house. She needs to be fucked good and hard cause trust me, a good fucking does wonders for the soul.

"If I tell you, I'd have to kill you and I kinda like you, so I really don't want to have to kill you."

"Well thank you, I don't feel like dying today so I appreciate that. And for the record, I like you too, Alani Thomas."

"So kiss her," some jerkwad from behind shouts, my guess is Rian. Flipping the bird behind me, I ignore the fucker, but someone grabs my finger and bites it.

"Flip that at me again and I'll bite it harder next time," Reign says, coming around and leaning on my desk.

"Bite me again and I'll snap your dick off."

"You won't," he matter-of-factly states.

"And why won't I?"

"Because you want to feel it sliding into your cunt."

I feel brave so I lean into his ear and whisper, "It's fine, I have Hudson's dick for that." He swallows audibly, hunger flaring in his eyes so I decide to test the waters. "You should join us sometime." Pulling back, I stare into his gorgeous eyes, and I see they are blazing now. *Holy shit*, he's thinking about me and Hudson and him together. "What do you say, huh?" But before he can reply, Mrs. Plunkett calls for everyone to take their seats.

Reign just stands there, staring at me.

"Mr. Vanderbelt, unless you want a lunchtime detention, I suggest you take your seat and open up *Romeo and Juliet* to where we left off yesterday and begin to read. There will be a pop quiz in fifteen minutes."

Everyone moans and groans. No one likes a pop quiz.

Seems Mrs. Plunkett was dicking with us because there was no pop quiz, but she did tell us that for our assessment, we need to write a thousand-word essay and discuss how the individual characters of *Romeo and Juliet* are presented in Acts

1 and 2 and how this forms their relationship. We are to use relevant quotes from the play to support our discussion, but we are not to regurgitate the play word for word. That earns a groan from the guys behind us.

"Wanna meet in the library after school and smash this out?" I whisper to Remy.

"Yes, but this is easy. I love R and J."

"I love Leo as Romeo in the remake."

"Oh. My. God. Yes, he was so hot in that film."

"Right? I also loved him in *Titanic* and I wanted him and Kate Winslet to get married in real life. They are perfect for each other."

"True, but sometimes your soulmate is your best friend and not your lover."

"That's very philosophical of you," I tell my new friend.

She shrugs. "It is what it is."

"You are very peculiar, Remy Hearst."

"Why thank you, Alani Thomas."

After class, I watch Remy as we step into the cafeteria. Her eyes widen as she takes in the room. As with all things at Crestwood, everything is over the top. Our cafeteria reminds me of a 3-star Michelin restaurant. The tables are covered with white tablecloths and the chefs, yes chefs, here are top-notch.

With our food in hand, Remy and I make our way to a table. I can feel him staring at me, but I do everything I can to ignore him, but I have to face them when Remy asks, "Who are they?" Nodding her head toward the back corner.

Looking over my shoulder, I take in the four assholes. "The Lords of Crestwood Prep," I whisper, not wanting him to know I'm talking about him.

"The Lords, really?" she questions, her reaction is like every new student who arrives here. You watch those movies with the preppy assholes who rule all and you think that only happens in TV land but unfortunately for us, it happens here too.

"Really, really. Thatcher, Hendrix, Reign, and Saint Vanderbelt, they run this school. Nothing happens without their say-so."

"Who died and made them king shit?" Another million-dollar question.

Shrugging at her, I pick up a fry and take a bite. "The Vanderbelts have reigned over this school and town for eons now. My advice, ignore them, Remy. Run if they approach you but whatever you do, stay the fuck away from them." She nods but she glances back over at them and a look washes over her, she's intrigued, clearly she's not heeding my warning. "I'm serious, don't get sucked into their vortex." Looking back over at them, I find myself staring at Reign. He gives me a look that has my insides thrumming. Shaking away that thought, I focus back on Remy, who is still focused on them, Thatcher in particular. "Remy, they will suck you in, chew you up, and spit you out without blinking an eye."

"Speaking from experience?" she asks me.

"Kinda sorta," I reply with a nod. "But let's not focus on that, just stay away from them." Not wanting to talk about the Lords anymore, I jump up to get more fries, standing up to join the line. Of course, he decides to join the line too and being a Lord, he cuts in behind me. No one says a word about the line cutting because a Lord does what a Lord wants but this one will NEVER do me again.

"You look beautiful today," he purrs from behind me. The comment is a little confusing. If I'm just 'a place to stick it' why does he give a flying fuck what I look like? Just fuck me from behind and you don't have to worry about what I look like.

"I always look beautiful," I inform him, not looking back at him, even though the urge to glance over my shoulder at him is strong. Don't do it, Alani, don't give him the satisfaction of seeing how much he affects you.

"That you do. We should catch up later."

"I'm busy ... washing my hair."

"I'm happy to help. You know, help wash you in those hard-to-reach places." He slides his hand down my side, reaching around to cup me between my legs but I grip his hand, stopping him.

Swallowing deeply, I'm finding it really hard to ignore him right now, but I need to be strong, girl power and all that shit. There's a pull between us and even through the hurt, my traitorous body and vagina still want him.

"What do you say," he leans in and whispers. His heated breath fans over my neck. "Wanna get wet with me, Red?"

REIGN

I'M SO hot for her right now. Ever since she laid into me, I have thought about her nonstop. About her wanting to angry fuck me. I'm tempted to throw her down on the nearest flat surface and fuck her senseless, the fact we're in the middle of the cafeteria isn't even crossing my mind. All I can think about is sinking myself deep in her cunt. Hell, her hatred for me right now is such a turn-on.

Speaking of hatred, Thatcher is currently glaring in Remington and Alani's direction, but the two of them pay him no attention. If looks could kill, right now, those two would be dead and turned to ash, and then for added pissedoffness, he'd piss on their decaying corpses. Grabbing my lunch, I head for our table. Watching Alani talk to the new girl and befriending her isn't going to end well. From the grinding of his jaw as I drop down next to him, my big bro doesn't like this, not one fucking bit.

Before I dive into my fettuccine carbonara, I throw the folder down in front of him that I brought with me, then take a bite of my pasta. As I chew, my eyes find her, and fuck, I can't get her out of my head.

Thatcher ignores the folder and his burger and continues to glare at Remington Hearst.

Surprising me, it's Hendrix who breaks first. "She has a lot of fucking nerve laughing like her family hasn't caused us shit." He glares at her and it rivals Thatcher's stare. Pushing his chair back, he growls, "Fuck this, I need to find Quinn." And like the caveman he is, he grabs her, pulls her out of her seat, and drags her toward the hall. Taking off with her, most likely to fuck her wild somewhere.

Not that I'm jealous per se. Okay, I'm totally fucking jealous because the girl sitting across the room from me has occupied my mind since the first time I kissed her and I want, no I need fucking more. And the other person currently occupying my thoughts, stands up and places his tray on the wash-up counter—no grimy trolley here, we have a busboy on hand to take the dirty dishes and immediately wash them. He then turns toward the exit and heads through the cafeteria doors.

Scoffing my carbonara down, I stand and leave my shit to follow Hudson. Without a goodbye to my brothers, I chase after him but I see Red in line for more food so I make a slight detour ... maybe I can get her to join Hudson and me, fuck, that would be all my fucking dreams coming true.

Cutting the line, I stop behind her and lean into her personal space. After breathing her in, I say to her, "You look beautiful today."

She turns on her heel and says, "I always look beautiful."

And her sass turns me the fuck on. I was ready to fuck her when I saw her earlier, but now, that need has intensified. When I notice some freshmen motherfucker staring at her, I force a glare his way, making him cower into himself. I know I don't want anyone else to see what's mine, so I do the responsible thing and I don't fuck her in the middle of the cafeteria. "We should catch up later," I whisper after agreeing that she's always gorgeous.

"I'm busy ... washing my hair," she snaps, she's still pissed at me it seems. Not exactly sure what I did to deserve this but whatever the case, my dick is still hard for her.

"I'm happy to help. You know, help wash you in those hard-to-reach places."

The need to touch her overwhelms me, I slide my hand between her thighs cupping her pussy. I can feel the heat of her cunt through her skirt, but she grabs my wrist and stops me. I know she wants me, I can tell from the way she's breathing, I wish she'd look over her shoulder at me. No doubt, her eyes will be glazed and her cheeks pink with desire.

Stepping closer to her, I press my cock into her ass. "What do you say, wanna get wet with me, Red?"

"Not a chance in hell, asshole." But I can tell she's lying. Her breaths are labored and her cheeks are flushed.

She thrusts her ass at me—not in a good way—grabs her fries and marches away from me. Standing here, I hold up the food line and watch her swing that delectable ass from side to side as she storms away.

Readjusting my dick, I shake off the rejection just now and exit the cafeteria in search of Hudson, hoping that he and I can talk ... or more, especially since Red got me so hot and bothered just now.

When I exit the cafeteria, he's nowhere in sight, the halls are empty.

"Fuck," I hiss.

Turning around, I head to the library to see if he's there. He always seems to be there but after a quick search of the place, I don't see him so I head back inside to finish my lunch.

That afternoon, my brothers and I are standing in a circle, discussing Grayson Hearst. Thatcher is once again on edge, he wants to know what happened to Arlen and he has it in his head that Grayson knows. I want to know what really happened too because I don't for one minute believe he jumped. But how the fuck can his brother, who wasn't even here, know anything? I know we're missing something but what?

As they all discuss various ways to get Grayson here, my mind goes to the place it always does. I'm so different from my brothers. Where they all have dark hair and eyes, I'm blond with blue eyes. They are all angry assholes and me, I'm the softie with a side of angry asshole when it's called for.

It's something that's always bothered me, why am I so different than my brothers?

"We need to get him to visit. We get him here and then we take action," Saint says, snapping my attention back to the present but a gasp echoes through the halls, making us all turn in the direction it came from.

Remington Hearst is peeking around the corner. Her eyes are wide and before any of us can react, she takes off. Surprising me, Saint is the one to take off after her.

Fuck, this isn't going to end well. Thatcher is already willing to kill our classmate Brennan for just talking to her, so hopefully Saint is prepared to feel his wrath for talking to 'his Peach' too. A smile graces my face at the thought of seeing

Thatcher and Saint get into it, their tussle might pull me out of this funk I find myself in so I take off after them. Fighting or fucking is my outlet and since fucking is off the table until I figure my shit out, fighting it is. When Saint comes back, it's fight time.

"The fuck you chasin' her for?" Thatcher growls, gripping Saint's shirt and shoving him into the lockers beside us.

Before Saint even opens his mouth, I just know whatever he's about to say has me fearing for his life because where Remy is concerned, Thatcher is psychotic.

"Just warning your little peach to forget what she heard and to fuck off."

Three.

Two.

One.

"She's off-limits," Thatcher snarls at him.

Saint clearly has a death wish but surprising me, he bites his tongue. Ignoring him, he shoulder checks Thatch and storms off. Him not picking a fight with our brother is not Saint-like at all. Something is off with our brother and like the rest of us, he's not open to talking. Must be a family trait. I almost scoff at my thoughts.

Thatcher looks ready to end Saint, but the warning in Hendrix's voice is clear when he says, "Leave him be. Something's up with him."

We know he's right. When it comes to Saint, he needs to explode and self-destruct before we can help him, but this time, I think we need to intervene before that happens. "We need to deal with whatever he has going on before he explodes."

Thatcher nods but right now, Thatcher is all about his peach, so I know it's going to be up to Hendrix and me to fix our brother, and that thought is confirmed when he says, "Let's deal with one thing at a time."

Sighing, I nod and focus back on problem number one. "You know he's right, Thatch. She heard something."

"I don't trust her," Hendrix growls.

"She's a Hearst. What do you fucking expect?" Thatcher snarls.

"Regardless of what she heard, none of what we just said is incriminating in any way whatsoever. But what do we do?"

Thatcher looks over at Hendrix and me. "We stick to the plan. We keep an eye on her." Thatch reaches out and squeezes my shoulder. "Reign, you take command, befriend her but don't be too friendly and whatever you do, don't let her out of your sight."

Saluting him, he nods and then takes off to who knows where. Me? I head to the library. I drop my books down on the table and sigh, doing this assignment is the last thing on my mind, but I know unless I want detention it needs to get done. I'm waiting for Rian to get here since he's my partner, but I have no doubt that I'll be doing most of the work. Rian likes to pay people to do his work for him. I mean, he's a Vanderbelt. Why not use it, and his charm, to get what he wants?

Opening *Romeo and Juliet* to the first act, my eyes already hurt from staring at the words. Thank fuck we don't speak like that anymore.

"You are some piece of work, Reign Vanderbelt," Hudson snarls over me. His arms are crossed over his chest and his glare while intimidating to some, just has me smiling.

"This isn't funny," he snaps, and my smile widens. "Why the fuck did you run?"

My chair knocks over behind me when I stand. Gripping Hudson's arm, I drag him into the corner, out of earshot of the other students here before he opens his mouth about my personal shit.

"Do you fucking mind?" I sneer, clenching my teeth.

Hudson shakes me off and it causes his shirt collar to

move, showing me his neck. My gaze drops to where I left my mark on him.

"Yes I do, Reign, what are you afraid of? Why did you run like you fucking regretted me and why the fuck—"

Reaching up, I snap and wrap my hand around his throat. He doesn't get to speak to me like that. "I don't regret it, you asshole, I'm fucking scared."

"Of what?" he asks and from his tone, I know he means it. He genuinely cares about what I have to say.

"I'm scared of people knowing my shit."

"And you think I'm going to blast it to the whole school that you're gay?"

"I'm not fucking gay, okay? I'm not, I mean, fuck. I'm bi but I don't need you forcing me to come out, and I certainly don't need this fucking pressure from you. Okay?" Releasing my grip on his neck, I begin to pace back and forth. My fingers twist in my hair, tugging at the ends in frustration. "Fuck," I hiss.

"I'm not trying to out you, Reign. I'm trying to help," he says, and his words really hit home. I struggle to breathe for a moment, I can't do this.

"Hey." Hudson pulls my hands from my hair, stopping me from pulling it out in chunks. He takes my hand in his and squeezes. Dropping my gaze, I stare down at where our hands are joined. Hudson's thumb rubs over my palm and a jolt runs through me, I know he feels it too.

Lifting my head again, I smirk. "I like seeing my mark on you." Reaching up, I touch the side of his neck, he gasps when my finger begins tracing over the red mark on his skin.

"Reign," he whispers, his voice breaking.

"I just need more time." I swallow the lump building in my throat.

Tears fill my eyes and I know if Arlen hadn't gone maybe this wouldn't be so hard. Of course, it wouldn't because he and I would have finally come out as a couple.

"I like you," I tell Hudson and swallow again. "I really like you."

"I like you too," he repeats.

Silently, we stare at one another and then he pulls me to him. Wrapping me in his arms, he holds me like I'm a small child, running circles over my back while his other hand runs through the back of my hair.

Lifting my head up from his chest, I turn my lips toward his, needing him right now. Slipping my hand between us, my fingers fist the bottom of his shirt, tugging him closer to me.

Our lips brush together. Our tongues clash as our kiss heats up. Thrusting my hips into his, I reach down, gripping his cock but Hudson pulls back, pushing me away from him and putting way too much fucking space between us. "I wanna fuck your ass so fucking bad."

My words cause his eyes to widen. "This isn't about getting laid, Reign," he growls, he's angry and pissed off at me. "It's about you owning who you are. Once you accept who you are, only then will I let you fuck my ass, until then, I'm sorry, I can't."

His words are a slap to the face, but I know he's right. I can't keep using him to make myself feel good. I need to figure my shit out before I possibly ruin the best thing to happen to me since Arlen.

Really not in the mood to do this assignment now, I text Rian and tell him I need a rain check. Not that the fucker cares since he isn't here, but he takes my cancellation as code for I'm getting laid because his reply tells me to 'wrap it before I tap it.'

Taking a walk, I head up to the cliffs and when I get there, I see Remy. She's so much like Arlen, it sometimes hurts to be around her.

"I miss you, Arlen," she whispers into the night sky and before I can stop myself, I murmur, "I miss him too."

The sound of my voice startles her. Taking a step back, I stay hidden in the shadows. No one can know my secret, least of all her, but being up here with her makes me feel close to him. "He loved you so much," I tell her, confused as to why I'm engaging with the enemy.

"And I loved him dearly," she whispers and once again, I speak before I can stop myself.

"Me too."

I need to get out of here before I say something that will incriminate me, but at the same time, I don't want to. I feel at peace up here with her. "Who are you?" she asks, breaking the silence.

"I'm your worst nightmare," I tell her before I spin around and vanish into the shadows.

Heading back to my room, I climb into bed but sleep eludes me. My mind is a jumbled mess right now and I keep asking myself the same questions. What do I want with Hudson? Alani? Did I really love Arlen or was it just a thrill to do something that would piss dear old Dad off?

Eventually, I drift off, but when I wake the next morning, I'm still confused, and when I meet up with my brothers, I become even more confused.

When I enter English class, I smile when I see Alani with her head in her book, paying no one any attention. Bending close to her ear, I can't help myself and whisper, "You look so fuckable today."

She jumps, but when she sees it's me, she shoves me away from her. "No," she hisses and drops her focus back to her book.

"Come on, Red." I pout. "Just a little taste," I whisper.

Leaning into her ear, I bite down on her earlobe. "You know you want it. You want my cock to slide between your lips, face or cunt, and you want me to fuck you until you are a breathless panting mess."

Her head snaps up and she looks around the class checking our classmates haven't heard our X-rated conversation. "Reign Vanderbelt, you have a one-track mind and unluckily for you, your dick isn't coming anywhere near my lips, face or pussy. Now, sit the fuck down and leave me alone."

Fuck, she's hot when she's bossy. Leaning toward her again, my cock at half-mast, I growl, "Yes, Miss Thomas."

She slaps her hand on my bicep and I laugh, taking my seat right behind her. Leaning back in my chair, I stare at her. She peeks over her shoulder at me, her red hair falling to one side.

Winking at her, I place two fingers over my lips then use my tongue in a swiping motion back and forth until her cheeks turn the cutest shade of fucking pink.

Mrs. Plunkett enters, halting my explanation of what I'd like to do to her, but I'm happy to pick this up later.

The teacher starts rambling about today's class, but I'm not paying attention to her. My attention is locked on Hudson as he enters and takes the only seat free, which just so happens to be across from me.

Leaning my head on my hand, I peek under my arm looking over at him, the hickey I left still sits permanently on his neck. The thought that in a few days it'll start to disappear makes me want to mark him again, ensuring he always walks around with my mark, showing everyone he's off-limits. But Hudson won't let me near him again, not until I sort myself out and I haven't the slightest idea on where to fucking start with that.

REIGN

… a few weeks later

FUCK. Is any of this real? Is he real?

If I didn't see him with my own eyes, I never would have believed it, but Arlen is here. Alive. When I stepped into this room, I never fucking expected to find Rem with her brothers, one of which was supposedly dead.

I'll be honest, when Remy went missing and that fucker, Brennan, locked us in the secret room, I didn't have high hopes that we'd find her alive and I'm sure Thatch thought the same. With the two of them now a couple, they were inseparable and now we know that she isn't the enemy, we got to know her. Some of us more so than others, much to Brennan's disgust. He was trying to get into Rem's pants from the beginning but Thatcher beat him to the punch and, well, he went crazy after that. I always knew the fucker was unhinged but him teaming up with Rochelle Hearst and doing whatever she demanded, that was next level psychotic. Never in my wildest dreams did I expect that.

My fingers itched to touch him just to be sure I wasn't hallucinating, and the moment our gazes connected, a lump formed in my throat and with a few blinks of his eyes, I knew I wasn't lost in a dream, he was really there.

He didn't end his life.

Arlen is here.

I know I kissed him a few hours earlier but I'm still in disbelief. It can't be real. No way, there's no way I'm looking at him right now, no fucking way. I must be dreaming. If it wasn't for the cops and my brothers around us, I wouldn't believe it.

The pounding in my chest makes it hard to breathe as he stares at me.

Everything stills.

He's alive.

Arlen's alive.

Slowly coming toward me, Arlen walks with so much fucking swagger that I almost remember how good we were together.

"Hey," he murmurs.

"Hey," I breathe softly.

Lifting his hand, he sweeps his thumb under my eye, catching the tear I hadn't realized was falling.

"I'm so sorry," Arlen murmurs.

His hand drops the moment mine wipes across my face. He's here.

The loss of his touch brings back so many memories, so much pain.

Our fingers brush again, but the jolt that used to zap through me every time he touched me is absent.

I feel nothing. Nothing except pain.

The pain of losing him is still there but it's different now.

He's not the same, even I can see that. He's changed and so have I.

I can't do this. I can't be around him and not hate him for leaving me, for making me believe he'd done the unthinkable when in reality, he was alive the whole fucking time.

Taking a step back, I need to get away from him. I can't do this right now. I go to move around him, but my steps falter when his fingers brush against mine. His touch yet again doesn't spark anything inside me, and instead, it brings back all the hurt of losing him.

"One day I hope you'll let me explain." His voice rumbles, and without another word, he walks away from me, leaving me confused and hurt.

It's funny, it hurts more now than when he 'died' and I don't know how to process my feelings. Watching him walk away, I don't know how I feel, but we need to focus on the now and the fucked-up mess of what just went down.

A few hours later, we're all in my room, just hanging out. Thatcher has just returned from the hospital and was given the all-clear. Thankfully, Brennan didn't do any major damage, but he will be sore for a few days. Remy, Arlen, and Grayson are still at the station, awaiting Rochelle's arrival.

We're passing a bottle of tequila around because tequila is needed right now. Hendrix takes a swig and then looks at me, and I know what's coming as soon as I see him open his mouth. "Anyone else want to know why Reign and Arlen sucked face back there?" All eyes turn to me, but before I can answer, he asks the other question I knew would follow. "Are you gay? What about girls?"

"My sexuality is a story for another time," I tell him. Snatching the bottle from his hands, I take another swig.

"Will there be tequila?" Saint questions, causing me to laugh and snort tequila through my nose. Trust him to make a joke regarding something serious, but it also eases my apprehension over telling them.

"No doubt there will be." I pause and wonder if tequila will make it all better, but I know it won't because all tequila does is make you do stupid things and give you a killer hangover the next day. "I just wanna say, I'm still me ... I just—"

"No need to explain, bro," Thatcher says, squeezing the back of my neck in that 'it's all good' kind of way. "Just know we're here when you're ready to talk."

Nodding, I take another mouthful and pass the bottle to him.

Leaning back, the rest of them start talking about the events of the night, the focus no longer on me and I'm thankful for that. I still have a lot to process—Arlen, Red, Hudson. Me. So much to process. Looking around at my brothers and friends, I notice that we're still us, that kiss they witnessed hasn't changed a thing. I don't know why I'm so scared to share my secret with them because deep down I know they'll accept it, and me. But before I confess all, I need to figure a few things out and I know exactly what I need, I need to talk to Mom again.

It was another week before I got the chance to sneak away to see Mom. After discovering Arlen alive, things took another sinister turn when Remy's mom took Thatcher and tried to Fight Club him away, and then we discovered some things about Dad that shocked us even more.

Even from the grave, he's fucking with us, asshole. You'd think when someone dies—thank you who ever murdered him—life would move on smoothly but no, Thornton Vanderbelt is still fucking with us. I bet he's down in hell laughing at all of us, as we uncover all his secrets and betrayals.

With life beginning to get back on track and Thatch finally out of the woods, after his *Fight Club* ordeal, it's time to focus on myself so I head over to Mom's place for that chat I need.

It's still mind-blowing that Rem's mom was the leader and mastermind to an illegal underground cage fighting ring. I thought our family was fucked up but man, the Hearsts are fifty shades of fucked up—and if you mention to anyone I referenced *Fifty Shades of Grey*, I'll deny it ... and then kill you.

Pulling into the driveway, I realize that that sense of dread is no longer there. I know I should be upset that Dad died, but I'm not. The fucker who killed him did us all a favor.

Walking inside, Lisette is coming down the stairs and I'm greeted with a smile and a hug from her. "She's in the sitting room," she tells me, "and before you ask, she's doing good. Real good." She squeezes my hand and heads toward the kitchen, no doubt to fix me a snack because Lisette knows what I like. Guess that happens when she pretty much raised me.

"Baby," Mom coos and stands up to wrap her arms around me when I walk over to her.

"Hey, Mom," I say, kissing her cheek and dropping onto the sofa next to her.

"This is a nice surprise." Mom smiles, and you can actually see it in her eyes, and I find myself smiling back at her. Lisette was right, she IS doing well. Who knew we just needed someone to murder Dad for that to happen? "What are you doing here?" she asks, pulling me from the gleeful thoughts of my father's death, and reminding me I need to swing by and piss on his grave. Yes, pissing on a dead man's grave is abhorrent, but the man was the devil incarnate so I think I'm allowed to celebrate his passing.

"I umm," I begin but stop the moment I realize I have to say everything out loud, "I ..."

"Reign, sweetheart, what is it?" Mom asks. She sits up straighter and reaches over to take my hand and squeezes it.

Squeezing it in return, I take a deep breath, "I ... I have to tell you something and I also need some advice."

Before I can tell her anything, Lisette returns with a snack for me, a pitcher of iced tea, and two glasses. She places the tray down, and Mom goes about filling up our glasses. It's nice to see Mom drinking something non-alcoholic in the middle of the day for a change. Mom hands me my drink and then she sits back and stares at me. "Okay, what do you need to tell me? And then we can get on to the advice of your dilemma."

Without thinking, I just blurt it out. "I'm bisexual, and I'm in love with two people and the two someones I told you about, it's a girl," I pause, "and a guy."

Mom nods, processing my words. The silence is unnerving, but I can't begrudge her for that, it's a lot to process and take in. She leans forward and places her glass down. "And these two people, they make you happy?"

"Yeah, Mom, they do," I reply with a nod and a smile. "Really fucking happy and together, I think we could be everything." Mom shakes her head at my swearing, but my brothers swear all the time. Hell, I'm pretty sure Thatcher's first word was fuck, or maybe it was Saint. Either way, swearing came to us as easily as the ABCs.

"I love it when you smile like that." She reaches over and cups my cheek. I love these moments with her. Even when she was drinking heavily, she and I always had our moments together. I don't remember smiling much when I was little, and Father never gave us any reason to smile the last few years, but she's right, since admitting my feelings for Alani and Hudson, I have been smiling and I want to take what I have separately with them and bring the three of us together. But is that even possible?

"You used to smile all the time when you were younger, it's nice to see it back on your handsome face again." My cheeks heat at her words, no man wants to hear his mom tell him about his looks. "You are a very handsome young man, it's no wonder you found two people. Now, tell me all about them."

"Just like that?" I question. "No, the Bible is a man and a woman, not a man, man, and woman."

"Do I look like the Bible abiding type of woman?" I shake my head. "Exactly, and at the end of the day as long as you're happy, that's all that matters to me. I don't care if you have a harem of men and women. Your happiness and theirs is all that matters. Now, tell me all about them."

"Well, their names are Alani and Hudson. We all individually care for one another, but I think the three of us together could be amazing, but I don't know if I will get that."

"Why do you say that?"

"Because I'm scared. I've done things that inadvertently hurt them but, Mom, I need them, I need them to calm me. I need them to tell me they feel the same way I do. I just need them."

"Well, there's only one way to find out, Reign. Be honest with them, but you have to understand they may not want to share and may not need you in the way you need them."

"And that's what I'm scared of, Mom. I lost the first person I ever loved. Well, now they're back, but we can never be."

"You were in love with the Hearst boy, weren't you?"

Her question shocks me, but at the same time, it doesn't. Mom knows me better than anyone. Even when she was in la-la land when Dad was alive, she still cared about me and my brothers. "How did you know?"

"I'm your mother, I know more than you think. Whenever the Hearsts, and specifically him, were mentioned, you'd clam up. You'd get this look on your face, and I can vividly remember the time your father made a comment when he died, well apparently died, you were crestfallen at how callous he was. He was always saying harsh things about other people but on this day, it affected you deeply. You were crushed. I was hoping you'd come to me, but you never did, until now." Nodding, I take in her words, she really is a good mom, all things considered. "I'm guessing you and he will never be?"

Shaking my head, I bite my lip. "He doesn't want me anymore, and to be honest, I don't know if I can get over the betrayal of him faking his death. I thought we had something special, but he left me and now he's back, he still can't be honest with me. He just keeps saying sorry, like those five letters will fix the hurt."

"Maybe he needs time, Reign. Something major must have happened for him to walk away and fake his death. He not only left you, but he also left his family."

"I guess you're right."

"Give him time, and I'm sure when he's ready, he'll talk."

We both fall silent, and the silence is broken when the alarm on Mom's phone goes off. "I'm sorry, baby, but I have to get going. I have an appointment at the spa this afternoon."

"I'm glad you're doing things for yourself again."

"Me too, and maybe you should take your own advice. Voice your wants to Alani and Hudson. You might be surprised by what the outcome is."

"Thanks, Mom." I lean over and hug her. She hugs me back, and I somehow know everything will turn out. "Love you, Mom," I whisper.

"Love you too, baby. Once you have everything sorted, I want to meet the lucky lady and guy who have stolen your heart."

"Will do, Mom."

We say our goodbyes and as I drive back to school, I feel much lighter. I should have spoken with Mom long ago. As I pull into my spot at school, I decide I will broach the topic of a three-way relationship … soon … or when I grow a pair. After all, you can't rush love.

ARLEN

SITTING IN THE LIVING ROOM, my family all stares at me. My brother and sister want answers and Dad, well, he can get fucked. Our mother wasn't the only cunt in this family. He's not as bad as her, but he comes in a close second. Our father is a lying piece of shit but without him, I never would have been able to pull off my suicide, and it all would have been fine if that Brennan fucker and Mom hadn't discovered me. That was an unforeseeable hiccup in my plan, but I think now I can make it work to my advantage, as long as dear ol Dad sticks to the plan.

"I don't understand. Why didn't you talk to me?" Remy

mutters softly.

"Or at least me," Grayson dejectedly adds.

I know I hurt them, and it's evident by the looks on their faces they are still angry, but they don't know the real me. No one does. Sure, when we were all living under the one roof we were close, but there was also an invisible wall separating me from them.

This distance now, it's for their own good. I can't have them getting caught in the crossfire of my actions, actions that saw me do something I never thought I would do but I think it was for the best.

"I'm sorry." I swallow, staring at my brother and sister.

Dad clears his throat, and it irks me that he's here, but to keep up appearances, I need him by my side. After all, he was the one to 'help me.' "He did what he thought was necessary," he says, but his coming to my defense pisses me off.

"I thought I had no other option," I cry, my tone somber. "Being who I was, I felt …" but I drift off and stare into the distance. I know exactly who I am, but for what I have planned, I need everyone to think the opposite of me.

"You never have to hide who you are, Arl, not from us." Remy looks over at Grayson, and he nods in agreement.

"I know," I mumble, *but the voices told me I had to.*

"We love you," Remy tells me, coming over to sit next to me. She takes my hand and I know she's telling the truth. Jellybean sees the good in everyone, and when the corner of my mouth lifts into a grin, she returns it.

"Love you too, Jellybean," I say. Her smile widens at the use of the nickname I gave her when we were kids.

We fall into easy chatter, and before long, it's time for them to go when Grayson looks at Remy. "We need to get back, Rem." Grayson hates getting deep with anything so this will be overwhelming for him—*Us too,* the voice confirms in my head.

Nodding, she leans toward me and wraps her arms

around me. She holds me tightly. Knowing I hurt my sister, that the lies I spun hurt her, hurts me. *But it was for her own good*, the voice says, repeating that statement for the millionth time since I put this plan into action all those months ago.

"Please call if you need anything," Remy tells me. "Don't fake die on me again, otherwise, I really will kill you and we both know, I don't look good in orange."

We all laugh. Trust Jellybean to calm my inner voice.

"I will," I tell her but it's a lie. We both know I won't.

Grayson pulls me into his arms. "I'm always here, Brother."

As the oldest, he always felt he needed to protect Remy and me, he just never knew how bad things had gotten. No one did, and thankfully Dad fucked up and I could use him to my advantage.

Slapping my arm in that brotherly way, he and Remy say bye to Dad, and they make their way to the door. Leaving me alone with the asshole.

"It's easier this way," my father says, "they won't get hurt if you push them away this time."

Turning a glare toward him, he cowers. *Pussy*, the inner voice chortles. "Just remember what I know, old man. If you don't want your own secrets spilled, I'd shut your mouth."

"Arlen. I—"

"Just keep your mouth shut and maybe I'll keep your secret about the embezzlement," I growl.

My father's look of panic makes me smile. He has just as much to lose as I do, therefore, I know my secret is safe … for now at least.

"We have a deal, father. Stick to it or I'll have no choice but to take you down too."

My father may have helped me, but I won't hesitate to turn him in, just to save myself.

I'll be damned if I don't see this through until the end. I've been given a second chance, and I will not fail this time.

HUDSON

… four weeks later

SITTING in the diner downtown across from my sister, Lauren, I listen intently as she tells me all about the academy and life in New York while we wait for lunch. Lauren is an amazing dancer who attends Stepz Academy in New York. It's a prestigious dance academy that only accepts the best of the best, and my sister just so happens to be the best of the best dancers around, and I'm not just saying that because she's my sister. Lauren has danced for as long as I can remember. Mom and Dad did everything they could to harness her talent, and when she was offered an all-expenses paid scholarship to Stepz, she moved, and it was great for her and her dance career. For her, at least, it was amazing but it meant it was just me at home, and my parents and I do not have the best relationship all because of one conversation …

… Dad and I are out in the boat, something we do together whenever we get the chance. I need to tell him about me, he's bound to find out, and I'd rather it come from me than anyone else.

I've always been open about who I am. When I wanted to dance instead of playing football, I told him, and he made it happen. When I became obsessed with girls, and Wendy Waterson in particular, he arranged for the two of us to hang out together, but now that I've moved on from Wendy to her brother, Warren, I'm scared to tell him.

Dad has always been vocal about his feelings when it comes to gays and lesbians, but what about people who are bisexual? Surely, because it's me he'll understand, right?

"Dad," I finally say, the courage to be honest filtering through me.

"What's up, Hudson?"

"I … I'm bisexual."

Easing back on the throttle, he turns his attention to me. "What did you say?" he sneers, and I can tell from his tone, he's not happy.

"I … I'm bi, I like Wendy … and Warren."

"I'm sorry, did you just say that you like the Waterson boy? And his sister?"

Nodding, I swallow the lump sitting in the back of my throat.

"Liking boys isn't how I raised you, Hudson. A man and a woman are meant to lay together, not two men. The Bible is Adam and Eve, not Adam and Steve. You will forget this nonsense and never utter a word to anyone again. If it got out that my son was one of those queer boys, we'd be ruined."

"But, Dad, I can't help who I like."

"You can and you will. You like Wendy, not her brother, end of story." He pushes down on the throttle again, ignoring me and the conversation we just had.

He guides us back to shore, cutting our boating trip short, and as we come to a stop at our dock, he looks at me. "I have never been more disappointed in you, Hudson. Get the fuck out of my sight."

Climbing out of the boat, I hang my head in shame and walk along the jetty, dejected my own father won't accept me for who I am. His last words to me are, "Don't let that affect your grades."

Things between us have never been the same since, and I have no doubt if things with Alani and Reign pan out how I hope they do, I will be ostracized from the family even more so.

Lauren is home visiting because she's helping to plan Mom and Dad's upcoming twenty-fifth wedding anniversary party. I was shocked when I received an invitation, but it'll all be for show. I'd love to fuck it up and arrive with Reign or both of them, but I refuse to subject either of them to my parents, no one needs that. The less they have to do with my family the better.

After breakfast with Lauren, the two of us walk around town. We bump into Arlen on the way back to our cars and he scowls at me, mumbling something about not deserving him and he'll make us pay.

"Who was that?" Lauren asks.

"Arlen Hearst," I tell her.

"The guy who came back from the dead?"

"Yep," I reply, nodding, "no one knows the exact details, but I'm sure his psycho mom was involved somehow. That woman was into some crazy shit, and faking her son's suicide falls right into that crazy category." Lauren looks at me confused. "You heard all about the events recently?"

She shakes her head, so I proceed to tell her everything

that went down with Mrs. Hearst and Brennan, the kidnapping, and the underground fight club thing.

"No fucking way, that's something straight out of *Days of Our Lives*," she states, taking another sip of her green snot-colored smoothie that's 'great for bone strength and energy' but I'll have to believe her on that, I ain't drinking snot.

"I think it's even more fucked up than *Days of Our Lives*," I tell her, and then I decide to come clean with her. "I'm bi, Lauren, and I think I'm in a poly relationship."

"No shit," she scoffs, smacking me on the arm.

"You knew?" I question her, shocked.

"Mmmhmpf." She nods. "Dad wanted me to try and sway you away from 'sinning' after you confessed to him." She air-quotes sinning. "And I've been waiting for the day you come out, as such, to me."

"Ohhh," I reply, shocked.

"Yeah ohh, but, dude, over breakfast, you've mentioned Reign and Alani fifty million billion times, so I put one and one together and got threesome."

"I did not," I refute, but when I think about it, I think she's right.

"Uhm, yeah, ya did, and now that it's out in the open, when can I meet Mr. and Mrs. Hudson?"

"How about I make it official with them first and then you can meet them?"

"Deal, and for what it's worth, I'm happy for you. Dad will come around. You know family means everything to him."

"He will never accept having a bi son, and there's no way in hell he'll accept me if I'm in a throuple. And that's the cold hard truth, but I won't change who I am for anyone."

"And so you shouldn't. He'll get over it, and if he doesn't, it's his loss 'cause you, Hudson Finley, are fabulous."

"As are you, Lauren Finley."

Lauren and I finish wandering around town, and I drop

her off at the hotel she's staying at. She was asked to stay else-where so our aunts and uncles could stay at the house, but I think she's okay with that. No one wants to be stuck with 'old' people all weekend long.

After dropping her off, I head back to school in search of Reign and Alani. It's time we have 'the talk.'

ALANI

TODAY IS party day and I cannot fucking wait. It's been too long since we had a party and with the recent events, we all deserve a night to let our hair down and make dumb decisions. No doubt the Lords will pull their holier-than-thou bullshit at the beginning of the night, but as long as I end the night with Reign or Hudson or both—wishful thinking—I'll be one happy lady.

I'm sitting in the cafeteria nursing a coffee when a body drops into the chair across from me, and I smile when I see it's Reign. Not two seconds later, someone drops into the seat next to him, and my smile widens when I see Hudson.

"My two favorite guys," I coo. "To what do I owe the pleasure of your company?"

"We need to talk," they both say in unison, their tones rough and meaning business.

"Should I be worried that you two are in sync right now?" They both shrug in sync, and my eyes widen. "This same-same thing is getting creepy, and now I'm scared what you both have to talk about is bad."

"It's not," Reign says, while Hudson just shakes his head.

"Okay, shall we discuss it here? Or somewhere private?"

Then the three of us say, "private," at the same time, causing us all to laugh, giving me a boost that all will be okay with our little 'chat.'

"Well, let me finish my coffee, and then we can head up to my room." I offer my room because it's my safe space and if this all turns to shit, I don't want to have to walk in public with my heart bleeding on my chest for all to see. I want to be able to break down in private, with no one around to witness my heartbreak, because that's what I will be—heartbroken—if these two guys walk away. Sure, nothing's official, but deep down, I know the three of us could be something special. Maybe I need to grab the proverbial balls in my hand and make the move. Put on my big girl panties instead of a G-string and make what we, well what I, want official—make us an us-us-us.

Both of them stare at me intently, watching my every move, but I can't stand not knowing so I chug back my coffee which, FYI, I do not recommend. Zero stars because I burn my esophagus by swallowing the black liquid gold also known as coffee in one mouthful.

"Let's go," I say to the guys once I feel like I can talk again.

Hudson grabs my mug and drops it off to be washed. Reign takes my hand and drags me toward the exit. Hudson joins us and he takes my other hand and the three of us, hand in hand, walk toward my room.

The closer we get, the faster my heart beats. It's so rapid by the time we reach my room, I'm worried it's going to burst out of my chest, or I'll have a heart attack and die before getting my happily ever after.

The door to my room closes, the sound of the lock engaging echoes throughout the space, and the only sound is our heavy breathing and the still rapidly beating of my heart.

The three of us awkwardly stand in my room, our gazes darting back and forth. "Soooooo," I draw the word out. "Who's going to go first?"

My nerves are frayed right now. With the tension building in my room, I kick my shoes off, walk over to my bed, sit down, and shuffle back, leaning against the wall. I cross my ankles over one another and stare up at the two men before me. Pride filters through me when I realize, I really am a lucky girl. These two guys are hotter than hot, and from the searing looks on both of their faces, I just know whatever is about to happen is going to be good.

Really

fucking

good.

And like earlier in the cafeteria, they both speak at once, saying the same thing, "We need to discuss us." And then Hudson adds, "I want it to be exclusive."

"You mean the three of us exclusive or just me and you exclusive?" I ask to clarify because I'm not quite sure what he's getting at, but I really hope he means the three of us.

"I mean, the three of us. I … I really like you both, but I think together I could even love you guys."

His words hang in the air. No one utters a word as we process what he just said. Reign steps up to Hudson, grips his cheeks, and slams his lips to his. The two of them passionately kiss before me, and I find myself smiling as I watch my two guys make out in front of me. Rising to my knees, I shuffle to the edge of my bed, so I can get a closer look. Lifting my hands, I place one on each of their shoulders. They break their kiss and turn their heads toward me. "Don't mind me," I sheepishly say, grinning like I've won the lottery, and I have because these two men want me like I want them. All my dreams and desires are about to come true, and I could not be happier than I am right now at this moment.

I move my hand from their shoulders and cup their cheeks. Running the pad of my thumb along each of their defined jawbones. "So, we're doing this? We're really gonna give this three-way thing a go?"

They both nod and my grin widens. "Soooooo, should we seal this with a threesome kiss? A blow job? All of the above?"

"And that, Alani Thomas, is why you are fucking perfect for us," Reign states before he turns to face me on the bed. He grips my cheeks like he just did to Hudson only moments ago and covers my mouth with his. My eyes close as his tongue pushes into my mouth and languidly sweeps around, wrestling with my tongue as he devours me. I feel a presence to the side, and when I open my eyes and turn my gaze, Hudson is watching us intently. Lust and desire are written all over his face. Pulling my lips away from Reign's, I press mine to Hudson's and kiss him just like Reign kissed me.

Breaking the kiss, I stare at my guys, *my guys*, I love that. "So, we're doing this?" They both nod. "Really, really?" I can't believe this is actually happening, sure, separately we all talked about it, but I never in a million billion years thought it would actually happen.

"Really, really," Reign confirms, reminding me of that scene in *Shrek*.

"Did you two just *Shrek* yourselves?" Hudson asks.

"*Shrek*, yeah we did," Reign and I say at the same time.

"It's freaky how in sync we all are," I tell them, smiling

like a carnival clown. "But it shouldn't surprise me since the three of us have been pining for this for a while now."

"Ohh, have you been pining to be dicked three-ways from Sunday?" Reign teases me but from the heated look on his face, he wants this too.

"Excuse me, Reign Vanderbelt, I know for a fact *you* want to be dicked three-ways from Sunday, as you so eloquently put it, and I think tonight, we make that fantasy a reality."

"Real—" Hudson presses his finger to Reign's lips, shushing him.

"No more *Shrek* references." He shakes his head. "But to confirm, yes. Tonight we all get dicked three-ways from Sunday."

We all nod. "So," Reign says, with a sexy, sinister smirk on his face. "Are we going to confirm our dicking three-ways from Sunday commitment with a blow job or something?"

"How about we just watch *Shrek*, and if you're lucky, I will blow you both to seal the dicking three-ways from Sunday deal." I smile cheekily and then add, "Or I could just make you both wait until tonight, delayed gratification and all that."

Reign nods and Hudson, the cheeky man that he is, smirks. "Really, really?"

The three of us collapse into laughter, and then we make a bed on the floor in my room and snuggle, watching *Shrek*.

Well, *Shrek* plays in the background as we kiss and fondle before I blow my guys and they finger me, getting me good and ready for my dicking tonight.

REIGN

TO SAY the events of recent months have been a mind fuck is the understatement of the century. Dad is dead and his killer is still out there. Remy's mother is also dead, but the most fucked-up revelation, Arlen is alive. That's the one thing I don't know how to process. Before his 'death' I thought he was the love of my life, but now, well, I'm in love with two people and I have never been happier.

After chatting with Mom, I knew what I wanted. I wanted Alani and Hudson with every fiber of my being, and after the chat with them just now, it's all confirmed, we are officially a throuple. I should be focusing on tonight. Focusing on the party of all parties to celebrate life getting back to normal, well, as normal as life at Crestwood Prep can be. Instead, my head is a fucking mess, but with Red and Hudson on my team, I know I will get through this.

"Dude, what the fuck is up with you?" Hendrix asks, dropping down next to me and bumping my shoulder to get my attention. "You've been off in la-la land … again."

"I'm fine," I hiss at him, bringing the bottle of beer to my lips and taking a swig. I'm pissed off because I had to leave Alani and Hudson earlier when I wanted nothing more than to stay and lose ourselves in each other. But because I'm a chickenshit asshole, I want us to be secret until I tell my brothers that I'm bi.

Maybe Mom is right, and they won't care, but what if they do? What if they are disgusted with me and I ruin our relationship? I need my brothers just as much as I need Alani and Hudson.

This is all so hard, and not in a good way.

"You know, if you were a chick and said that, it would mean you are anything but fine AND since you're my baby brother, I know right now that you're not so, spill."

"I'm …" Fuck, how do I tell my brother all my secrets. They've been mine for so long now, and I don't know how to deal now they are possibly about to be exposed. My brothers and I have always shared everything but not this, this has always been my secret. My burden. My demon to bear. Don't get me wrong, I want to shout how I'm feeling from the rooftops, but it's not just my secret, there are others to consider.

Him.

Her.

Him.

The three of us.

I think we're all on the same page, but will we be able to handle all the scrutiny when it comes out?

"You're what?" he questions, and it's on the tip of my tongue to tell him, but something is holding me back. Maybe it's the unknown between us or the non-closure with Arl. Whatever it is, I need to pull my head out of my ass and get my head in the game.

"I'm excited for tonight," I tell him instead of the truth. "We need a night to let loose, get fucked up, make questionable decisions but most of all, we celebrate that we made it through the last few fucked-up weeks and months."

"That's the spirit," Hendrix cheers, "let's get fucked up."

"Dids schumeones sayd fuscked up?" Rian singsongs as he staggers into the room. He's already fucked up going by the half-empty tequila bottle in his hand, and the sway he has while walking, but he deserves to be. His whole world has been rocked. He's not coping at all, and like me, he's not letting anyone in. Whereas, I've gone quiet while trying to get on with things, he's doing the complete opposite. Dear old Rian has turned into a manwhore, an even bigger one than Thatch was before Rem came along and tamed the manwhore. We were so wrong about her, she isn't the bitch we were led to believe her to be, and I'm happy she and Thatch are together now. Nothing like an enemies-to-lovers romance.

Rian is drinking excessively and fucking his feelings away with anything that moves, male or female. We've all tried to get him to open up, but he's locked up tighter than a nun's cunt.

"Wanna ease up there?" Saint says to our cousin, trying to take the bottle from him. That move pisses him off, and he tries to take a swing at Saint, but Saint is quicker than the drunk fucker and he pushes him, causing him to fall.

"Whaytchs da fuck meansd?" he slurs.

"Get yourself together, man," Saint hisses. "Tonight is about celebrating life getting back to normal."

"Mys tids never bes normal gan."

"It will be if you let someone in, you stubborn fuck." Saint shakes his head at him, lost as to what to do. He turns and pokes his head out into the hallway. "You," he growls at someone, "get your ass over here."

A few moments later, Conroy walks in. "You're on Rian duty."

"But—" he protests, but Saint gives him 'the look' that makes anyone shit their pants. "Fine," he huffs, giving Saint one of his own looks before turning to Rian. "Come on, drunky, let's go."

"Wheresch?" Rian squints to look at Conroy. "Hey, I knows youd."

"No shit," Conroy hisses, then he looks to Saint. "You owe me, fucker."

"Add it to the tab," Saint nonchalantly says.

"You know, one of these days, I'm going to grow a set and tell you to get fucked."

"Can't wait for the day, now get him to bed."

"Bedsh disd goodsch," Rian agrees.

"First time you've spoken sense all night," I tell him. He tries to flip me the bird, but in his drunken state he gives me a thumbs-up. Then he squints and focuses hard on his hand and finally manages to sideways bird flip me.

Conroy wrangles him out of my room just as Thatch and Remy arrive. "Do I wanna know?" Thatch asks, pulling Rem onto his lap after pulling out my desk chair. The said chair Alani fucked me on the other night. I can't help but smirk at the memory, my cock twitching when I think about Red's nails digging into my shoulders as she rode me like a bucking bronco.

"Probably not," Saint says, and the sound of his voice snaps me back to the present.

"He's really struggling," Thatcher says, stating the obvious. "I wanna help him but how?"

"Find his sister … and we just have to hope she's still alive because I don't think he'd handle it if she isn't."

"Sounds like a plan," Thatch states, "but for now, let's head to the cemetery so we can party like it's nineteen ninety-fucking-nine."

"Dude, we weren't even fucking born then," I scoff at him.

"Fine," he growls, "let's party like …."

"Rock stars," Remy adds, "just without the cocaine and threesomes."

At the mention of threesomes, I get a vision of Alani, Hudson, and me together. Our limbs entwined. His cock in my mouth, my cock in her mouth. Her glossy red hair caging us in, fuck, I'm hard again. I've never had a threesome before, but after discussing it with her the other week, it's been at the forefront of my mind.

… "Have you ever had a threesome before, Red?" I ask out of nowhere. "Huh?" I question like a doofus.

"Threesome. Ménage à trois. A three-way. Two dicks, one vag."

"What about two vags, one dick?"

"Not my cup of tea but sure, two vags, one dick … I'm guessing you have had two vags, one dick ménage?"

"Nope, only ever one dick or one vag for me, but if the opportunity arose, I'd be keen for two dicks, one vag. What about you?"

"I'd be keen for two dicks, one vag, but I want it all."

"How so?" I ask, throwing my pen down and giving her all my attention.

"Well, I want to be spit-roasted. I want to be double-stuffed, but I also want to see them together. Nothing would be hotter than seeing two guys losing themselves in each other."

"You've really given this some thought, Alani Thomas, and here I thought you were a sweet and innocent girl."

"There's a lot you don't know about me, Reign Vanderbelt." She looks over at me and fuck, she has never looked so beautiful. Her

cheeks are stained pink. Clearly, she's aroused from our ménage conversation. "Now, let's finish this paper, and then I'll let you fuck me before I leave your room."

And we did.

We finished our paper and then she rode me on my desk chair, while I thought about Hudson taking her from behind before I took him in front of her like she wants to see.

"Dude, you good? You're off in your head again." Saint slaps my thigh, getting my attention.

"Yeah, I'm all good. I'm just looking forward to partying like a rock star and letting my hair down."

"That's the spirit," Saint states as he jumps up. "Let's go get your drink on."

ALANI

THIS PARTY IS off the charts tonight. Don't get me wrong, a party hosted by the Lords is always amazing but tonight, there's something in the air. It feels like something massive is going to happen, but something massive in the most amazing massiveness of ways. Enough shit has gone down recently, and we are due for a night of unbridled fun and drinking and debauchery.

Hudson has been by my side all night. Always touching me and my body is abuzz with desire, want, and need. All I can think about is being taken by both Hudson and Reign later. Hell, I fucking woke up this morning with my hands in my panties after the most erotic dream ever of Hudson and me with Reign.

Like, what the fuck?

I've been messing around with them separately for the last few months, it's been nothing serious, just how I want it but now we are official, I want them both at the same time like I need my next drink.

Seems my 'I don't share' mantra is now moot, but let's be honest, I would only share Hudson with Reign, and I will stab a bitch if anyone tries to steal my men.

But officialness aside, they are both mine and mine alone. I don't know when I became so protective of them, but I have, and now I can't fucking wait to have them both, together. Me the cream in a Hudson and Reign sandwich will be sweeter than sweet. Can you imagine the bliss that those two fine-ass men will bring me together? I'm dripping just thinking about it … but then I think of my parents and there's no way in hell they would allow me to be with two men out in the open. Hell, there's no way they'd allow me with either of them … period. Guess, lucky for us, Reign wants to keep us a secret for now.

"You all right, Bitsy?" Hudson asks.

"What have I said about calling me Bitsy?" Yes, I'm short, well tiny, compared to Hudson's six three, but it's not my fault and no matter how much I protest the nickname, it's stuck.

"Deep down you love it when I call you Bitsy, especially when I moan it while your sweet, sweet pussy is milking my dick." *Dammit*, the asshole has me there so I ignore him. "You can ignore me all you want, but you and I both know, deep down you love it, but I will let it go for now as long as you tell me what's up?"

"I'm fine, why?"

"You just shivered but it's not cold."

"Ohh, yeah, I'm … I'm fine," I stammer. As much as I

want him and Reign, it's never going to happen outside of our bubble so I need to bite my tongue. Maybe I just need to drag him off to the woods for a quick fuck so I can get a sexual release and clear the sexual fog in my mind. It's like since we agreed to this earlier, I've become a wanton whore, I can't stop envisioning what's going to happen later tonight. My panties are soaked and that's just at the thought of later. I'll be a Slip 'N Slide once I get the two of them naked later.

"Are you blushing?"

"No," I hiss, but I think I might be. I'm so turned on right now.

"Red. Hudson," a deep voice says from behind us and my body zings alive. Spinning around, I come face to chest with Reign. Lifting my gaze up his body, I swallow when I take him in. In the moonlight he's sexy as fuck, just as sexy as the man standing behind me. He steps toward me, and I take a step backward, bumping into Hudson's rock-hard chest. He rests his hand on my hip and his touch sparks through my body and ends up exploding between my thighs. I choke back a moan but at that exact moment, the current song playing ends and it's dead quiet, well, except for my moan.

Reign's eyes widen, and I feel Hudson's breath hitch from behind me as Reign steps closer. Pushing me closer to Hudson and I'm now the official filling in a Hudson and Reign sandwich. "This, right now, the three of us here together, it reminds me of a conversation we all recently had."

Nodding, I bite my bottom lip, unable to form words as I remember that conversation. I'm ready to combust and who wouldn't with two extremely hot guys making you the meat in their sexy AF sandwich?

"What conversation might that be?" Hudson asks from behind me, knowing full well what Reign is referring to. I mean, said conversation happened only a few hours ago.

"The one from a few hours ago where Red here confessed to getting dicked—"

"three-ways from Sunday," I murmur, butterflies taking flight in my stomach at the thought of the dicking that's coming my way.

"That's right," Hudson whispers into my ear. "If I remember correctly, you want to feel Reign's dick in your vagina while I take your sweet, sweet ass. Or we could go with my cock in your cunt and his dick in your throat."

"That works," I breathlessly pant.

"But what I think you really want, Bitsy, you want to watch my dick slide into Reign's ass while you finger yourself, and once you've made yourself come on your fingers, Reign will fuck your cunt while I come in his ass."

"Yes," I pant like the wanton hussy I am. "Yes, to it all."

"What do you say, Reign?" Hudson growls. "Should we give our girl what she wants?"

HUDSON

"WHAT DO YOU SAY, Reign? Should we give her what she wants?" My heart races as I ask Reign this question. I have wanted this for longer than I care to admit, and I'm now full of apprehension that my secret desire is about to possibly come true. What if it's terrible? What if we hurt her? But then my thoughts turn to, what if we love it and it's everything and more than we hoped for? That's the what-if I want to be true. I care deeply for these two, and I'd be devastated if I lost them both.

Alani is perfect in every way, and Reign is stronger than he realizes. Together as a throuple, I think we'd be perfect and with one question, it will either be perfect or we end before we even have a chance.

Reign's gaze locks with mine, and I see the same desire I'm sure is in mine staring back at me. "It would be ungentlemanly for us to not give this sexy woman what she desires."

Leaning down, I nuzzle her neck. "What's it gonna be, Bitsy? Option one, two or three?"

"I-I -" she stammers.

"You what?" Reign questions, stepping closer to us. He rests his hand on top of mine on her hip and when his skin touches mine, an electrical current shoots directly to my dick. I'm harder than I have ever been before, and we are all still clothed. We're caught in an erotic trap right now and there's no place I'd rather be. "Tell us what you want, Red? Tell us so we can make it happen."

"I want you both."

"That's inevitable, babe, but how do you want us?" Reign growls. "Cunt and ass? Or cunt and mouth?"

"I don't know, I just need you both."

We all fall silent, processing the enormity of what's about to happen. The air around us is thick with desire and arousal. A silence wraps around us, even though we are standing in the middle of a party. The quiet is not awkward, it's what we need. Each of us processing now it's go time. Truth be told, I want whatever Bitsy wants and, even though we're all on the same page, she still needs a little push in the right direction. It's not like any of us have ever done a three way before, well, maybe Reign has but like sex, it's always different with a new partner and adding in a third, may prove awkward. I think we're all excited but nervous. I'm the one to break the silence when I voice what I want. "I personally would love to see Reign's cock slide into that tight ass of yours while you ride me."

"That," she pants, "I want that."

We both lift our gaze to Reign, and he nods. "We need to

go somewhere private so this can happen." He takes Bitsy's hand in his, she takes mine, and then the three of us slink into the darkness. We're racing along the path in a line when my foot catches on a stray branch and I trip, pulling everyone down with me.

"Sorry," I murmur, "I tripped," stating the obvious. "But I think here's as good as any place," I add on, causing Bitsy to laugh and the sound is music to my ears.

"I'd much prefer a bed," Alani says, "but going by Reign's hard dick that's currently digging into my stomach I think he's happy for it to happen here too."

"Are you sure?" Reign asks.

She nods and then looks over her shoulder at me. She beckons me to her and while I shuffle over, she bites her bottom lip. Reaching her, I lift my hand and pull her lip free before I lean forward, close my eyes, and cover her mouth with mine.

Alani moans softly, sending the sound straight to my cock. Reign shuffles forward and my eyes flicker open. I watch him sweep her hair over her shoulder and lower his lips to her neck. He begins kissing a line down her neck, causing her to shiver. Our gazes connect and it's full of desire for the moment, seeing the heat in Reign's eyes, knowing it resembles my own is such a fucking turn-on. I'm not sure how long I'll last before I'm ready to explode.

Reign's fingers slide Alani's shirt strap down, freeing her boob. The plump mound is right in his face, begging for attention. Without hesitation, he takes her nipple into his mouth, sucking hard. Alani's breaths quicken. With my lips still fused to hers, I trace my fingers down her side and lift the hem of her skirt up. Pushing her panties aside, I slide two fingers through her wetness. A groan slips free at feeling just how turned on she is. "You're soaked." I mewl against her lips.

Breaking the kiss, I watch her as she gives herself over to

the pleasure building. Reign's fingers wrap around her throat, tugging her toward him, and he slams his lips on hers.

Alani moans once again, making both of us growl.

"Fuck, Red, I'm about to fucking burst hearing those sounds come from your pretty little mouth."

Alani pouts when I remove my fingers, but when she sees me sliding my zipper down, her face lights up like a Christmas tree. She helps me pull my pants down to free my cock. With my eyes flicking between the two of them, I begin to stroke myself. Both Alani and Reign watch intently as I fist my cock, squeezing the head before sliding my hand down my shaft.

"Bitsy, come take my cock, baby," I demand.

Alani crawls toward me. With her ass in the air, she drops her head taking my cock in her mouth. I almost shoot my load down her throat when she wraps her lips around the head. Her tongue swirls around the tip before she sucks me into her mouth, hitting the back of her throat. "Fuuuuuck," I hiss, my body is in sensory overload right now. Never have I felt immense pleasure like this before.

Reign moves in behind her, gliding his hand between her thighs. She moans around my shaft when he pushes his fingers into her.

"Fuck, Red, you're so wet for us. You're fucking dripping, baby," he growls.

Alani hums and nods in agreement.

"Fuck, fuck, fuck," I chant, "I'm going to come." Pulling her head from me, I grip her chin in my fingertips. "I … I need you to stop, Bitsy, or I'm going to fill that mouth with my cum."

Leaning back on my elbows, I take a minute to collect myself and watch the pleasure on her face as Reign continues to finger fuck her. She's completely on fucking edge and she's never looked sexier.

Alani gasps, and from the chuckle and smug look on

Reign's face, it tells me that he just pushed a finger inside her tight little ass.

"Fuck, Red, your ass is so tight around my finger. I can't wait to feel it choking my cock."

Alani whimpers and moans, giving a slight nod at the thought of Reign's cock in her ass. I know how good that cock feels in an ass and I'm slightly jealous she's going to get it tonight. Seeing her lose control is erotic in itself. Pushing myself up, I cover her mouth with mine again, swallowing her cries of joy when I slip two fingers inside her pussy next to Reign's. She explodes at the intrusion, gripping my shoulders as her cries of pleasure fill the night around us.

Reign pulls her up, her back to his front. With his eyes locked on me, he leans into her ear and hisses, "We're not done with you yet, Red. I wanna see you ride him, baby. Show us how good you can take Hudson's cock."

She spreads her legs and allows me to slide between them. She shimmies up my thighs, straddling me. She's still wearing her panties but in the blink of an eye, Reign grips the material in his hands and tears them from her body. Bringing them to his nose, he inhales deeply. With his eyes locked on mine, he smirks. "Fuck her, Hudson. Fuck her like she's never been fucked before," he demands. His words are such a turn-on and I willingly comply. Gripping her hips, I pull her forward until I can feel the head of my cock pushing against her entrance. She begins to lower herself down just as Reign begins to lower his zipper. The sounds of the teeth opening echo through the night air. He places his legs on either side of mine and positions himself behind her, smacking her ass as she slides the last few inches down on me.

Alani and I both groan as I fill her to the hilt.

"So fucking hot," Reign grumbles.

Leaning around her, I watch as he takes his cock in his hand and guides it toward her. I pull out of her pussy, and he slides in, lubing his dick up. When he pulls out, I push back in. "One day, you're going to take both of our dicks in your pussy."

"Yes," she moans, "yes, yes, yes." I know the moment he pushes into her ass because her eyes widen and she gasps.

Leaning forward, I cover her mouth with mine, kissing her and making her forget about the sting of him entering her forbidden hole. Her pussy clenches around me as Reign moves slowly back and forth, working his cock deeper inside her. Kissing her neck, I bite down before sucking, soothing my mark. My tongue works over her quickening pulse.

Reign grunts as he thrusts all the way in. The three of us fall into a rhythm, I thrust in. He thrusts out. Repeat. Over and over.

Alani cries out as we both fill her. "Oh, oh God. So full," she murmurs. "Fuck," she cries out in ecstasy.

Moving in sync, Reign and I work Alani right to the edge. My balls tighten, my spine tingles, and I know I'm close.

"So close," I pant as Reign groans, "Fuck, Red, I'm going to fill this ass. You ready, baby?"

"Yes, yes. Please give it to me, please," she demands.

Riding me like a goddamn pro, my fingers dig into her hips while she clamps around me. I come so fucking hard I almost black out, grunting and hissing like I can't fucking breathe. Holding her to me, I fill her up just as she explodes. Crying out our names as her pussy clenches around me, milking every last drop out of me.

"Hudson, Reign, oh, God," she cries out. She's still seated on me when Reign lets out a guttural growl, the sound of him thrusting into her is the only sound I hear as I come down from my high.

"Fucking hell," Reign voices as he pulls out. He flops down next to me, breathlessly panting. Reaching up, he pulls Alani down to him and kisses her hard, his tongue tangling with hers. Then he turns to me, grips my head, and does the same and all of a sudden, my cock, which is still inside Alani, begins to harden again.

"That was so hot." Alani pants, her gaze fixed on Reign and me. "Next time, I want to see the two of you fuck."

"Yeah, is that what you want, Red?" Reign smirks, looking over at me.

The silent question is in his eyes, and I nod my agreement.

"I don't care who takes who, but I want one dick in me while the other fucks one of you," Alani says.

"I think that can be arranged, Red," Reign says in agreement.

That thought has me hard all over again. I want to make it happen right now. I want my cock inside Reign while our girl rides him.

Fuck, we need a re-do because that is so fucking happening.

REIGN

AFTER FUCKING IN THE WOODS, we redress and make our way back to my room. Unfortunately, we didn't recreate Alani's fantasy, but we will, that's for damn sure. Tonight was the beginning of something beautiful and for the first time in a long time, I feel happy and content. Nothing can burst my bubble.

After showering, we fall into bed. Alani is sandwiched between Hudson and me, her back to my front but above her head, Hudson and I hold hands. The three of us promptly fall asleep, exhausted from our earlier fucktivities.

My phone beeping at stupid a.m. wakes me, and when I see who it's from, confusion fills me.

ARLEN

I need to see you. Our place, when you can get there.

Staring at the screen, all the joy I felt last night dissipates. Arlen was my first love, he'll always hold a piece of my heart but these two, they've taken up residence there too. I'm not sure it's love just yet, but I know I care for them deeply. As corny as it is, Hudson and Alani complete me.

"Why are you thinking so loud?" Hudson complains into my pillow.

"Sorry, I—"

"Shhhh," he whispers, covering my lips with his finger. "Go do what you need to do and bring breakfast back with you."

"How did you know?"

"When you get a text at stupid a.m., and then lay there and stare at your phone, it's something important. Now go, and then bring breakfast back but if you take too long, I'm having Alani for breakfast."

"I like the sound of that," she sleepily mumbles, then adds, "but shut the fuck up before I smother you both with a pillow. I'd hate to kill you because I can't wait to have a re-do of last night."

"Well, we could always do that before I have to go."

"I need sleep … and coffee before I let you two at me again."

"Is that your way of saying you want a coffee?"

She lifts her head and gives me a dazzling smile. "You catch on quickly, Vanderbelt. Now, leave so I can sleep more." And with that, she snuggles back into Hudson and promptly falls back to sleep.

Climbing out of bed, I pull on my jeans and a black Henley. Leaning down, I press a kiss to Alani's temple. She smiles in her sleep, leaning over, I go to do the same to Hudson, but he surprises me when he grips my shirt and slams his lips to mine. His tongue pushes into my mouth, and what was only meant to be a quick kiss goodbye turns into so much more.

"Hurry back," he murmurs against my lips.

Nodding, I smile at him and quickly exit my room. A few moments later, I find myself standing before Arlen in the secret spot that was ours. We used to spend hours here and it was in this very spot Arlen and I made love for the first time. I remember how nervous I was, but he made me relax and it made the moment special.

"Hey," I offer in greeting, sliding my hands into my pockets. I smile down at him sitting on the floor in a room I haven't been back to since he 'died.' "I haven't been here since the last time I was here with you. I thought it would be a mess."

"It wasn't too bad," he tells me, "but I did clean it up a little." A chuckle slips out. Arlen is Mr. Clean in person. "When I returned, I needed somewhere to just be, and this was the first place I thought of." Nodding, I stare at him. I'm not sure what to say but the urge to know what happened surges to the surface. Like he's in my head, he shakes his. "I'm not ready to discuss that," he says, in a tone of voice I have never heard him use before. It's like a different person is before me.

"Then what did you want to discuss?"

"I … I wanna discuss us."

Nodding again, I shuffle on my feet, unsure how I tell him I'm with Hudson and Alani, and after last night, I will not give them up. But on the other hand, I miss him. I miss what he and I had. He was my first love, that's not something you easily forget. When he 'died' life went on and now, now I don't know what's going to happen with us. But one thing I do know, I'm pissed he 'died.' I'm pissed the fuck off he didn't love me enough to tell me the truth, hell, he's still not telling me the truth.

He taps the floor next to him. "Sit," he demands, and like the puppy I am when I'm with him, I comply. Dropping down next to him, I lean against the wall and let out a sigh as silence falls over us.

"I'm so angry at you right now."

"I deserve that," he agrees with a nod. He picks at the invisible lint on his leg, something I remember he did when he was anxious.

"I'm so confused right now," I tell him, resting my head on his shoulder as we sit in our secret place.

"Why are you confused?"

"Because you're here and I'm …"

"I'm what?" he asks. It's still surreal that he's alive, but there's something different about him. But then again, would I be the same if some psycho kidnapped me, at the behest of my mother, with the sole intention to sell me off?

"I … I still love you but I also hate you. But that love—"

"Please don't," he interrupts me, "a lot has happened, and … I … understand." He drops his voice. "There's a lot you don't know about me, but what I can tell you is I'm not who I was before I went away. And I don't think you are either." He pauses, and I lift my head to stare at him. He shuffles around to face me, but I can't look at him right now so I lower my gaze to my legs. He takes my hand in his. "I will never stop loving you, Reign, but I'm not the one for you. You need to move on."

There's an edge to his voice that is not Arlen-like at all. He's Arlen but not, and I don't know how I feel about all of this. On one hand, I'm so fucking happy he's alive but on the other, I've moved on, and I'm finally happy. So fucking happy, but where does that leave him? Us? I feel guilty for continuing to live but I also feel anger. "You lied to me," I sneer at him, my tone harsher than I intended but I don't give a rat's ass.

"I didn't lie."

Pulling my hands free, I run them through my hair in frustration. "So you didn't fake your death and let me grieve."

"Well, yeah, okay, I did that."

"And you're still lying to me, Arl. You aren't giving me anything, I thought … I thought I meant something to you."

"This isn't about you, Reign. Not everything revolves around the Vander-fucking-belts. You need to move on … with them and forget about me and us."

Lifting my head, I shimmy around to face him, and through my anger, I realize he said 'them.' "But—" He presses his finger to my lips, and I notice that there's no spark like there used to be between us when we touched.

"We're different people now, Reign. You, you've … moved on … and I don't blame you for that and to be honest, I'm glad you did." He swallows deeply. I hate seeing him so broken. So aloof. Reminds me of when he 'died' and I couldn't show my true feelings, and then Thatch discovered all that fucked-up shit about his mom and our dad and then life really took a turn. "Reign, I'm not the man you think I am. I can't and will not ever be who you remember I was. I still have shit to work out and do, shit that you can't be a part of but they, they can give you what I can't. Knowing you have them makes me so fucking happy."

He takes my hands in his again and squeezes. I stare at the man who used to own my heart and I see he means what he just said. He doesn't want me in that way because he still has whatever caused him to fake his death to deal with. I'm not good enough for him and that hurts. I don't know this version of Arlen, but maybe I didn't know him at all. But the shitty part of all of this is I still want him in my life. "I don't know you at all, do I?"

He shakes his head. "No one does, Reign."

Silently we stare at one another. As I take in the man who was once my everything before me, I see a broken person. My heart and I want to get to know the real Arlen. "You really mean that, don't you?"

He nods. "They are my secrets to bear and mine alone, but I never lied to you when we were together." I eye him. "Well, okay, I kept some secrets from you, but I did from everyone. I think I'll always love you, Reign, but I'm not in love with you."

"I'll always love you too, Arl … but I'm not in love with you either."

After that declaration, Arlen gets up and leaves. I sit here for a few more moments and process what just happened. Arlen is still lying, and it hurts that he was never completely honest with me. The old me would go get shitfaced and maybe if I did that, I could have Hudson like I did that one time. I smile as I think about that …

…"Whats choo wants?" I slur.

"You okay, man?" Hudson asks me. Walking over, he squats down in front of me. Even in my drunken state, I can see he cares.

"Depenshs onds zee defsnicin ofds oskays."

"And according to your defsnicin?"

"Drunksd. Sads. Confused."

"Well, how about we start by getting you back to your room? The Dean is on the warpath tonight." Ever since the news of Arlen broke, the faculty has been on edge. I cannot tell you how many teachers have asked 'are you okay' or 'I'm here if you need to talk.' Where was all that when clearly Arlen needed someone. Hell, I didn't notice, and I was fucking him. He stares at me, waiting for my reply so I nod. "Osdkayd. Eisd bed nowd."

I try to stand up, but I'm struggling due to the liquor coursing through my body right now and Hudson chuckles at me, I like the sound. Squinting, I look up at him. "Would you like some help?" he asks, offering me his hand.

"Pleased." When I place mine in his, a spark jolts between us and I quickly pull my hand back. Silently we just stare at one another, something passes between us, but I don't know if it is the booze talking or if it actually did.

"Come on," he says again, offering me his hand again. I take it and I notice our hands fit together perfectly. It's as if our hands were formed in the same mold. "Let's get you to bed."

"I betsd youd saysd dhat toods allds da girlsd."

"And boys," he adds.

"Ands da boyds," I slur as he pulls me up into a standing position. I stumble and fall into him. He holds on to me tightly, and I feel comfort in his arms.

"I got you," he reaffirms as we begin our stagger to my room. My heart kicks up at his words, I've been so alone these last few days but here now, drunk in Hudson's arms, I feel content and at peace.

Reaching my room, I just stare at the door.

"Keys?" he demands.

"Pocket," I reply.

He slides his hand into the pocket of my jeans, trying ever so hard not to brush my dick but it's hard—pun intended.

"Dats snotsd myd keys," I slur. With his hand in my pocket, I lift my gaze to his and see him hungrily staring at me. I'm pretty sure I have the same look on my face, just with a drunken tinge. Licking my lips, I reach up, grip his cheeks, and press my lips to his. Before I have a chance to kiss him deeper, my body goes lax, and I mumble, "Fuck."

One minute I was kissing Hudson and the next, I feel the softness of my bed behind me. "Thanksd youd whaatchs yourd namesded," I drunkenly mumble when I hear the rattle of the door handle.

"Good night, Reign," he whispers back before slipping out and leaving me to pass out.

· · ·

After my trip down memory lane, I get up and head out. I have breakfast to get and two amazing people waiting for me in my bed.

Swinging by the cafeteria, I grab three coffees and three breakfast sandwiches and make my way back to my room.

When I step in, I close the door behind me and look to the bed. A calmness like never before washes over me when I see Alani and Hudson sound asleep, wrapped in each other's arms.

Placing the drinks and food on my desk, I strip down to my boxers and climb back into bed with them. This is where I'm meant to be and I could not be happier.

ARLEN

IT HURTS to push him away, but I need to do this for my plan to come to fruition. I didn't fake my death for it all to fall apart now. Watching Reign walk away hurts now, but what pains me more is knowing those feelings we shared are gone.

What we were is nothing but a memory now.

Knowing what I've done, I know Reign would never be able to look at me the same again, and I'm okay with him getting his happy ending, even if it's not with me.

Making my way to the cliffs, I drop down onto the seat and listen to the waves crash against the rocks below. Pulling my medallion from my pocket, I play with it.

Flipping it over and over between my fingers as I look out over the horizon, I remember the last time I was here. It was when I 'killed' myself and set my plan into motion.

"Arlen." The sound of my sister's voice pulls me from my thoughts. Turning slowly to face her, I see she's only a few feet from me. Wrapping her arms around herself, the breeze up here tonight is strong and there's a chill in the air.

"Are you okay?" Her soft voice filters between us.

My mouth lifts slightly and nodding slowly, I stand up and take a step toward her. "I'm fine," I mutter and begin my trek back to Crestwood Prep.

"Arl," Remy yells, "wait." Her footsteps are heavy behind me as she runs to catch up. Gripping my arm tightly, she forces me to stop. Spinning to face her, I stare into my sister's frightened face.

"Talk to me," she pleads, "please."

"I can't." I swallow, cupping her cheek. Her eyes well with tears and I hate seeing her upset. I pull her into me, holding her to my chest. Her arms wrap around me, and she holds me tightly. It's as if she senses the change in me.

Breaking our hug, I take her hand and tug her with me as I lead us back to the school, knowing soon enough lockdown will begin.

We walk through the doors to the residence hall and Grayson stops at the bottom of the steps. It's as if he was waiting for us.

"You good?" he asks me.

I nod to appease our brother, but again it's all an act because am I truly okay? Hell fucking no, but I'm not dragging Remy and Gray down with me. If keeping my secret means they stay safe, then so be it. Mother almost fucked this up for me and now that she's gone, I can get back to the task at hand.

"There you are, Peach." Thatcher Vander-fucking-belt tugs

Remy away from me and into his arms. He kisses her like he hasn't seen her in days.

"Damn, man, let her breathe," Gray grumbles as I yank Remy from his arms. Thatcher glares at him over her head.

"Don't tell me what to do with my woman," Thatcher snaps, getting in Gray's face. Internally, I'd love nothing more than to see Gray knock the fucker out, but we need to play happy, for now at least. Forcing myself between them, I play the bigger person and shove them apart.

"Take him away, Jellybean," I tell Remy. She nods and wraps her hand around Thatcher's wrist, pulling him along with her.

"Fucking Vanderbelts," Gray grumbles again, storming toward the front doors. It's late and we need to head back to the hotel.

Yeah, I agree, *fuck them*, I think as I watch Gray storm off. Well, I mean, I used to fuck him, not all of them but I wouldn't mind taking any of the Vanderbelt brothers for a ride. Yes, I hate the other three with a fiery passion, but hate fucks are always good. But now he belongs to someone else. Two someones actually.

Gray turns around to face me. "You coming?"

Shaking my head, I throw my brother a smile. "I just need to grab something," I tell him. "Meet you at the car in ten."

He nods and turns back around, heading for the exit. Why he and I keep hanging out at Rem's school, I don't know. Probably because we are both living in a hotel right now. With everything that went down, he and I are displaced because mother fucked up our lives.

Leaving me alone, I slip through the empty halls and make my way toward the library.

It's quiet, the bodies of students are long gone. Of course it's empty, it's close to midnight, still, I look around to be sure I am in fact alone. You can never be too careful in this godforsaken place.

Once I'm sure I'm alone, I move to the last row at the end. Bending down to the bottom shelf, I take my screwdriver from my pocket. I winch the edge of the wooden shelf, prying it open just enough to reach my hand in so I can feel around for what I'm looking for. When my fingers brush against the cloth, I'm relieved to know it hasn't been tampered with.

Pulling it out, I check the coast is clear one last time, but this is the perfect hiding spot because hardly anyone comes back here, it's why I chose it.

Unwrapping the cloth, I smile when I see his medallion sitting next to the piece of evidence that can never be found, it will be my downfall if it is. My fingers twist around the metal and I feel a connection to *him* and his last moments. A smirk touches my lips and all I can think about is *him* as the light left his eyes for the final time. Nothing felt better than pulling that trigger.

Closing my eyes, I lift it to my nose and breathe in, the smell of the gun infiltrating my soul. Hearing a noise, I quickly wrap the gun in the cloth again and place it back into the shelf cavity before I gently push the edge closed.

Someone curses out loud and drops something. "Fuck it," they mutter. The voice is familiar, but I can't place it right now.

Sneaking a peek from behind the shelf, I see someone stumbling in the dark lifting a bottle to their lips.

Eyeing them cautiously, I watch as they stumble into a table nearly falling face-first onto the floor.

"Who's pud tat tere," the drunken voice slurs before they take another sip. He swallows loudly, downing half the bottle before he comes up for air. I shake my head at the damn idiot.

Finally, he turns toward me, giving me a view of his face. "Fuck," I whisper-hiss. It's Rian Vanderbelt. Of fucking course, it had to be another Vander-fucking-belt, didn't it.

Slipping past him unnoticed, I head for the door. Opening it, the hinges creak slightly and I cringe at the sound.

"Whod's here?" Rian slurs, his footsteps begin to move. Not wanting to be caught, I slip out the door and into an alcove just as the door opens. I hear him walk out but I'm sure in his inebriated state, he won't find me. Crouching down, I hide in the dark and watch as Rian staggers past me. He trips on his feet a few more times before he's far enough away that I can head for Grayson's car before the drunken idiot spots me.

Opening the passenger door, I drop into the seat, expecting him to grill me on where I've been, but instead, he's fast asleep, snoring loudly.

Leaning my head back, I let out a harried breath. Tonight was close, but I've got work to do, I can't afford any more distractions.

ALANI

WAKING UP, a smile graces my face when I realize where I am. That smile widens as I remember the events of last night. Lifting my arms above my head, I stretch my muscles out, moaning as the ligaments pull and contract. The sheet slips down, baring my naked chest. My nipples pebble in the cool morning air. The soft peaks stiffen when I feel a fingertip circle around my areola. Looking over, I smile when I see Reign staring intently at my boobs. He's on his side, resting his head on his palm. Then I feel lips wrap around my other nipple and a moan slips free. Turning my head, I see the top of Hudson's head as he lavishes attention to my breast.

Not wanting to be left out, Reign takes my nipple into his mouth. Having two mouths on you at once is an indescribable feeling. "Mmmhmpf," I moan as my clit begins to throb.

Hudson removes his mouth, lifts his head, and watches Reign for a few moments. He reaches over and pulls Reign off my boob, I whine in protest, but when Hudson slams his lips to Reign's, that whine turns into a guttural groan. Watching the two of them kiss is so sexy. Lifting my hand, I cup each of their cheeks and continue to watch. Reign pulls away first, his eyes ablaze with lust and his lips puffy from Hudson's kiss.

"That was hot," I tell them. They both turn their attention back to me.

"You think so, huh?" Hudson asks.

Biting my lip, I nod. The air around us crackles. Reign lifts his hand and cups my cheek. "Tell us what you want, Red?"

"Everything," I murmur, "I want everything."

"Everything we can do, but you need to be more specific." They both stare at me. Hunger is in their eyes, and I can't tell if it's for me, for each other, or both. "I … I want to watch you two kiss again and then, I … I want to watch and help each of you give each other a blow job."

"I'm sure that can be arranged," Hudson agrees. He flicks his gaze from mine and over to Reign. His eyes peruse his face, he lifts his hand and slides it behind Reign's head. Leaning forward, he presses his lips to Reign's, and I lie beneath them and watch as each of their eyes close and they lose themselves in the kiss.

One minute they're above me kissing and the next, Reign is on his back next to me and Hudson is sliding down his body. He situates himself between Reign's legs and lifts his gaze to mine. Molten hunger reflects back at me. "You want to join me?"

Nodding, I lick my lips and quickly move and join Hudson between Reign's legs. Reign shuffles into the middle of the bed, his cock is hard. The tip is glistening, and I need to taste it. Leaning forward, my tongue darts out and slides over the head. He hisses and I moan as the tartness of his precum dances over my tongue. Placing a kiss on the head, I turn and look at Hudson. Gripping his shaft in my palm, I offer it to Hudson. He smiles and lowers his head, where mine was a little lick, he opens his mouth wide and lowers his head. His lips sliding down and engulfing Reign's girthy member has me dripping. Reign hisses and at that sound, I lift my gaze to his. My eyes dart between Reign's pleasure-filled face and Hudson sucking his dick, I have never seen anything more beautiful. Reign's eyes are closed and there's nothing but pure desire etched on his face.

He opens his eyes and our gaze connects. "Kiss me," he demands and like a moth to a flame, I shuffle to my knees and kiss him. He slides his hand into my hair, gripping the strands. There's a gentle pull and it kind of hurts but when his tongue slides into my mouth, I forget all about the pain and focus on the kiss.

It's my turn to hiss now because Hudson is now finger fucking me while sucking on Reign's cock. "Mmmmmmmgh," I mewl against Reign's lips when he inserts another finger. The angle isn't quite right, so I remove my lips from Reign's and pull away from Hudson. Shuffling to the side, I throw my leg over Reign's stomach so I'm straddling him. Leaning forward, I press my lips to his once again and I push my ass toward Hudson.

"This view is stunning," Hudson says from behind us. "Your cunt up close is perfect, and you know what will make it more perfect?"

"What?" I pant like a wanton hussy.

"Reign's cock sliding into it."

"Do it," I demand, and before I've even finished saying that, Hudson grips my hips and slides me down onto Reign's cock. His thick shaft spears deep inside. "Fuuuuuuuuuck," I groan, drawing the word out.

"Ride him, Bitsy. Ride him hard."

Resting my hands on his chest, I push myself up and do exactly that. I ride him like my life depends on it. Reign lifts his hands and massages my breasts. Hudson grips my hip and with his other hand, slides it around to my front and rubs my clit. It's pleasure overload.

"I'm gonna come," Reign hisses and Hudson, the asshole, lifts me off his dick. I groan in protest but when I look behind me, I see him cover Reign's cock with his mouth and he sucks him to release. Reign's body shudders beneath me and he grunts as he empties himself into Hudson's mouth. Hudson sucks and swallows every last drop. Reign's cock pops out of his mouth and it hits my ass.

Hudson lifts his gaze to mine and as if he's in my head, he lifts himself up and kisses me. I can taste myself and Reign mixed together as he pushes his tongue into my mouth to kiss me deeper. A gasp escapes me when I feel Reign thrust two fingers deep inside of me. His fingers thrust in and out in sync with Hudson's tongue and before I know it, I'm screaming into Hudson's mouth. I'm pretty sure the whole boys' floor just heard me, but I don't care. All I care about right now is these two men and the pleasure coursing through me.

My body goes lax and I collapse forward onto Reign's chest. "A girl could get used to waking up like that," I pant into Reign's neck.

"Duly noted," Reign nods in agreement, "but we still have a job to do." Lifting my head, I stare down at him in confusion. "Hudson hasn't come yet."

"And Hudson won't get to. Hudson has to go, I have a study session to get to."

"Can't you blow it off so we can blow you off?" Reign asks, chuckling to himself at his corny joke.

"Rain check," he replies.

He climbs off the bed and picks through the clothes on the

floor. Finding his, he gets dressed. Once he's dressed, he leans down and kisses Reign goodbye and then kisses me too.

"Catch up later, guys." With that, he leaves Reign and me.

"Is it weird that I miss him?" I ask Reign.

He shakes his head. "Not at all because I do too. Last night started something between the three of us and whatever that something is, I'm going to treasure it with everything I have."

Smiling at him, I snuggle into his side. This is where I'm meant to be and it's perfect in every way, but my bubble of happiness pops when I'm invited, well summoned, to my parents' place that night for dinner and a chat. A last-minute invitation to dinner is never a good thing, nor is a chat. My parents and I are polar opposites in that they have sticks up their asses and look down on everyone. Whereas me, I love everyone and I don't have a stick up my ass—well, sometime soon I will have something shoved up my ass. I cannot wait for that to happen with my boys. After one night, they've turned me into a cockwhore and I could not be happier.

After dropping Rem back at school, I turn my car back around and head toward my parents' house. On the drive over, I try to think of what they'd want to 'chat' about. For once, I haven't been in trouble so I don't think it's anything I've done wrong, but any one of my past misdeeds could be coming back to bite me in the ass. To my parents, Gerald and Portia Thomas, I'm the epitome of a doting daughter and prize student. Little do they know their little angel loves to drink, break the rules, and right at this moment, she loves to fuck two guys at once. Ohh the scandal if that was ever to come to light.

Pulling into the circular driveway, I notice there's a silver

Mercedes parked here too, a surprise guest at a last-minute dinner can't be good.

Taking a deep breath, I climb out of my car and walk to the door. Before I reach it, it swings open and Mom peruses me. "Alani, you could have at least dressed better." Looking down at my outfit, I scrunch my face in confusion. I'm wearing a navy and white polka dot off-the-shoulder blouse —that SHE bought for me—dark skinny jeans, and heeled boots—that she also bought for me. I think I look hot but obviously, looking hot isn't good enough for Portia Thomas this evening.

"Hello to you too, Mother," I say, ignoring her barb at my outfit because it's not worth the argument. "I'm fine, thanks for asking," I add on to be bitchy.

"Yes, yes, hello to you too." She steps aside and lets me in. She looks nervous and it immediately puts me on edge.

"Alani," Dad says in greeting when I walk into the sitting room.

"Hi, Dad," I greet him with a kiss on the cheek and that's when I notice a couple and I'm guessing, their son, waiting for us in the formal living room. "Alani," he says, "this is Pamela and Bert Blanchard and their son, Raymond. They just moved here from Philly."

"Nice to meet you all," I reply with a smile as I take a seat next to Dad. Mom returns and hands me a glass of iced tea. "Thanks, Mom." Taking the glass from her, I take a sip and wince when she's not looking. Mom is a good cook but when it comes to iced tea, she sucks, and iced tea happens to be her favorite drink. This is so sour it's not funny. Dad grins at me and I roll my eyes, he clearly knew this was horrible.

"Your father tells us you're a student at Crestwood, Raymond will be starting there next term. They wouldn't take him mid-semester so I'm homeschooling him for now."

Hmmmpf, I think to myself. They took Remy mid-semester earlier this year, wonder what that's all about? Ohh right, she's a Hearst and before the recent events involving that family, they, along with the Vanderbelts, could have gotten away with murder and I guess they did, per se, because I still have my suspicion that Momma Hearst killed Daddy Vanderbelt making Rem and Thatch all the more interesting.

When I look up again, everyone is staring at me. Offering a smile to them, I tell them all what they want to hear. "It's a good school, you'll like it there."

"Only the best of the best attend that school," Mom adds like that means shit and her version of best of the best refers to last names only. Most of the kids who attend that school are stuck up pretentious assholes or backstabbing bitches and then to prove my point, she says, "Was such an unfortunate thing that happened to that boy," Mrs. Blanchard says, shaking her head in disgust. "Rumor has it he was one of the gay ones,"

"Probably couldn't live with the fact he was one of them and that's why he jumped," Mom states.

"But he didn't jump," Mrs. Blanchard states, "He just went into hiding, according to what I heard."

"I think he just wanted attention and that's why he faked it," Mom adds, her tone full of disdain and for the first time in my life, I realize just how conceited my mother is. "Those gays are always wanting attention. They are disgusting, the lot of them."

"Mom, what the hell," I hiss, "that's my friend Remy's brother you're talking about."

"Watch your tone and language," Dad berates my use of hell and Mom sneers, "You're friends with a Hearst?" Her tone alludes to the fact that she's not happy at hearing about my friendship with Remy.

"Yes, I am. The Dean asked me to show her around on her first day," little white lie but whatever, "and we clicked. She's really smart, hoping to get into design school after she graduates."

"Design School?" Dad scoffs. "No career in that."

Mom looks at the Blanchard's. "Alani is going to be a lawyer."

My eyes widen at that, I haven't wanted to be a lawyer for a few years now. As of today, I don't know what I want to do. I was saving that conversation for the future, but I guess the future is here now. I've been happy for twelve hours, that seems to be the quota for me. *Fuck you, Universe.*

"Actually, Mom, I'm not sure what I want to do when I graduate. I've been thinking of taking next year off to travel before I decide what I want to do with the rest of my life."

"I don't think so, young lady," Dad admonishes me. "This is something we can discuss when we don't have company." He looks at Mom. "Portia, how far away is dinner?"

"It shouldn't be too much longer, Gerald," she says, tapping his hand in the condescending way she does.

"I'll go check," I offer and before anyone can say anything, I jump up and race into the kitchen, needing to get away before I say something I will regret. I can't believe they spoke about Arlen and Remy like that, but most of all, I can't believe I let slip what my plans are for next year. That was meant to be kept quiet until I graduated, and I had my ticket in hand, at least I didn't say anything about Hudson and Reign.

This dinner will be interesting now and one I really do not want to be attending.

HUDSON

THE NEXT FEW days are amazing in every way, and I can't stop smiling.

Reign and I walk Alani to her classes and then we all grab lunch together and spend the afternoons studying. Once we are all studied out, we then reward our academic efforts with an orgasm … or three. And to top it all off, I aced my last history exam. Not even the shitshow that will be my parents' anniversary party tomorrow night can dampen my mood. Life is perfect and nothing can bring me down, but those were famous last words because no sooner has that thought left my mind, my phone rings and this call changes that happiness.

Picking it up off the side table, I smile when I see it's my sister, Lauren. She flew in yesterday for the anniversary party this weekend. No doubt she'll be calling for the gossip about Reign, Alani, and me. She's been dying for an update and the gossip queen that she is, will want all the deets before tomorrow night. No doubt so she can tease me for being happy and in love. "Hey hey, sissy," I say as I bring the phone to my ear.

"Huddy," she says, her voice breaking as she utters my name.

"What's wrong?" I demand, sitting up in bed. My heart is racing as to what she's going to say next.

"I ... I need you. Sssssomething hhhappened and I nnnnneed you."

"I'm on my way, I need to hang up so I can order an Uber, my car is getting fixed." Some dickwads keyed my car and slashed my tires yesterday.

"I'm already here in the parking lot. I need you, Huddy." She swallows. "I need you. Please."

"I'm on my way." Putting the phone onto speaker, I pull on my joggers. "Talk to me, sis, you're scaring me."

"I ... I ..." She's so upset she can't talk. "I need you," she repeats again.

"I'm coming," I tell her. Picking up my phone, I bring it to my ear and race out of my room and down the hallway.

"No running," someone shouts. Flipping them the bird, I race down the stairs, two at a time, hoping I don't slip and fall. Pushing the front doors open, I see my sister sitting in her rental car in the parking lot and I pick up my speed, the need to get to her takes over.

"I see you," I tell her, and she lifts her head from the steering wheel. Even though she's across the lawn from me, my heart breaks when I take in her state. Mascara tracks stain her cheeks and her eyes are red and puffy. Her hair is a mess. Flinging open her door, my eyes widen when I see her torn dress. Her lip is split. "Lauren," I whisper, dropping down to her level. Reaching out, I take her hand and squeeze.

"Huddy," she cries. "He … he tried to but … but I got away."

"He's fucking dead," I growl. "What's his name?"

She shakes her head. "I just wanna forget, please, Huddy, make me forget."

For the moment, I forget all about the fucker who did this to my sister and just focus on her. I can plan his death once I know she's safe. "Come on." I offer her my hand. "Let's get you inside and cleaned up."

She nods and takes my outstretched hand. Pulling her out of the car, she takes a step and then collapses. She's in shock, her body is shutting down. Scooping her into my arms, I race across the lawn and back into the building.

"What the fuck?" Quinn hisses when she sees my sister and me. Looking at her, I open my mouth to ask for her help, but she beats me to it. "What can I do to help?"

"Can you help me get her cleaned up?"

She nods. "Follow me."

Following Quinn up to the girls' floor, we race into the bathrooms. "Out," she growls at the girl at the sink. She opens her mouth to protest but when she sees me with Lauren in my arms, her eyes widen and she quickly scampers away, leaving us alone.

The door clicks closed just as I lay Lauren down on the ottoman in the middle of the room. She comes too when I stand up. Her eyes widen as she takes in the room. "Hey," I offer, dropping down next to you. "You're safe here, Lauren. Quinn is going to help me get you cleaned up."

She nods and I step back, allowing Quinn to take over. Leaning against the vanity, I stand here and listen as my sister breaks down in the shower. Quinn steps out.

"How is she?" I ask.

She shrugs her shoulders. "She wasn't raped if that's what you're asking." Relief washes through me as she confirms that, I thought Lauren just said that earlier to appease me. "She's shaken up, but she'll be fine, trust me, I know." My eyes widen at that revelation, as do hers, I don't think she meant to say that. "Forget you heard that." I nod. "Do you have any clothes your sister can wear?"

"Yeah, I'll go grab some things for her." Looking at the closed shower stall door, my heart hurts for my sister. Turning around, I unlock the bathroom door and head up to my room. Grabbing a hoodie and some sweatpants, I race back out. Rounding the corner, I smash into a hard body. His smell hits me, and I know it's Reign. "Excuse me," I say, stepping around him. I try to get past, but he reaches out and grabs me by the arm. "Let go," I snap, I need to get back to Lauren and he's holding me up and pissing me off.

"You okay?" he asks, his tone laced with concern but right now, all I can focus on is Lauren.

"Let go," I repeat, "please."

He lets me go and as soon as I'm free, I head back to the girls' floor. Pushing the bathroom door open, I smile when I see Lauren is sitting on the ottoman engulfed in a bright orange towel. She looks up and just stares at me. "You look good in orange," I tell her, "but let's stick to towels and not prison jumpsuits." Lauren smiles at my joke, but it doesn't reach her eyes. Dropping to the ottoman next to her, she rests her head on my shoulder and takes my hand. Squeezing it, that little squeeze lets me know she's going to be okay. Us Finleys are tough. We stick together, no matter what.

"I think she'd rock one," Quinn says, lifting up the brush in her hand. Lauren nods and Quinn steps behind her and begins to brush Lauren's hair. I have never seen Quinn so ... nice before. It's disarming but I'm thankful she's here right now. "You on the other hand, Hudson, you could not rock the orange. Plus, you're too pretty for jail, you'd become some-one's bitch for sure."

"More like he'd make someone HIS bitch," Lauren adds.

"Seems you and I have different opinions when it comes to your brother. I see him more as a lover than a fighter."

"When it comes to those he loves, he's a fighter all the way. He—" The conversation is halted when the door flies open, it slams into the wall with a bang, shaking and rattling.

We all turn our heads and see Reign in the doorway.

"Out," Quinn growls at him, she's definitely a fighter and not a lover.

Reign just stands there, his gaze flickering between the three of us. His fists are clenched and he's angry, what the fuck for I have no clue.

"Get out, Vanderbelt," Quinn sneers at him again.

"What's going on?" a sweet voice says and then from behind Reign, Alani appears.

"Nothing," the three of us all state at once.

"Right, nothing," Reign spits. His face is red with anger, his jaw clenched, like his fists. His gaze keeps flicking from me to Lauren to Quinn.

He's about to say something else when Alani tugs on his arm. "Come with me," she says, but he just stands there. His eyes are locked on Lauren's hand in mine. "Now, Vander-belt," Alani growls. For a little thing, she sure is a spitfire and it makes all the feelings I have for her bubble to the surface. Then again, she is a redhead, and we all know what they say about redheads—and that carries over to between the sheets. She pulls again on Reign's arm and this time he follows her. A few seconds later, she darts back and gives me a look that says, 'I'm here for you too.' Then she closes the door, leaving me alone with my sister and Quinn.

"She likes you," Lauren says, bumping my shoulder and then under her breath adds, "he does too."

"Me too," I mutter in reply, Lauren's eyes widen when she

realizes I mean both of them. "Do you want me to drive you to Mom and Dad's place?"

She shakes her head, "No ... I don't want to be alone tonight. Mom and Dad are out for a romantic dinner, I don't want to ruin their night."

"You can stay with me then." I know girls aren't supposed to stay in your room, but fuck that, my sister needs me. I'll take all the detentions they can throw at me if it means my sister is safe. "Can't believe I'm saying this, but I can't wait to go back to New York, I fucking hate this town."

It hurts to hear her say she wishes she'd stayed in New York but if she did, she wouldn't have been attacked. All I know is, I need to find out who did this to her and when I do, that fucker is dead.

REIGN

"YOU NEED to calm your fucking farm, Vanderbelt," Alani hisses as I continue to pace back and forth in her bedroom.

"Don't tell me to calm my fucking farm, I don't even own a fucking farm, I'm not Old McDonald." She rolls her eyes at me. "Who the fuck was that chick?"

"That's what you're focused on right now, the chick?" I nod at her, once again earning an eye roll from her. "For your information, farmer boy." I smirk at her name for me. "That chick is Hudson's sister, Lauren."

"Hudson has a sister?"

"Duh," she replies with a headshake as if I should know that about him.

"Why doesn't she go here? Is she dumb or something?"

"Don't be such a judgmental dick. She's a dancer, an amazing dancer. She attends the Stepz Academy in New York."

"Huh," I say, the rage I felt at the thought of him hooking up with another chick dissipates. "Why was she in one of Quinn's hideous towels? And why was Quinn there?"

"It's none of our business, Reign."

"But—"

"Nope, no buts. Not. Our. Business. He knows we will be here for him when he's ready. Now, sit your ass down and come watch a movie with me."

"You wanna watch a movie with me? Now?"

"Yep, now either sit down or get the fuck out." She flicks her finger toward the door.

"Fine," I hiss, "but it better not be a chick flick."

It was worse, she made me watch a Disney-fucking-musical, at least it had Emma Watson in it. "You know what I love most about this story?"

"What?" I ask, pulling her to my side and snuggling with her.

"Belle fell in love with the beast when he was a beast. She loved what was on the inside, regardless of what he looked like on the outside. That there is pure love."

"Hmmmpf," I nod, "I never thought about it like that before."

"Of course you wouldn't because you are a guy and you look at the world differently than us."

"But the same can be said for you too because not many chicks think like that about this movie."

"Touché, Mr. Vanderbelt, touché. Now, get the fuck out of my room, I need my beauty sleep."

"You are beautiful regardless of how much sleep you get," I honestly tell her.

"Did you just Belle theory me?"

"I guess I did," I reply with a nod. "Think I can get a good night kiss before I go?"

"I think I can manage that." She beckons me to her with her index finger. Caging her underneath me, I press my lips to hers. Her tongue pushes into my mouth, slipping and sliding against mine. She breaks the connection and pushes on my chest. "Good night, Reign."

"Seriously? I'm just getting a goodnight kiss?"

"Yep," she states matter-of-factly. "My va-jay-jay needs a rest, who knew fucking two guys would wear a vag out?" She pushes on my chest again, indicating for me to get off her. "Call it payback for leaving me high and … wet that one time."

My lips lift in a smirk as I remember her on her knees before me. Her lips glistening with my precum, fucking Dad and his dinner demands cockblocking me. "Fine," I relent. "But next time you make me watch a Disney movie, there better be at least a hand job … and popcorn."

"Alani, make note … no more Disney movies with Reign … and stock up on popcorn."

Shaking my head, I climb off and stare down at her. She looks stunning with her red hair fanned out beneath her. "You really are fucking gorgeous," I tell her.

"Thank you but just so you know, your sweet words aren't getting you laid tonight."

"I didn't think they would." Leaning down, I press a quick kiss to her lips. "Good night, Alani."

"Good night, Reign."

Exiting her room, I make my way back up to mine with a goofy grin on my face. Before I reach my room, I bump into Hudson. He looks like shit. "Everything okay with your sister?" He shrugs at me, and I hate seeing him like this. Stepping to him, I slide my hand around the back of his neck and bring his head to mine. Resting my forehead on his, I murmur, "Red and I are here if you need anything." He nods and smiles, but it doesn't reach his eyes.

He kisses me quickly on the lips before stepping around me and heading toward his room.

Spinning around, I watch him walk away. I don't like seeing him like this but as Alani said, it's none of my business. He knows I'm here and that's all there is to it. I just have to be patient and let him deal with whatever is going on with his sister. Patience isn't a virtue of mine but for the man I love, I will try. I will do anything for him and Alani, anything.

ALANI

WALKING into the cafeteria just after lunch, I smile when I see Hudson, Lauren, and Reign sitting at one of the tables in the back chatting. The boys are laughing and Lauren, well, she's there but there's a glazed-over look on her face. She looks broken, I have never met her in person before, but right now, all I want to do is envelop her in my arms and make it all go away. I don't know what went down last night, but it looks like she needs some female company, so I grab a coffee and two brownie slices and make my way over to them.

"Hey," I say in greeting. Placing my drink and the sweet

treats down, I drop into the chair next to Reign. "I'm Alani," I say to Lauren, "and you look like you need a brownie."

Lauren's gaze flicks back and forth between the decadent chocolate slice and me. Her mouth opens and closes. "I really shouldn't, but ..."

"We all deserve a treat every now and then," I tell her. Picking up my brownie, I slide the plate over to her.

"I'll take it," Hudson states and reaches for it. Lauren and I both reach out and slap his hand away. "Ohh," he hisses, "you two are vicious."

"Duuuuude," Reign draws the word out, "you never get in the way of a woman and her brownie. That's like Girl 101."

"Where's the 'I got your back bro' code?" Hudson whines, looking butthurt that Reign is siding with Lauren and me.

"Sorry but 'girl who we're fucking' code, trumps that."

"At least he didn't get jealous over your sister," I unhelpfully state. My comment causes Lauren to laugh and when she smiles, it lights up her face.

Reign sneers, "I don't have a sister," while Hudson deadpans, "Huh?"

"Our fella here thought you were cheating on us with your sister, and he got all growly after you kicked us out of the bathroom last night. It was highly entertaining. He was sulking until I put him in his place and informed him Lauren is your sister and not another secret lover."

Lauren breaks out laughing, like full-on belly laughing. "Oh. My. God," she stutters between breaths, "that is the funniest thing I have ever heard. I mean, did you not see the resemblance between us?" And she's right, Hudson and Lauren could be twins.

"No, I was focused on the hideous towel of yours."

"Yeah, it was quite hideous, wasn't it?"

Quinn Ellis is known for her hideous towels, it's been a running joke on the girls' floor for as long as I can remember, and speak of the devil, she sashays into the cafeteria and when she sees us, she turns and makes her way over.

Lauren jumps up and immediately hugs Quinn. They whisper together and then Lauren looks at us. "Back in a sec." The three of us sit here and watch her walk out of the cafeteria with Quinn.

Before Lauren returns, Reign's brothers and Remy arrive. They make themselves at home and our quiet catch-up is now not so quiet.

Lauren and Quinn return, but Lauren and Hudson have to leave to get ready for their parents' anniversary party. Going by the look on both their faces, that party is the last place they want to be.

We end up having a movie night in the lounge and it's fun, but I miss Hudson, as does Reign. He and I spend the night acquainting ourselves with each other's bodies. And because we are such good partners, we film ourselves pleasuring each other and send it to Hudson. Earning ourselves a short video back of his fist wrapped around his dick before he comes all over his hand. FYI solicited dick videos from one of your partners is hot, unsolicited ones from strangers, not so much.

Before drifting off to sleep, Reign and I make plans to pick him and Lauren up in the morning for her flight back to New York.

After dropping Lauren off at the airport, the three of us head to Lockhart Falls for a secret breakfast together. I long for the day we can be all touchy-feely and kissy-kissy in public, but Hudson and I are respecting Reign's wishes to be secret until he officially comes out to his brothers. He's apparently spoken to his mom, which I think is way too cute and she thinks he should tell Thatcher, Saint, and Hendrix. She's sure they will be accepting but I get his reservations. I still need to tell my parents I'm with two guys and I just know that it won't be received well. Mind you, I could be dating the president and they still wouldn't be happy.

The waitress delivers our breakfast and as soon as she walks away, Reign asks the one question that's been on the tip of my tongue for the last twenty-four hours. "So, you guys really don't have a clue who attacked her?"

"Nope," he sneers, shaking his head, "but I'm glad she's going back to NY and school. And if I know my sister like I think I do, now she's gone, we will never talk about it again and her attacker will remain a mystery forever."

"Does it not worry you?" I ask him. "Her being alone after what happened?"

"Naaah," he shakes his head, "if she was still here, yeah I would be, but she's safe in New York."

"New York is the least safe city in the world," I deadpan, stealing a strip of bacon off his plate.

"I think Crestwood takes that honor, babe," Reign states and then he reminds us of all the shit that has occurred in Crestwood recently. "Need I remind you of a murder, in which the killer is still on the loose. Child trafficking. Kidnapping. A fake suicide. And I'm sure there's more shit that we don't know about."

"Fair enough," I agree.

"And the biggest of all," Hudson interject, "the three of us being whatever the fuck we are."

"A throuple," I tell them and they both look at me with blank faces. "Three in a couple, throuple."

"I like it," Hudson says with a grin. "So, when do we go public?" I kick him under the table, especially when Reign's eyes nearly bug out of his head.

"I … ummm, shit, fuck hell," he stammers, clearly upset with Hudson's question.

"When we are all ready," I state, placing my hands palm up on the table where each of them places theirs in mine, and Reign offers his to Hudson. "I don't want to hide us forever because I am deliriously happy and I just wanna sing it from the rooftops, but we need to take everyone's feelings into consideration, it's what throuples do."

"Me too," Hudson agrees. "I don't want to hide us. I mean, just so we can have breakfast together and show our affection for one another, we had to drive to Lockhart Falls, forty-five minutes away." Reign looks crestfallen and as if sensing his turmoil, Hudson adds, "But for you, Reign, I will keep this secret. I'd go anywhere for breakfast with you, Reign. And that extends to you too, Bitsy."

"I'm sorry," he dejectedly says. "It's just, what if my brothers shun me when I confess? They already have an inkling I like guys after I kissed Arlen in front of them but when I tell them straight and confirm it, it's a whole different thing."

"They won't," I reassure him. "And if they do, you'll still have us." And I mean that, I will fight to the death for my guys and no one better get in my way.

HUDSON

… one week later

BY THE TIME CLASS ENDS, I'm ready for today to be over and thankfully it nearly is. One more class after this and then I can just lie around with Alani and Reign on my bed. We can watch a movie together or maybe explore each other's bodies again. I keep thinking about last weekend, our night together. The morning after together, it was everything and more.

This week has been tough, Lauren is still lost in her head, and I hate seeing my vibrant sister not so vibrant anymore each time we FaceTime. She returned to New York after the party and she still refuses to go to the cops, which I think is a mistake, but it's her choice. I haven't told Reign or Bitsy the specifics of what went down, it's not my place to, and they understand. I love they're letting me deal with this in my own way. Just being with them is comforting enough.

The bell finally rings, and excitement simmers beneath the surface but the second my phone rings and I glance down to see my father's name before me, I groan. My day is about to turn to shit.

Swiping accept, even though the temptation to hit decline is strong, I bring the phone to my ear. "Hello, sir," I say in greeting.

"Hudson," he tersely says my name and then I'm met with silence.

"What can I do for you?"

"I expect your grades haven't slipped." That's not a question, it's a statement. "And I expect you're thinking with your head?"

"Yes, sir," I tell him. "Always doing my best." *And you'd know this if you actually spoke more than two words with me at the party on the weekend.*

"Is that sarcasm I hear in your tone, Hudson?" he snaps.

Yes, I internally shout while also flipping him the bird and smacking him in the face with a frying pan. There is no love lost between my father and me. "No, sir, just stating the truth."

"I don't pay for you to attend Crestwood to be worrying about getting laid or whatever next phase you're into." And there it is, the dig at my sexuality. Gripping the phone harder, I clench my teeth so I don't fly off the handle in the middle of the corridor. "Have you come to your senses yet?"

It still hurts to hear him call my sexuality a phase and ask me if I've come to my senses. From the moment I was honest with my father, he has never accepted I'm bi and our relationship has deteriorated. To Benjamin Finley, being into boys is the devil's work and I should be shunned because of it. I can only imagine what he's going to say when it comes out I'm in a throuple relationship with Alani and Reign. If I'm honest, I'm secretly happy Reign is keeping us a secret because I'm not looking forward to the day my dad finds out.

"I expect you to direct all your attention to your studies, Hudson. I raised you right and normal and I'd like to hear this phase of yours has passed. I look forward to the day you and I have another conversation and you inform me of the nice young lady you are courting and until that happens, you are not welcome at home. No son of mine will be with a man under my roof. If you want to be a part of this family, you will do as I order." And with that, he hangs up and for a few more moments, I stand still in the middle of the corridor with my phone glued to my ear.

Breathing deeply, I repeat his words over and over, *'you are not welcome at home. No son of mine will be with a man under my roof. If you want to be a part of this family, you will do as I order.'*

Students file past me unaware my father once again shunned me because of who I am. Emotion, another trait not to be shown in public, begins to build. Taking a deep breath, I force myself not to break down in the middle of school, couldn't have that getting back to him. Pushing through the crowd of students chatting with each other, I make it to the restrooms just before I crumble.

Not at all eager to get to my next class, I lock myself away in a stall. Slamming the door shut, I knock the toilet lid closed and sit down just as the first tear falls. I take a deep breath trying to collect myself, but it doesn't work, it never does. My father's words are always a hurtful reminder of what I am and what I will never be in his eyes. He and I had a great father-son relationship until I confessed who I really am.

As the conversation from that fateful day plays over in my mind, I realize, apart from the party the other night, I haven't been to the house since that day, or in the boat with him either.

Not a day goes by that I don't play his words over and over in my head, *"Liking boys isn't how I raised you, Hudson. A man and a woman are meant to lay together, not two men. The Bible is Adam and Eve, not Adam and Steve. I have never been more disappointed in you, Hudson. Get the fuck out of my sight."*

Our relationship has never been the same since I was honest, and I find that funny. He always told me to be honest and the one time I am brutally honest, it bites me in the ass.

A toilet flushes and I sit here and hold my breath. I was so in my head, I didn't even realize I wasn't alone, and right now, I don't want anyone to see me falling apart. I hear them open the cubicle door and wash their hands. I see their shadow beneath the door, but they don't say a word before the main door opens, creaking loudly before it clicks shut behind them.

Once I'm alone again, that's when I realize tears are still tracking down my cheeks. I wipe furiously at my eyes, knowing I'll have to skip the next class because my face will be red and puffy, and I just don't have it in me to face anyone right now.

My phone beeps from within my pocket, I'm worried it's my father so I ignore it. One lecture from him is enough per day, and right now, I can't handle more from him. I'll forever be the disgrace of our family, but I am who I am. I hate he'll never accept me but at the same time, I'm not going to change who I am for anyone.

Would my life be easier if I only liked Alani? Fuck yes, life would be easy breezy for me if that was the case, but just to fuck things up with Dad further, right now, I'm with Alani AND Reign. I can only imagine how Dad will take his son being in a throuple, he didn't take me being bi very well. This might just push him over the edge. Pulling my phone out, I send off a message to Alani.

HUDSON

We need to talk.

I hope she replies straightaway because I really need to talk to her, and I need to talk to her now. I need her to reassure me it's going to be okay. That we'll all be fine.

REIGN

SOMEONE DROPS into the seat beside me and when I look up, I see Rem. Looking around her, I search for Alani, but I don't see her. I don't know why I assumed they'd be together, school only finished half an hour ago.

"What's up, Re-EIGN?" she says, she's in a chipper mood.

"Not much, and you, Rem-E?"

"Same," she replies with a shrug.

"Where's Alani?" I ask her and then I immediately realize my mistake because why would I care? But thankfully, she doesn't seem to notice my faux pas.

"Not here," she nonchalantly states, and then she utters two words that confuse me to no end. "I know."

"You know what?" I throw back at her, but she gives me 'the look' and my eyes widen. Surely she doesn't know what I think she knows. "How?"

"I've had an idea for a while, but when you guys found us at the cabin and you kissed my brother, it piqued my suspicion. But what really confirmed it and added a whole other layer of 'now it really makes sense' was when I, umm, ahh," she drops her gaze and then quickly spits out, "I-saw-you-guys-together-in-the-woods." Those last words flow into one another and as I process them, my eyes widen at her words.

"Please don't tell anyone. I ... I still have a few things to work out before I tell my brothers but I'm, well, we're going to confess all soon."

"It's not my secret to tell but, Reign"—she reaches over and squeezes my arm in that comforting way she does—"don't hide who you really are. You're an amazing guy and I want you to be happy. Actually, I want you all to be happy."

"I am happy, Rem, it's just ..."

"I get it, but just know I'm here for you if you ever need someone to chat to. So is Arlen." *How did she know about Arlen?* I didn't think anyone knew but then again, she's close with her brothers, he's probably spoken about me since his return from the dead.

"I know, I've already spoken to him."

"You have?" she questions, shocked at this revelation.

"Yeah, he was my best friend, no, he was more than a best friend and I'll always love him, Rem, but ..."

"But you love—"

Nodding, a goofy grin appears on my face, but I think she's right. "Yeah. I think I do. And again, please don't say anything because I haven't said it yet."

"Your secrets are safe with me, but for what it's worth, I'm happy for you guys."

"Thanks, appreciate it."

We fall into mindless chatter about last night, but my mind is all over the place and sensing my inner turmoil, Remy doesn't hang around. She takes off and leaves me with a now cold coffee and my thoughts, and to be honest, I'm thankful for that. After my conversation with her, I need time to decompress before I see my guys.

My guys.

I love saying that, but one thing is for sure, I need to come clean with my brothers about who I really am. I know they'll have my back, but there's that teeny tiny niggling that when I tell them everything they'll shun me. Turn their backs on me and I can't lose my family. They are my everything, just like my guys are.

Dropping my head into my hands, I sigh in frustration because now I have even more secrets, and secrets always come out … just like I need to.

ALANI

STARING AT THE TEXT, I keep reading those four words over and over.

HUDSON

We need to talk.

Receiving that text from Hudson with no other context is unnerving. Everyone knows when someone says they need to 'talk' it's never good news. Is he wanting to end what we have already? I'll be gutted if he walks away because as much as I like each of them separately, I need them both together. Three is my new favorite number, it will never be two again.

My focus on this lesson is gone and while I wait for the bell to ring, I swear time drags by. The hands on the clock click slower and slower with each movement around the clock face.

Finally, the bell rings and before it's even finished ringing, I'm out of my seat and racing from the other side of the school to the main hall. I race up to the boys' floor and without knocking, I storm into Hudson's room.

"What the fuck is wrong with you?" I breathlessly shout at him, slamming the door behind me. "Don't you frickin know when a girl, hell, even a boy, receives a text saying, 'we need to talk' they immediately think the worst?"

"I'm aware, and that's why I sent a follow-up text."

"Nuh-uh." I shake my head. Digging my phone out, I thrust it into his face. "See nothing."

He scrunches up his face and grabs his phone off his bed, and when he opens his messages his eyes widen. "Ohh fuck-balls, I didn't press send." He turns it to face me. "As you can see, I was to follow it up with 'I've had a fucked-up day and I just need you.' And now 'cause of my fat finger moment, my fucked-up day just got even more fucked up. I'm so sorry."

"It's fine," I tell him. Walking over to him, I cup his cheek. "What happened?"

"My dad," he quietly says.

"Is he still being a dickwad asshole about you?"

"Yep," he replies, letting the 'p' pop, and that one word popping is full of sadness.

"Well, as I said, he's a dickwad asshole. Personally, I think you're fan-fucking-tabulous, Hudson Finley. So fan-fucking-tabulous in fact, we're going out. Tonight, I'm going to take you and Reign out to dinner and then I'm going to have you guys for dessert, and you'll forget all about senior Fuckwit Finley."

"Fuckwit Finley, I like that. But do you think I can have a dessert sampler before we go out?"

"That could be arranged, I mean, everyone deserves a treat every now and then."

"And you, Alani, are the sweetest treat of them all." We stare at one another, the temperature in the room rising with each breath we take. "Kiss me, Bitsy."

Leaning forward, I press my lips to his. Throwing a leg over, I drop down and straddle his lap. My tongue pushes into his mouth and I begin to grind myself on him. Breaking the connection, I pull back and grin. "For the record, I kissed you 'cause I wanted to, not because you demanded me to."

"Mmmhmpf." He nods, a smirk on his gorgeous face. "One more kiss, then shower, then dinner, and then my favorite ..."

"Dessert?"

He shakes his head. "Your pussy."

"I thought Reign's dick was your favorite."

"I have two favorites now."

"So greedy," I tease him.

"Says the woman who, if I remember correctly, was gagging for two dicks just yesterday."

"What can I say, I know what I want and after dinner, I want to be sandwiched between you and Reign as you both fuck me into next year."

"I like the sound of that."

"Perfect, I'll text Reign and tell him our plans for the evening."

ALANI

You, me, Hudson, dinner then a nightcap of you, me, Hudson where you both fuck me into next year.

"Invite sent," I tell him, "and I mean actually sent." I wink at him, and he just shakes his head. Reign texts back a winky emoji and then asks where we are, I tell him we're in Hudson's room.

"Soooo," Hudson drawls, "what shall we do before dinner?"

"I don't know about you, but I need to beautify myself. I have a hot date with two sexy assholes."

"You don't need to do a thing, Bitsy. You're beautiful just the way you are."

"I know, I am," Reign states as he walks into the room. I was so lost in Hudson and his words that I didn't even hear the door open. "And for the record, I think you're both fucking amazing and that's why I can't come to dinner tonight." He kisses Hudson on the lips and then me and then drops down next to us.

"Huh?" I deadpan, totally confused right now.

"I'm going to tell my brothers everything tonight. I don't want to hide us. I've done the hiding thing and I don't want to do that again. You both deserve better than to be kept as a dirty little secret."

"Are you sure?" Hudson asks, beating me to the punch.

"I'm sure." He nods. "Secrets always come out and this is one I want to reveal myself. I owe it to my brothers to be honest, they've always been honest with me. It's about time I did the same."

"Do you want us to be there with you?" I ask him, resting my palm on his thigh, reassuring him that I am definitely here for him if he needs me.

Again, he shakes his head. "I'd love nothing more, but I think this is something I need to do on my own, but I am definitely keen on this nightcap about fucking you into next year that you proposed."

"I propose we skip dinner and get right to the nightcap," Hudson suggests, his dick hardening beneath me.

"No," Reign and I both shout at the same time, causing us to laugh.

"You two are mean," Hudson whines.

"Just think about how amazing the end of the night is going to be. Delayed gratification, I think, is what they call it."

"Fuck delayed, I want it now," Hudson whines, and the pout on his face right now is priceless.

"Will this tide you over," Reign says before he grabs Hudson by the neck and pulls him in for a kiss. It's all teeth and tongue and from my view on Hudson's lap, it's sexy as hell. Breaking the kiss, Reign smiles brightly at Hudson. "Better?"

"No, 'cause now my dick is harder than stone and I have to wait a few more hours before I can relieve myself."

"Then this probably won't help you," I tell him. Gripping the sides of his head, I cover his mouth with mine. My tongue pushes into his mouth, sliding and caressing with his. My hips rock on their own accord, grinding his dick with my pussy. When I pull away from him, I lean over and kiss Reign in the same manner, just without the dick grinding, well, I keep grinding on Hudson and now I, well, my pussy, is all whiney like Hudson. It wants more too.

"You don't play fair, Bitsy," Hudson complains when I pull back from kissing Reign.

"Never said I did, but for the record, I'd totally jump you both right this second, but we all have work to do so, Reign, you go see your brothers and, Hudson, you go shower for dinner."

Climbing off his lap, I pick up my bag and before I exit his room, I look over my shoulder. "I'm thinking of a nice juicy steak for dinner. K?" He nods, and I walk out to start getting ready for my date with Hudson.

An hour and a half later, hand in hand, Hudson and I walk into the local steakhouse. I wish Reign was here with us but tonight, he's off telling his brothers everything. I'm so proud of him for doing that, it must be hard hiding something so big from your family.

The hostess escorts us to our table. Hudson pulls my seat out like the gentleman he is and then takes his across from me. He orders us a glass of wine each, even though we're only eighteen and I don't even know if I like a cabernet, hell, I don't even know if he ordered us red or white. I've never been on a date like this before, and I feel like a little kid who gets to stay up late on New Year's Eve.

As far as first dates go, this one is off to an epic start, and I can't wait for the bang—pun totally intended—at the end of the night. My date is a total gentleman, if only tomorrow wasn't a school day because then we could laze naked in bed together in the morning.

"Why do you look like your puppy just got run over?" he asks me, never missing a thing when it comes to my emotions. He and Reign can read me like a book, no one has ever been able to do that with me before. Not even my parents. They see what they want to see, and that's to follow the path they have set forth for me, but after giving into my desires with my guys, I think it's time I stood up to my parents too.

"I was just thinking I wish tomorrow wasn't a school day, that way we can snuggle and laze naked in bed together."

"What if I promise, come next Saturday morning, we can wake up and laze like that?"

"Personally, I'd like to wake up with your tongue between my thighs or maybe even your dick. Or even better, seeing your lips wrapped around Reign before you both turn your attention to me."

"I'm sure I can arrange something like that for you."

My clit begins to pulsate, and I have to squeeze my thighs together and lean forward to clench the sensation.

"You're horny right now, aren't you?" Nodding my head, I bite my bottom lip. He links his fingers with mine on top of the table and pulls me toward the center. He leans forward and rests his chin on our clasped hands, while lifting his index finger to beckon me closer. Shuffling forward, I stare intently at him and swallow back a moan, in this position the extra pressure on my clit is teasing. "Bitsy, I want you to remove your panties and hand them over."

"Are you Fifty Shadesing me right now, Huddy Boy?"

"Huh?" he deadpans, confusion written all over his face.

"Never mind," I tell him, shaking my head. "After I hand you my panties, then what?"

Before he can direct me on what to do next, the waitress arrives to take our order and before she looks at us, she places our wines in front of each of us. She's a girl from school and when she finally lifts her gaze and sees Hudson and me, she smiles brightly. "Oh. My. God," Nicole screeches. "Are you two, like dating?"

We nod and she squeals again but then schools her expression. "I thought you liked dudes?" she asks Hudson.

"I appreciate all things fine," he replies, throwing me a wink.

"Oh. My. God, that's so romantic." She looks at me. "You are so lucky, you bitch."

"Yeah, I am," I tell her and imagine how she'd react if she knew I was also with Reign. It might sound cocky to some, but right now, in the middle of this restaurant with Hudson sitting across from me, looking like he wants to devour me, I feel a million bucks.

"So, what can I get you both?" she asks us. Hudson and I both order a steak, medium, with a baked potato and side salad. "I'll also bring you a bottle of this amazing red from

Australia, it pairs so well with that steak and will complement the glass you're about to have."

Before we can say it's fine, she hurries off to get our order in and deal with other customers. We sit here and watch her race away.

Averting my gaze back to Hudson, I realize he's still staring at me. Hunger reflects back at me. "So, Huddy Boy, you were saying something about doing this?"

Reaching across the table with my closed fist, I drop my G-string on the table in front of him. He picks up my discarded underwear, balls them in his fist, brings his hand to his nose, and inhales deeply. "Fuck, you smell divine." He licks his lips and then slides them into his pocket.

"You know, this is pretty unfair, I'm sitting here with no panties on, and you're fully dressed."

"Who said I'm wearing any?" he throws back at me, and the thought of Hudson sitting across from me commando has my pussy dripping.

Nicole returns with our bottle of wine, even though we haven't finished our first glass. She and Hudson talk about wine as she opens the bottle and lets it air, whatever the hell that means. I can't tell you what they spoke about because I was too focused on watching Hudson. For someone who was so down and broken earlier, he's shining brightly right now. He doesn't seem to have a care in the world, but I know the truth, underneath that gorgeous smile, is a boy who just wants his dad's approval.

Nicole leaves and Hudson picks up his wine. "A toast." Nodding, I pick my glass up. "To the most beautiful woman in Crestwood and an amazing night."

"I'll drink to that." We clink glasses and I take a sip. My eyes widen when the robust wine dances across my taste buds. I moan at the taste because that's the most delicious red wine I have ever drunk.

"I love hearing you make that sound," Hudson informs

me before taking another sip of his wine. "Makes me want to throw you down on this table and feast on you, but I don't want any other fucker, male or female, to see what's mine."

"Well," I counter, "there's one person you wouldn't mind sharing me with." I wink at him. "But to be honest, I'm not one for public fucking." He eyes me about the other night. "That doesn't count. But right now, the urge to drop to my knees, crawl under the table, and free your briefless commando cock has me dripping even more than I was before."

"Fuck, Bitsy, you cannot say shit like that to me. My cock is going to pierce through this table in a minute."

"Fair's fair, you cannot say shit like that to me when I'm soaked for you and want nothing more than for you to slide that dick of yours into me."

"I thought it was my tongue so I can have you for dessert?"

"Dick, tongue, fingers, I'm not fussy. I just need you to relieve this ache between my thighs."

Once again, the moment is interrupted when Nicole returns with our meals and it's probably for the best, considering how X-rated our conversation just got.

She places our meals down, refills our wine, and leaves us be. The steaks look amazing and with gusto, I cut into the juicy fillet before me. It's cooked to perfection, it's ohh so tender and just melts in my mouth. I think my mouth is as moist as my pussy right now, and that's saying a lot considering how wet I am for Hudson.

Looking up, I see him staring at me, "What?" I ask, wiping at my face in case I have food on it.

"Those sounds you're making are making it very hard for me to concentrate."

"Is that so?" He nods. "Well, I propose a game."

"A game?"

"Yep, a game." I nod and pick up my glass. Slowly, I bring

the glass to my lips and take a sip, building the anticipation for what's to come. Placing the glass down, I stare intently over at him. "I want you to take your hand, free your dick, and make yourself come while I slide my hand between my thighs and finger myself. First one to come loses."

"Sounds like a win to me," he nonchalantly replies.

"I guess in this game, there are no losers. So, wanna play with me?"

"Fuck yes, fuck yes I do." He picks up his wine and chugs it back, he winces as he swallows and after placing the glass back down, he moves his hand under the table.

Picking up my glass, I leisurely take another sip and then I slide my other hand down between my thighs. Brushing past my clit, I hiss. That tight little bud is so sensitive right now. What I really want is for Hudson to duck under the table, crawl over, and suck and nibble on it.

"I want to bite and suck on your clit," Hudson tells me as if he knew exactly what I was just thinking about.

"Well, I want to lick the tip of your dick like an ice cream before sucking it into my mouth and sliding my lips down to the base. The head hitting the back of my throat causing me to gag and choke."

He hisses at that thought, I really wish the table wasn't in the way. I want to see his hand gripping his shaft. Squeezing and pumping.

My X-rated vision is interrupted when a shadow looms over the table above me. I manage to drag my eyes away from Hudson to see who's standing there. My eyes widen, and all sexy sensations dissipate in an instant, but my hand is frozen between my thighs as I stare up at the person before me.

HUDSON

THIS IS the most erotic thing I have ever done. Considering I've only just turned eighteen, it's not surprising, but the moment is interrupted when an older man stops by our table. Quickly, I shove my dick back into my pants and I sit here, hoping he can't tell what I was just doing. My heart is racing, I knew doing this in a restaurant was risky, I just didn't know how risky.

My dick is safely back in my pants when Alani utters one word that instantly deflates my dick, "Dad?" Alani says, her voice laced with shock, and fear flashes behind her eyes. "Wwww … what are you doing here?"

"I could ask you the same thing," he sneers. He turns his attention to me and looks me up and down. From the disdain on his face, I can tell he thinks I'm a piece of shit on the bottom of his shoe.

"Having dinner with my boyfriend," she hisses.

"Boyfriend," he growls. "I thought you were going to date Raymond Blanchard. That was the whole reason for dinner with them recently."

My eyes widen at this revelation. Alani never said anything about the dinner with her parents. I knew it didn't go well but this, I didn't expect. Is she just playing me? Playing us? Tiding herself over until this Raymond fucker swoops in.

"No, Dad, I will not be dating him. If you or Mom even bothered to ask about my life, you would have known what was happening." She stands up for herself and seeing her like that causes me to push my chest out with pride.

Pulling my hand out from under the table, I offer him my precum-covered hand. "Hudson Finley, Mr. Thomas, pleasure to meet you."

Her dad takes my hand and Alani's eyes almost bug out of her head when she realizes what hand I just used.

"Gerald Thomas," her dad informs me. "Pleasure to meet you. I presume you met at school?"

"Yes, sir, in detention." I can't help but mess with the asshole.

"Alani, is this true?" he growls at Bitsy and I hate the tone he's using. With four words, she crawls into herself, and I feel like a dick for making a lame joke.

"I'm only joking, sir. We share a few classes together and last year after doing an assignment together, I was smitten. Took me a few months to man up and approach her, but it was the best decision I ever made." I look up at him, really look at him. "Your daughter is amazing, sir."

"She takes after her mother." He beams but Alani scoffs.

"Dad, Mom and I are nothing alike. She—"

But before she can finish, a round, robust lady joins us. "Gerald, what's … Alani," she says her name in a tone I don't like, "what are you doing here? Are you here with Raymond?" When her eyes land on me, that shit stain look I felt from Gerald is nothing compared to the contempt reflecting back at me from the lady I'm guessing is her mother.

"Hello, Mother, and no, I'm here with Hudson. My boyfriend." She looks over at me and smiles. "Hudson, this is my mom, Portia."

"Pleasure to meet you, Portia." Fuck using niceties with her, she wants to be a bitch to her daughter, well, I'll be a bitch right back in said daughter's honor.

"Portia, Hudson here was just telling me how smitten he is with our daughter," Gerald beams as he says this. This man is hard to keep up with.

"Yes, yes, but what about Raymond?"

"What about him?" Alani snaps. I notice her other hand is still between her thighs, and for some reason, the thought of her with her fingers in her cunt while she's talking with her parents is such a turn-on. My cock comes back to life as I imagine her fingers sliding in and out. I wish her parents would fuck off so we can get back to our game. "This isn't the eighteen hundreds you can't dictate who I date. Raymond is a nice guy and as I said, when he attends Crestwood next year, I'll show him around, but I will never date him. Hudson and I are dating now and I'm happy."

"But—"

"No buts, Mom. If you had even asked me anything personal the other night or anytime for that matter, you would have known. Instead, you ambushed me with a setup. Luckily, Raymond is a nice guy and when we spoke, I told him all about Hudson." Hearing that causes my heart to flutter. "So please, either take interest in me and my life or butt out."

"Alani, what has gotten into you?" *Me. Reign. Both of us*, I think and smirk as her mom covers her chest in fake hurt. "I don't think this man is a good influence on you." Her mom looks at me. "No offense."

Not giving her an out, I stand up and tower over her. "Offense taken, Portia. As I was telling Mr. Thomas," I purposefully treat him with respect and address him properly, "your daughter is an amazing woman." Walking around the table, I stand behind her and rest my hand on her shoulder, reassuring her I'm here. She covers my hand, looks up at me, and smiles. "I'm proud to call her mine and that's what she is, mine."

"Gerald, are you going to let him speak to me like that?"

"Speak to you how? All I'm hearing is a young man singing praise for our daughter and that's all I want as a father."

Her mother huffs and storms off.

"Sor—"

"No, Dad, don't apologize for her. That's all you ever do, but I appreciate you sticking up for Hudson and me."

"I just want you to be happy, Alani. It's a dog-eat-dog world out there."

"Dad, I'm eighteen and still in school. I've got plenty of time to figure it all out."

"It'll fly by quicker than you think. I'll let you get back to it."

And with that, he walks away back to his table. I watch him walk to his wife and notice her arms crossed with a sneer on her face and her glare is directed at me.

Looking down at Alani, I can tell she's still smiling. She must sense me looking at her because she lifts her gaze back up to mine, and I see happiness etched on her beautiful face. "What?"

"You stood up for me and so did Dad. Am I drunk?" She picks up her glass and that's when I notice her hand is still under the table.

"Is ...."

"Yep," she nods, "I do believe I won."

"Uhhh uh, Bitsy, no one has come yet so the game is still in play," I remind her.

She raises her eyebrows and because I'm focused on her, I notice the subtle movement of her shoulder. Leaning over, I grab her napkin and drop it. "Oops," I playfully utter. Dropping to my knees, I duck down, lift the tablecloth, and look underneath to see her hand between her thighs. The squelching of her fingers sliding in and out echoes beneath the table.

Lifting my head, she's biting her lip. I don't know whether to look under the table or at her face, but I don't need to make a choice because she bites down hard on her lip and comes. She quietly moans and the sound has my cock coming back to life.

She opens her eyes when she comes back to earth, she has a sated grin on her face.

"I win," she tells me. "Well technically, I lost because I came first but as you said, this is a win/win game." She winks and then takes a victory sip of wine.

"I do like this win/win game and we are both definitely winners. I got to watch you come and as soon as we exit this restaurant, I will get to come in you," I tell her as I stand back up.

"Check please," she sings out while giving me a sultry look.

Shaking my head, I place a kiss on her forehead before I walk back to my side of the table and sit back down.

With the interruptions over, we finish our dinner. Our plates are cleared away and I take a moment to watch her, she really is something. "I can't believe you kept your fingers inside you when your parents came over."

"I can't believe you shook my dad's hand with the hand you just had wrapped around your dick."

"Yeah, that was kinda awesome."

She bites her lip, again, and I'm overwhelmed with the need to have her. I need her spread out on my bed and I need to see her fingers slide in and out of her cunt, and once she's come all over her fingers, only then will I slide my dick into her while Reign slides his dick into me. "What do you say, Bitsy, we take this game back to my room and we watch each other play?"

"Check please," she sings out again, and I can't help but laugh. Alani is a breath of fresh air and I'm so glad to have her, and Reign, in my life.

REIGN

… a few hours earlier

THE OTHER WEEK was a turning point for the three of us and I'm glad it happened how it did. I was worried my conversation with Arl may have affected what I'd been building with them, but somehow, it, and he made everything all the more clear. I'm glad that I'll still have him in my life, and I know that after our chat and what happened with Alani and Hudson after, I'm not IN love with him anymore. I'm unequivocally in love with them.

My stomach growls so I climb out of bed, pull my jeans and Henley back on and go in search of food. Running my fingers through my hair, I style it in that messy but together way. Grabbing my Chucks, I slip them on and head to the cafeteria to grab some lunch, well a late lunch since it's almost three.

Walking through the halls, it hits me, in a few short months, we will have graduated and be at college, away from this Godforsaken place and out in the big wide world. I still don't know what I want to do with my life, but as long as I have Alani and Hudson by my side, I know I can do anything.

Not wanting to be social, I grab a sandwich and a coffee and head back to the dorms to wait in the lounge so I can hopefully catch Alani and/or Hudson before they head upstairs, but little did I know, they were already in his room.

I'd love nothing more than to recreate what went down that first night but at the same time, I want us to take our time. I want us to explore each and every inch of each other's bodies, making it romantic and perfect. Not that it isn't already perfect, the three of us go together like, well, I don't know what three things go together perfectly, but it's perfect between us and I will do everything in my power to keep it that way. We all deserve to be happy. Fuck, I sound like a girl right now *make it more romantic.* Thank fuck my brothers can't hear me.

After my chat with Rem, I know I need to tell my brothers and it feels like this evening is the perfect time to do so, but when I get that text from Alani proposing her for dessert, I'm close to saying 'fuck it' but I know, dessert will be that much sweeter.

Swinging by his room, I tell them what I'm going to do. When she offered for them to be with me, I was close to saying yes, but I feel like this is something I need to do alone so I encourage them to go on their date, with a promise to take them out together as soon as possible. I can't wait to shout to the world that Alani Thomas and Hudson Finley are mine, but first, I need to come out to my brothers.

REIGN

I'M SO WORKED up right now, my palms are itchy. My heart feels like it's about to explode from my chest, and my mouth, it's drier than the Mojave Desert. My stomach is knotting tighter and tighter as the seconds tick by. Every time I think about what I'm about to do, I feel like I might throw up because I'm about to confess everything to my brothers.

Everything.

I'm finally going to admit to them that I'm bi-sexual and I'm also telling them about Hudson and Alani.

No more secrets and no more hiding who I'm with.

I'm so fucking nervous. What if they can't accept me? Us? Everything?

Biting the bullet, I grab my phone and send a group message.

REIGN

SOS

Those three letters will ensure they come straightaway, and they do because they are my brothers and they have my back.

My heart rate spikes further when a knock sounds at my door, the handle rattles and the knock comes again. "Unlock the door, asshole," a gruff voice echoes through the door.

Staring at the wood, I feel like I can't breathe. Swallowing the lump in my throat, I slowly make my way toward it. Inching it open, Saint and Hendrix meet my gaze and from the looks on their faces, they know something's up.

"You okay?" Saint asks as worry flickers across his face.

"Yeah yeah," I lie. "I'm fine, come in," I tell them and just as I'm about to close the door. Thatcher calls out, "Hey, wait up."

Waiting for him, he brushes past me gripping my shoulder in that reassuring brotherly way, and that one little touch eases my worries slightly.

"Everything okay?" he questions, his face just like Saint's.

"Yeah, I just need to talk to you guys." Swallowing again, I stand here by the door, thinking that being close to an exit might be a good idea.

"What's going on?" Hendrix asks.

They all stand around my room, arms crossed against their chests, each with concern and worry etched on their faces.

"Maybe you should sit," I tell them, nodding into my room.

"Reign, just tell us, man, I'm fucking dying here," Hendrix demands.

"I-I," I mutter, "Fuck."

"Reign, whatever it is, we have your back," Thatcher tells me.

I chuckle. "I'm not so sure," I whisper.

Saint comes toward me and places his hand on my shoulder. That feeling of panic starts to build inside me again. Gazing at my brother's intense stare, that urge to flee bubbles to the surface.

"Reign," they all say my name at once.

Tears prick my eyes and for the first time since Arlen died, I feel absolute fear. "I'm bi," I whisper, keeping my eyes downcast. I can't look at them. The thought of seeing disgust or hate on their faces is more than I can bear.

I can feel my brothers moving.

Each one comes closer.

Closing my eyes, I wait for the shove. Wait for the fist to my face.

But nothing comes.

Lifting my head, I stare at my brothers and I don't know what I see reflecting back at me.

"Did you say you were bi?" Hendrix repeats my declaration. It's as if he needs to voice it himself to be sure those are the words I spoke out loud.

I nod quickly.

The silence is deafening, and I know I need to tell them everything. I'm dreading their next words and before they can yell or whatever, I continue. Take the bull by the horns as such. "I was secretly dating Arlen when he, well before he fake died," I murmur, hating how softly the words leave my lips. I'm not ashamed, I'm just scared about how they will react.

"Arlen?" Saint asks.

I nod slowly.

"So, you and Arlen?" Hendrix sighs.

With a shake of my head, I swallow deeply. "Not anymore, we're different people now," I stammer slightly and lower my gaze back to the carpet. I almost choke on my words, knowing Arlen too is hiding something. I hate I can't help him but before I focus on him, I need to focus on me.

Lifting my gaze, I don't look at any of them. I stare at a spot on the wall above my bed. "I'm with Hudson now."

"Finley?" Thatcher asks.

Nodding again, I feel like a damn bobblehead.

"Okay," Saint says.

Swallowing I then mutter, "And Alani."

"Wow," Hendrix breathes. I'm unable to decipher his tone but I'm too scared to look at him. At them. Finally, I pull my gaze from the wall and look to my brothers, expecting to see hate or anger but I see nothing but acceptance. They're all smiling.

"You're with them both, like what, a throuple?" Thatcher checks with me.

I nod again. Working up the courage to continue. "We're all together and I care about them a lot."

"Are you happy?" Hendrix asks.

For the first time since they entered my room, I find myself smiling and those nerves are disappearing with each passing second. Nodding vigorously, I confirm, "I'm very muchly happy." *Very muchly?* Nice Engrish there Reign.

"Good," Thatcher states.

"You're okay with me …" I stop myself. For some reason saying it out loud again feels harder.

"With you liking boys and girls?" Saint says, smirking at me.

"Yeah, we can deal with that, I mean you could do worse," Hendrix says.

"I thought you'd tell me to leave too. Tell me that I'm sick and a disgrace to the Vanderbelt name."

"I think Dad takes the trophy for that one, dude," Hendrix says, causing us all to chuckle.

"Really?" I question again because they really don't care who I'm with … or that I'm bi.

"Fuck, Reign, you're our brother regardless of who you like. It doesn't matter to us, nothing will change that. Besides, if someone told me I couldn't be with Remy I'd go completely apeshit, and I'm guessing if you feel this strongly for Hudson and Alani, then it's the same for you too." He raises his eyebrows in the 'mmmhmpf' kind of way. "Am I right?" he says.

My lip lifts in a smile and I nod. "Yeah, it is. The heart wants what it wants and mine wants Alani … and Hudson."

Saint pulls me into him, hugging me tightly. "We love you no matter what, Brother, just remember that." He rests his forehead against mine and squeezes the back of my neck, just like we did when we were little.

For all the worry I had, I never expected my brothers to accept me and my confession so easily.

A soft knock on the door makes me turn. My heart begins to beat in that pitter-patter kind of way because I know exactly who is on the other side of this door. For once I'm not afraid to hide and from this moment on, I don't plan on hiding what they mean to me anymore, from anyone.

My brothers accept me and that's all that matters.

Hudson and Alani are everything to me and I don't plan on messing this up.

ALANI

AFTER DINNER, Hudson and I decide to head to Reign's room. He hasn't messaged us and I'm worried it didn't go well with his brothers. "What if they beat him to a pulp and he's bleeding out on the floor in his room?" I ask Hudson as he pulls into a parking spot back at school.

"You really think his brothers would do that?"

"I … I don't know. I mean, you saw how they treated Rem when she first arrived, they can be right royal assholes when they want to be so I wouldn't put it past them."

"Yes, they can be fucksticks when they want to be, but

Reign is their brother and those four have a bond like no other, I don't think this will break that bond."

"I hope you're right," I tell him as I climb out.

Lacing our fingers together, we head inside and without a word, go straight to Reign's room. Lifting my hand, I knock on the door. I can't hear anything on the other side and my heart gallops like a wild stallion running free.

The door opens soon after I knock, and I smile when I see Reign grinning back at us. I take a quick look over him and don't see any blood or missing teeth and relief floods my system but just to be sure, I ask, "It went well then?"

He nods and I let out the breath I was holding. "Thank fuck," I breathlessly woosh out, "I'd hate to have to kick your brothers' asses."

"I'd like to see that," a deep voice says from inside and my eyes widen when I realize they're still here.

Both Hudson and Reign laugh. I eye Reign and elbow Hudson in the stomach. He grunts and I push past Reign into his room. His brothers are grinning at me when I come to a stop. Thatcher is sitting on his desk chair backward, resting his arms on the back. Saint is lounging in the beanbag Reign fucked me on earlier today, and Hendrix is sitting on the floor, leaning against the wall under the window with his legs outstretched and crossed at the ankle.

"So, you think you can kick our asses?" Hendrix taunts.

"I don't think, I know. I brought your brother to his knees, and I can do it to you too."

"Look, I'm all for you and Reign and Hudson being all throupley, but I draw the line at adding myself to the mix for a multitude of reasons. For starters, Reign is my brother and I have no desire to see him fuck either one of you, solo or together. That's too close to home for me," Thatcher states, and I nod at him.

Hendrix is the next one to speak. "One partner is enough to handle—"

"Is Quinn keeping you on your toes, dear brother?" Saint teases Hendrix and everyone but Hendrix laughs.

"Fuck off," he sneers, punching Saint in the arm before turning his attention back to us. "As I was saying, how you manage the three of you, it's a true testament to you all but I gotta ask, how the hell did the three of you happen?"

"Well," I say, climbing onto Reign's bed and leaning against the wall. Both my guys join me, one on either side. "For me, it all started the day Arlen died. That afternoon, I found Reign at the cliffs. He was upset over Arlen but because no one knew about them, or him, he had to hide how he was really feeling. I saw something in him that day and I was compelled to help him."

"That was the day I first kissed you," Reign adds with a dreamy look on his face.

"It was." I smile at the memory. "And from that first kiss, I knew you were special." Looking over at him my smile widens because he's come so far since that day. He leans toward me and presses his lips to mine.

"That was a turning point for me too, Red," he mumbles against my lips. We pull apart when there's a knock at the door but before anyone can move, Thatcher jumps up. "That'll be Rem, I know she'll want all the story too." He opens the door to his girlfriend and the two of them kiss as if they've been apart for months and not just a few hours.

"Shit," I hiss, "I haven't said anything to her yet."

"Said anything to me about what?" she asks when she and Thatch stop sucking each other's faces off. She looks at the three of us on the bed. Her eyes dart across us several times and then they widen. She points her finger accusingly at me. "I knew it. I knew you were fucking them both."

"What? How?"

"Please, I have eyes. Anyone with vision could see that the three of you were smitten with one another, but the dead giveaway was that I saw the three of you together."

"What?" I hiss again, "When?"

"You saw what?" Thatcher growls in that moody way he does.

"Nothing," I quickly say while at the same time, Remy says, "I saw the three of them threesomeing in the dark. It was like my very own live porn show."

"Is that why you've been so randy?"

She nods.

"Fucking hell," I mumble, shaking my head.

"Whatever the case, I'm happy you guys are happy," she says, as if us being a throuple is no big deal. "Now, what are we discussing?"

"We're getting the story of how they became a throuple," Thatcher tells her, returning to his seat.

"Awesome." Remy claps and then drops down onto the floor and crosses her legs, crisscross apple sauce style. She rests her elbows on her knees and implores me with her eyes to proceed.

"To catch you up, Reign was sad over Arlen and I talked to him. We've just had our first kiss—"

"And she was already smitten," Reign cockily adds. "Me, on the other hand, I was a complete mess and later that night, I ended up in the library drinking."

HUDSON

"I FOUND you drunk as a skunk in the library," I say, taking over story time. "And that night, you drunkenly kissed me," I tell everyone with a smile. Turning to Reign, I ask, "Do you remember that? You were pretty trashed."

"I remember." He smiles fondly at the memory. "I also remember bits and pieces after that but it's all foggy. Guess I should thank you for looking after me that night." He chuckles. "The next morning, I remember thinking I was totally screwed because now I had feelings for both you and Alani."

Saint interrupts me, "So in one night, Reign lost Arlen, which by the way, we need the story of you two next please."

Reign nods. "I can do that, it's the least I owe you guys."

"You don't owe us shit, Reign. Get that idea out of your head … or I'll get Alani to kick your ass," Thatcher says, earning himself an eye roll from Reign.

"But getting back to the story of you three. In one night, you lost Arlen. You kissed Alani and Hudson and got drunk. How the fuck did we not know about all of this?"

"I only let you see what I wanted you guys to see."

"Dude," I interject, "you let everyone only see what you wanted them to see, but that night, I saw under your mask and that was the night, my feelings for you changed."

"Seems that night was pivotal to all of us," Alani adds. She takes each of our hands and squeezes them before resting them on her lap.

"Looks like you all have Arlen to thank for getting together. Him faking his death was the start of the three of you being a throuple," Remy states, smiling at that thought.

Everyone nods at that assessment and to tell you the truth, I hadn't thought of it like that before. I should find Arlen and thank him because without his 'death' I'm not sure that the three of us would have found each other.

"So, what happened next?" Remy asks.

"Well, that kiss was it for Reign and me—" He leans across Alani, slides his hand around the back of my head, and brings his lips to mine. Kissing me hard.

"Actually, it was just the start," Reign mumbles against my lips.

"Is it weird that seeing Reign kiss a guy isn't weird?" Saint says as Reign and I break apart.

"I find it hot," Alani breathlessly states.

"Of course you do," Remy teases her friend and then she looks to Saint. "I think it's not weird because it's meant to be."

"That's very philosophical of you," he says and then his eyes widen. "Hang on a minute. The next morning, I found you," he points at Reign, "vomiting your guts out…"

REIGN

NODDING, I purse my lips and shudder as I remember how I felt that day. "Yep. In my vodka hungover state, I was even more confused than the day before. I had so many emotions and feelings coursing through me at that time and I didn't have anyone I could talk to."

"Why didn't you talk to us?" Thatcher asks me.

Shrugging, I squeeze the back of my neck. "I was so confused myself. How could I articulate to anyone what I was feeling? And add in the fact none of you guys knew I was bi."

Saint smacks me in the foot. "Still can't believe you'd think we'd care."

"Dad would have."

"Fuck him," Saint sneers. "He never had our backs on anything so his feelings are moot."

"Moot," I tease him, "did you just say moot?"

He flips me the bird. "As I was saying, he doesn't count and you know what?"

"What?"

"No one's feelings except yours and Alani's and Hudson's matter. Fuck everyone else."

Nodding, I take in his words and realize he's right. I have never before cared about what anyone thinks and this is no different. I'm happy and they're happy and at the end of the day, that's all that matters.

"You're right," I say to the room. "I'm happy and they're," I flick my thumb to Alani and Hudson," happy. As you said bro, fuck everyone else."

"Deliriously happy," Alani says. "You both made all my dreams come true." Before I can agree with her, she leans over and kisses me. Her tongue pushes into my mouth but it's not enough. Sliding my hands into her hair, I deepen the kiss and fuck her mouth with my tongue.

One of my brothers groans and I remember where we are so I reluctantly break the kiss.

Her cheeks are flushed and I love seeing her like that. As much as I want to confess all to my brothers, the need to fuck Alani is strong, especially when she turns and kisses Hudson like she just kissed me. I hope I never lose this feeling at seeing them kiss. This happy feeling is foreign and now that I've had a taste, I'll do whatever it takes to keep it.

HUDSON

THEIR KISS STARTS OUT SWEET, but when he slides his hand into her hair, I'm expecting him to pull her onto his lap but surprising me, that doesn't happen. They pull apart and she turns to me and grins before she leans over and kisses me as well.

"Stop sucking face and tell us what happened next," Remy says, interrupting our kiss.

"Fine," Alani hisses and she snuggles back into my side.

"So, okay, it was a few days after I found Reign drunk in the library. I kept playing our kiss over and over in my head. I was positive it was just a drunken mistake on his behalf but deep down, I wanted it to happen again."

"Well, I am irresistible," Reign throws out at me. The look on his face is playful and it's moments like these that make me fall harder for him. Take away all the Lord's bullshit and Reign Vanderbelt is just a guy. He's the guy who has stolen my heart, well a part of my heart, and now that I have him, and Alani, I will do everything in my power to keep them.

"Someone thinks a lot of themselves," Hendrix teases.

"I find you irresistible," Alani and I both say at the same time, causing everyone to laugh at our synchronicity.

"Anyway," I continue, "after the drunken kiss, I couldn't find you anywhere. It was like you disappeared into thin air but I did keep seeing Alani and that pull to her was still there so I went after her."

"So you decided that you wanted to fuck Alani to forget about Reign?" Hendrix asks.

"Yep," I reply, nodding. "And I'm aware it was an asshole thing to do, but I was confused and messed up."

"And horny," Saint interjects.

"That, but I'm always horny around her and your brother."

"TMI, dude. TMI," Saint complains.

"Well, you were the one who brought up being horny," I throw back at him.

"Hang on, hang on." Hendrix raises his hand in a stop motion. "I remember that day," he says, nodding and grinning to himself. "I remember thinking it was awesome the nerd got the hot chick."

"You think I'm hot?" Alani asks him.

"Without a fucking doubt." That statement earns him a growl from Reign and a chuckle from me cause he's right, Alani is the hottest girl at Crestwood. Always has been, always will be. "Calm your tits, bro. I just think she's hot, I don't want to fuck her." He looks to Alani. "No offense."

"None taken," she states with a shrug.

"What about me?" Remy asks.

Hendrix opens his mouth to answer but Thatcher eyes him and growls, "It doesn't matter what my brother thinks, Peach, you are mine and mine only." And to state that fact, he stands up and leans over Rem. He covers her mouth with his in a kiss that is both hot and claiming all in one.

"We get it. Remy is yours," Hendrix says, then he looks back to me, "so, after I serenaded you guys, what happened next?"

"We continued up to Alani's room and well, you can all guess what happened."

"AAAAND," Bitsy adds, "that was the day I found out just how kinky you were."

"Who knew Huddy Boy here was so studly?" Saint says.

"Huddy Boy?" I question.

"I've heard Alani call him that and thought I'd try it out," Saint replies.

"I do call you that," Alani confirms, smiling brightly at me.

Saint has a 'see, I know shit' look on his face and then scrunches it up, "But it's a little weird so I'll stick with Hudson."

I just nod because what can you say to that? "Ooookay, where were we?"

"I said who knew that Hudson," he places emphasis on my name, "was so studly?"

"I did," Alani confirms, raising her hand with an even brighter smile than before on her gorgeous face. Her smile infuses my soul and brings my cock to life, but now isn't the time to get a hard-on.

"So, what happened after you two bumped uglies?" Saint asks. "Surely you three got your shit together?"

"Not quite," I say. "Reign was still all in his head and messed up over everything—"

"Was not," he sneers, interrupting me.

"You were and you know it, now stop being a dick," I chastise him.

Alani adds, "You know, if you weren't such a dick, you would have been part of the kinky sooner, but I will admit, while Reign was struggling with his identity, so was I. While all these kinky things were fun and exciting, I was also thinking that no good could ever come from being with multiple guys at once. Sure, Sara Cate and Tate James make it seem sexy and hot and perfect in their books, but this is the real world. Ohhh, and you" she points to Reign, "are a Lord and from what I'd witnessed over the years, nothing good ever comes from getting involved with a Lord."

"Famous last words," Rem interjects.

Nodding, I laugh. "Right, but I can say, being with a Lord and a—"

"Stud," I offer.

"Being with a Lord and a stud, is good in every way."

And I agree wholeheartedly with her, I have never been happier since the three of us gave in. I keep waiting for our bubble to burst because this is Crestwood and things never stay good forever.

Before I continue the story, I look around the room and smile. "This is the weirdest and most fucked up story time I have ever been involved in—"

Hendrix interrupts, "Yep, I think we can all agree with that." Everyone nods in agreement to what I just said.

"But at the same time, I love hearing our story from your guys point of view too."

"And," Remy interjects, "it's nice to hear a happy story for once. Life has been pretty fucked lately, so hearing a happy story is kind of refreshing and we all know it ends with a happily ever after since you're all here and snuggling on Reign's bed."

And Remy is right, I'm happier than I have ever been

before and that's due to the two people on this bed with me. "Okay, where were we?"

Reign reminds me and I smile as I remember. I regal our tale again. "… and then I headed to the cafeteria for dinner to meet up with Alani."

"Is that the night we discussed threesomes over chocolate pudding and realized that we both wanted him," she flicks her finger at Reign, "as our third?"

"That's the one."

"Soo romantic," Reign teases, "threesomes and pudding," he pauses and then adds, "we should try that later."

Alani raises her eyebrows at him, and I make a note to stock up on chocolate pudding.

"I'm never eating chocolate pudding again," Saint complains, and we all laugh.

REIGN

"SO, LET ME GET THIS STRAIGHT," Saint interrupts Hudson, motioning his hands in a timeout T. "You were all with each other separately, but you were all fantasizing about being together as a threesome. Hell, you two," he flicks his fingers at Alani and Hudson, "already admitted you both wanted Reign without the other knowing that you were all hooking up separately?" We all nod. "So then, how did you all finally happen?"

"Well, it wasn't smooth sailing, let me tell you that. I was fucked up over Arlen dying and—"

"Can we get that story yet?" Saint asks, earning himself a smack up the side of the head from Hendrix.

"That story can wait, dude, I wanna know how this," Hendrix flicks his finger across the three of us, "came about." Then he chuckles. "Rowan and Quinn are gonna be pissed they've missed story time."

"Speaking of stories," Thatcher speaks up, "we need those ones too."

Saint shakes his head and Hendrix flips him the bird and says, "There is no story there but there is one here, so, please continue with 'The Sexual Adventures of Reign, Hudson, and Alani' which we are all so deeply invested in." He pauses. "Reign, your turn to share. How did you feel about Alani and Hudson banging without you?"

Shaking my head, I roll my eyes at my brother's antics but at the same time, I'm smiling on the inside because it's just how it was before I revealed my secrets. "Well, to be honest, seeing the two of them together sparked a jealous reaction inside of me that confused the fuck out of me. Like, seriously, why did I give a shit if *they* were together? Why did seeing them holding hands like that, acting so carefree, have such a visceral reaction on my body? I'll tell you why, I wanted what they had. My cock was at half-mast every time we saw them. I was green with envy on the inside and as you guys pointed out on several occasions, I was bringing out my inner Thatcher. I was snippy, my responses were curt, and I'm sure I rocked the 'resting bitch face' look."

"It's called resting asshole face when you're a guy," Saint unhelpfully informs me.

I flip him the bird and continue, "It was that night we went to the cliffs that you," I point at Saint, "called me out on my shit."

"I remember that night," Saint says. "I was so worried about you and you wouldn't talk to me. I was hurt because we, the four of us, always talked. We didn't have secrets, but I guess you did. A massive one."

"I'm sorry, but I just wasn't ready to share that side of myself with anyone. Look what happened when I opened up to Arlen, he killed himself."

"Well, he didn't," Remy snaps, "and just like you, he had his own secrets." She raises her hand. "And no, he hasn't told me anything yet about how it all went down and why. He's still hiding something, I just don't know what it is."

"Give him time," Thatcher reassures Rem, squeezing her shoulder. "But if he hurts you, or you, again." He looks me dead in the eye. "I'll kill him myself."

Thatcher's words hang in the air, but Saint breaks the silence, "Clearly you left a lot of shit out when we chatted that night." He pauses. "You know, it really fucking hurts you didn't feel you could confide in us, but I get why you thought you couldn't. We can be cunts when we want to be and something like this must have been hard for you. I'm glad we finally know and I'm glad you found your penguins."

"What the fuck does a penguin have to do with this?" Thatcher sneers, confusion written on his face but then again, we're all confused by Saint's penguin reference.

"Penguins mate for life, and I think these three have found their pengui."

"Pengui?" I question.

"That's the plural of penguins, right?"

"Fucks me," I retort, "you're the one who seems to know all about them. Anyway," I say before I continue our story, "when I got back to my room that night, I found a note saying they know my secrets."

"Did you ever find out who left that note for you?" Thatcher asks on high alert.

Shaking my head, I shrug. "To be honest, I forgot all about it. The next day, I met with Mom—"

"You and she have always had a special bond," Saint says, smiling at me. "I'm glad you talked to someone."

"I may have 'talked' to Mom but I still kept my secrets." I fill them in on my chat with her and my run-in with Dad as I was leaving. I'm still thankful he didn't overhear us that day. He would have whipped me if he knew who I really was. Thankfully, the fucker is dead and I don't have to worry about suffering his wrath. I see how Hudson is when his father has a go at him. I wouldn't wish that on my worst enemy.

"So, Mom knew you wanted more than one person and she told you to follow your heart, which is obviously what you did since you are now here and shit," Hendrix states before getting up and stretching.

"Well, yeah, but it still took a while for us to get to the us part."

"Well, what happened next?" Remy asks.

ALANI

"WELL," I say, taking over story time. "While Reign was battling his inner demons, so was I. Sure, I'd admitted to Hudson what I wanted but on top of that, there was school, and my parents. Not knowing what I want to do when I graduate. I felt like I was drowning." I laugh and look to Reign. "Not sure if you remember but one day, you grabbed me when I was running late. You kept calling me Red—"

"Which you totally love," he taunts.

"Agree to disagree. Anyway, you pissed me off and I went from wanting to bone you both at the same time to wanting to stab you with a rusty fork."

"I think I remember that day, I wanted nothing more than to fuck you silly, but I draw the line at fucking within the school, unlike some." Reign eyes Hendrix accusingly.

"What can I say, I like the thrill," Hendrix nonchalantly replies, looking pretty smug with himself.

"What's the story there?" I ask.

"This is your story, Alani. My adventures can wait."

"So, you wanna stab Reign and FYI, we've all been there." Reign flips the bird at his brother. "How did you go from stabbing to fucking?"

Shaking my head, I laugh. "So, yeah, I was pissed off, but Reign has this way of making me forget things."

"Like the fact you were pissed at him?" Remy asks.

"Exactly. We ended up in the library—"

"Hold up," Saint interrupts me, "I thought you didn't fuck in school."

"Who said anything about fucking?" Reign waggles his eyebrows at his brother.

"Isn't that what's about to happen?"

"Zip your lips and you'll find out." Reign looks to me. "Continue, Red."

"So, we're in the library. Hands are roaming under my uniform. My body is thrumming with desire. It's getting hot and heavy. I drop to my knees, ready to blow him and then he leaves. He fucking leaves. I'm on the floor with my tits out, ready to suck him off and one text from you"—I point at Thatch and glare—"causes him to shove his dick back into his pants and leave."

"You just left her there?" Thatcher questions. "On her knees? Willing to blow you?"

REIGN

"WELL, YEAH," I tell him with a shrug. "You called and it was urgent, and family always comes first, well, it did back then. You call me now and I have Alani or Hudson or both of them on their knees and you'll be waiting till I'm good and ready."

"Dude, if I had Rem on her knees, you fuckers would be waiting till she was one-hundred-percent sated."

"Thanks, babe." Remy blows a kiss to my brother.

"So, Thatch cockblocked you, why?" Saint asks.

"Dad summoned us to dinner."

"THAT'S why you ditched me?" Alani growls at him. "You ditched me for a dinner invitation at home?"

"Well, yeah, but if it's any consolation, I remember being super pissed. First, you fuckers cockblock me and then Dad did too because I had plans to make it up to you, Red." I laugh, and then I remember. "You," I sneer the word 'you' and point at Hendrix. "You decided to be your annoying self and taunt me so I took off back to the library to hide out."

"Good times," the fucker jeers. "So, when are you getting to the Arlen stuff?" Hendrix murmurs.

"One story at a time, asshole," I spit, flipping him off.

Saint berates him, "Shut the fuck up and let him continue." I chuckle at how invested these guys are in our story, but at the same time, it makes me realize they do in fact have my back. "So, I was at the library and I ran into Hudson and well, we got hot and heavy like I did with Red earlier—"

"Whore," Hendrix cough teases but I ignore him.

"We almost got busted by Quinn and then Hudson ran out on me."

Hendrix perks up at the mention of Quinn and I make a note to question him about her. Those two have been on my radar for a while now and his reactions whenever her name is mentioned has piqued my interest.

"Oh my God, I remember that," Hudson agrees, rubbing at his neck, obviously remembering me marking him.

"It's always a good time with me."

"No one likes a gloater, baby," Alani says, smiling sweetly at me.

"Question." Saint states. "How the fuck did Ellis not spill the deets?"

"I guess she didn't see anything," Hendrix defends her, once again confirming my suspicions that something is indeed going on there. "So, Huddy Boy, what happened when you ran off with your tail between your legs?"

HUDSON

"I WAS ONCE AGAIN CONFUSED by Reign, and I remember cursing Bitsy out."

"Me," she shrieks, "why?"

"Ever since our fantasy chat, that was all I could think about. But Reign was still so shy and I had no clue how to make it a reality."

"Clearly you're quite persuasive, Hudson, since you're now a throuple," Remy states matter-of-factly.

"Clearly I am. It was still only a fantasy, but it did give me some great spank bank fodder that night in the shower."

"Ugh, dude," Remy protests, "TMI."

We all just laugh at her but really, we are oversharing when it comes to certain parts of our story.

"Why is it that hearing about someone pleasuring themself is super hot?" Hendrix drawls, readjusting himself.

"You realize I just told a story about getting off to images of your brother and THAT made you hot?" I question him and I see the moment it registers in his mind. Once again, we all laugh. He flips us the bird and crosses his arms, sulking. "Don't worry, dude, what I tell you next will deflate your dick."

"Why, what happened?"

"That was when I received that warning note telling me not to fall for your tricks and shit."

"Why did you not say anything about that note?" Reign asks me.

Shrugging, I shake my head. "Didn't really think too much of it, but now that we're sharing our stories, you getting a note and me also getting one is probably something we should look into."

"Do you still have it?" he asks me and again, I shake my head. "Yeah, me neither."

"Should we be worried?" Bitsy voices, and I hate hearing the hesitation in her tone.

"Nah, babe, it's all good. We each received those months ago. Nothing happened so it's all good."

Little did we know, those notes would come back to haunt us in the coming weeks.

"Okay, so what happened next? This is like the slow burn of all slow burns," Remy says. "It's like a new age romance novel. Full of unrequited love. Burning desires, and hot-hot threesomes and trust me, you three together is hot. I'm getting wet just thinking about what I saw."

"You better not fucking be getting wet to thoughts of my brother," Thatcher growls.

"Who said it's him? Maybe it's Alani who I'm hot for."

"I'd be down for a little girl-on-girl action," Hendrix singsongs, earning him a smack up the back of the head from Thatch.

"No one gets Rem but me."

"Such a caveman," she states with an eye roll. "For the record, yes, my girl Alani is hot but I'm all for the guys."

"And Rowan, don't forget you shared a smoochy smooch with her earlier this year," Alani adds.

"I forgot about that," Rem says with a look on her face that makes me think she loved kissing Rowan.

"With my Rowan?" Saint asks.

Rem nods. "Yeah, the night Thatch and Conroy and Theon left me high and dry in the crypt."

"How the fuck did we not know about this?" Saint hisses, grabbing his phone and shooting off a text message.

"'Cause you don't need to know everything," Rem deadpans. "Now, let's get back to the story."

"Where were we?" I ask.

"You had just wanked off to thoughts of you and me after I marked you and Quinn interrupted us," Reign summarizes.

"Seems you had a habit of leaving us high and dry," Alani states, "maybe we need to return the favor one time."

"Duly noted," I confirm, while Reign growls, "or not." Causing everyone to laugh again.

"We get it, I was a dick," Reign states.

"Dude, you've been one all your life, that's not news," Thatcher teases, causing the brothers to all chuckle and Reign to flip the bird, again. "I can't see that changing anytime soon ... but getting back to the story. When we left off, our baby brother had hurt Alani, marked you, you wanked off in the shower, and somehow, Reign left you both wanting more—"

"How the hell did we miss all these make-out sessions and unrequited stares?" Saint voices.

"'Cause we're self-centered assholes," Hendrix says, earning a nod from all the Vanderbelt brothers.

"Yep, assholes who only think of themselves sometimes. Am I right, Rem?" Alani asks her.

"Hell yeah … and a Vanderbelt asshole is the asshole of all assholes."

"Yet we love them," Rem states, looking lovingly at Thatch. Then she looks intently at Alani. "If I remember correctly, you lying whore, when I first arrived, you warned me away from them. Why?"

ALANI

"WELL, yeah, I did. At that point, I was fucking Reign, but I didn't think Thatcher deserved you because, well, Thatch, you were a fucking dickface before Remy came along. She molded you into just a dick."

"Keep your chick in line, bro," Thatcher sneers at Reign.

"What can I say, she's right." Thatcher flips him the bird. "Right, now get back to finishing the adventures of Reign, Alani, and Hudson."

"Man, you're a girl," Saint tells him.

"Well…" Remy raises her hand and waves. "I'm a girl and I'm fully invested in this story and don't tell me you guys aren't either." They all sheepishly nod, and I can't help but feel grateful to have them as friends, but when I look to Remy, she has a look on her face.

"You okay, Rem?"

"Yeah, I am, it's just …"

"Just what?" I ask.

"I thought we were besties. Besties don't keep secrets and they definitely shouldn't keep X-rated secrets."

"I'm sorry," I whisper and climb off the bed. Crouching in front of Remy, I take her hands in mine. "I promise it wasn't intentional. I told them I wouldn't tell and when I make a promise, I keep it." I raise my hand to stop her. "And I know girl code usually trumps that, but dick code trumps all code and when there are two dicks involved, it doubly trumps girl code."

"You realize you're penalizing me 'cause I don't have a dick? That's like dickscrimination."

"Sorry, babe," Alani shakes her head, "dems da dicks."

Climbing back onto the bed, I finish telling our story. "… and that brings us to now."

"Hang on a minute. Back the fucking truck up," Thatcher interrupts me, raising his hand in a stop motion. "Peach, you've known since the last party?"

"Umm yeah, why?"

"You just berated your bestie for keeping secrets, but you kept this from me?"

"Because Reign asked me too."

"Ohh, shit," Saint voices, "these two are going to fight now."

"Fuck off, dickwad," Thatcher growls. "We don't keep secrets."

"For stuff relating to us we don't, but this wasn't my secret to share."

"I … well, shit, you've got me there." He gets this non-

Thatcher-like look on his face. "Thank you for being there for my brother."

"Anytime, and for the record, I'd be there for anyone in this room. Day or night. You guys are my family. My chosen family."

Everyone nods in agreement and now that our secret is out and our story has been told, I feel freer than I have in a long time. Life is grand and I cannot wait to see what the future holds for us all. Now that story time is over, we all head to the cafeteria for dinner.

... a few days later

Sitting in the library, I'm trying to concentrate on the assignment before me, but my mind keeps wandering to threesomeland, the most magical place in the world. No clothes are required, and orgasms are aplenty.

The three of us are no longer hiding what we are and life is great, but that feeling of greatness evaporates when my phone begins to vibrate across the table and I see Dad's name on the screen. I ignore it. I'm not in the mood to deal with any of their bullshit right now. I want to stay in my happy bubble. It stops ringing and then it immediately starts again. This time, I send it to voicemail, hoping he'll get the picture that I don't want to talk, but Dad isn't the sharpest tool in the shed and he calls again.

"What?" I hiss into my phone after stabbing at the answer button.

"Alani?" he questions in confusion, probably because I haven't ever answered the phone like that before.

"Yes, Dad, it's me. What can I do for you?"

"I need you to come to the house." He waits for my reply but when I don't say anything, he adds in a forceful, "Now."

"I'm busy, Dad."

"Alani, I'm not asking." He pauses and it feels like my world is about to implode and that want of going to three-someland intensifies. "Something happened and I need to tell you in person."

"Dad, you're scaring me."

"Please, Strawberry Shortcake," he begs, and the use of my childhood nickname that he hasn't used in years has me on alert. High freakin' alert. "Please, Alani, come home."

"Okay, Dad. I'll pack up and head over."

"Thanks." And without another word, he hangs up.

Shoving my things into my bag, I stand up and head to my car. I'm almost at it when Reign and Hudson race toward me. Both of them enveloping me in a tight embrace, Reign at my back and Hudson at my front. "That was unexpected," I mumble into Hudson's chest.

"Are you okay?" Hudson asks, cupping my cheeks in his palm. Worry is all over his face and I haven't even uttered a word. It's crazy how in tune we are with one another. I've heard of couples, well throuples, doing this but I'd never experienced it before. It's like that saying, 'they hurt, I hurt.'

"I'm fine, just heading over to parents." Stepping around them, I continue to my car, but Reign grabs my wrist and when I turn to face them, the look on each of their faces stops me in my tracks.

"We're coming and I'm driving," Reign states, not leaving any room for argument, and that's when I notice the look on Hudson's face.

"What's going on?" I ask him.

"Don't you know?" Hudson questions and that same sense of dread while on the phone with Dad builds again.

"Don't I know what? What the fuck is going on?"

"Shit," Hudson scoffs. He takes a deep breath, steps to me,

and takes both my hands in his. "Bitsy, your mom, my dad, and Rem's dad have been arrested."

"What? Why? How? I'm so confused right now."

"You and me both. All I know is there was a breaking report just now on the news stating they've been arrested in regard to embezzlement, fraud, and a slew of other shit."

"What?" I hiss again. "Why didn't anyone give us a heads-up?"

"The news literally just broke."

"Well, let's get to my house. Maybe my dad has more information."

"I'll drive," Reign declares again and both Hudson and I nod.

The three of us turn away from my car and head over to his car. Hudson climbs in the back with me, hugging me to his side and whispering sweet nothings as I try to process what's happening.

Before Reign has even turned off the engine, I fly out of the car and race to the front door. Hudson is hot on my heels and before I reach for the door handle, he pulls on my hand and spins me to face him. "Bitsy, you need to calm down. Don't go in there guns blazing."

"But—" My protest is silenced when he presses his finger to my lips.

"You need to calm down."

"Dude, telling a chick to calm down will have the complete opposite effect," Reign pauses, "but, Red, he's right, you need to take a deep breath. Chillax a little and let your dad explain."

Nodding, I take a deep breath, but it does little to calm me. "Okay, fine," I snap, "but if he pisses me off, I make no promises that my inner redhead isn't coming out."

"We wouldn't expect anything less. Now, come give me a hug before we head inside."

On the front stoop of my childhood home, my two guys

hug me tightly and give me the courage I need to approach this. The sound of the door opening has the three of us pulling apart. Silently, the three of us stare at my dad and I reach out to take their hands, anchoring myself to them. My dad's gaze keeps flicking between our clenched hands and our faces.

"What's going on?" I ask him when the silence becomes too much.

"Come inside and I'll fill you in, and then you can fill me in on this." He circles his finger around the three of us.

Nodding, we follow him inside. The house is in shambles. "It looks like a tornado went through here," I state the obvious.

"Tornado police force did a few hours ago, just after they hauled your mother away in handcuffs."

"What happened, Dad?" I ask again.

He gestures to the sofa and the three of us take a seat, me in the middle of my guys. "Seems your mother, Mr. Finley, and Mr. Hearst have been embezzling money from the Crestwood elite."

"What?" Hudson and I hiss at the same time.

"From what I know, someone tipped the feds off about Hearst, but when they began digging, they struck gold. Hearst rolled over, gave up his partners and details on the whole operation."

"Holy fucking shit," I whisper. "And you knew nothing?" I incredulously ask him.

"No clue, Strawberry Shortcake." I smile again at the nickname used. "Hell, I didn't even know she was in business with these men."

"You haven't called me that in years and today you've used it twice."

"When the feds ransacked this place, they found this." He hands me a photo booth photo strip, and when I turn it over, my heart melts. It's of Dad and me. I think I was maybe five and we went to Castaway Grove for a family holiday. Mom was in one of her moods, so Dad took me down to the beach. We spent the day swimming and playing. Then we stopped in town for dinner and after eating our weight in ice cream we commemorated the event with the photo. "Seeing you so happy and carefree made me miss you and the good times we used to have."

"Why did our relationship change?" I ask him.

"Your mother wanted different things, and I guess, I blindly followed her and in the process, I pushed you away."

Staring over at my dad, I see nothing but regret in his eyes, but then I also feel kinda guilty, I made no effort either. Our non-relationship isn't all on him. "It works both ways, Dad. I should have been a better daughter."

"No." He shakes his head. "No, you're an amazing daughter, Alani. You seem so happy and confident and considering all the shit your mother and I put you through, it's a credit to you and you alone."

Hudson's phone rings and he looks at the screen and grimaces. "It's Lauren, I need to take this. Excuse me."

"Hey, sis," he says as he walks out of the room.

"So, I need to know, the three of you?" Dad asks, eyeing Reign.

"Sir—"

"And you are?"

"Reign Vanderbelt, sir." Dad shudders when he hears who Reign is, but my man doesn't buckle at that. "Don't let my last name sway you, I'm nothing like my father, may he burn in hell. I, well, we, Hudson and I, we're both in love with your daughter. As you said, she's an amazing woman and her heart is big enough for both Hudson and me."

"It's unorthodox, but who am I to judge? My wife was screwing over our supposed friends so I don't really have a leg to stand on, but if you hurt her, I will fucking kill you."

His gaze flicks between both of my guys since Hudson has just reentered the room. "Both of you."

"Seems I came back in at the right or maybe wrong time," Hudson says, taking his seat beside me again.

"I was just telling Reign here that if either one of you hurts my daughter, I will fucking kill you."

"If we hurt her, I'll load the gun myself," Hudson tells my dad.

"Same here," Reign confirms.

Hudson tells us about his call with Lauren while Dad puts together a light dinner. Then, over meatloaf, we regale him with how we became a throuple. He even goes as far as to tell a story about when he, my mom, and some guys at college drunkenly got it on one night. That is an image that later that night was wiped away—thankfully—and replaced with one of myself, Reign, and Hudson.

Today my world may have imploded but with my two guys and my dad on my team, I know we can face whatever comes our way.

REIGN

"YOU OKAY?" a sweet voice asks and when I look up, I see Red standing beside me in the lounge. Smiling at her, I realize that I am indeed okay. Alani came into my life when I needed her the most, and Hudson, well, he was right before my eyes and I just didn't know it. The two of them complete me, as corny as it sounds, but it's true. They brought me back to life when I thought it was over and I will be forever grateful for that, but most of all, I found the ones for me. I may only be eighteen, but Alani and Hudson are it for me, and I'm going to hold on to the two of them and never let them go. I know what loss feels like and I never want to feel like that again.

"Yeah, I'm okay," I tell her with a smile, and I mean it. My brothers took my news better than could be expected. I should have trusted that they would but I was scared. Being bi is one thing, but being in a throuple is a whole other can of worms.

"Good," she states matter-of-factly. For a chick, Alani sure is feisty and that's one of the things that drew me to her in the first place.

"Question is, are you okay?"

"I am." She nods. "I really am. We're happy and out in the open, I'm starting to have a relationship with my dad again, and my bitch of a mother is rotting in prison, getting what she deserves."

A laugh escapes me because, yes, the last ten days have been chaotic, to say the least. Sitting here, I stare at the amazing woman who owns half my heart. "What?" she self-consciously asks. "Do I have something on my face?"

Shaking my head, I smile. "No, there's nothing on that beautiful face of yours."

"Then what?"

"I just realized it's all going to be okay. There are no more secrets. Everyone I love is safe. Life is good because as you said, I've found my chosen family."

She smiles at me. "Weeeeeell," she draws the word out and beckons me forward with her finger. "If you come with me, your life is about to get doubly good." She raises her eyebrows seductively.

Nodding, I jump up and make my way over to her. Taking her in my arms, she presses her lips to mine and kisses me deeply. My tongue pushes into her mouth and what started out sweet and soft turns hurried and carnal.

A throat clears from behind her and when we pull apart my smile increases when I see Hudson standing before us. "Room for one more?"

"Always," I tell him.

He walks over to us and just like Alani did only moments ago, he presses his lips to mine. His tongue pushes into my mouth, mine pushes into his. It's the complete opposite of my kiss with Alani, this one is sloppy and messy but just as passionate.

"Fuck, it's hot watching you two kiss like that," our girl breathlessly pants. I bet if we slipped our fingers into her cunt right now, they'd effortlessly slide in from how wet she is.

"How hot?" I ask her, sliding my arm around her waist, and pulling her into me. Hudson steps behind her, sand-wiching her between us.

She looks up at me. "If I was wearing any panties," she lifts to her tippy-toes and whispers in my ear, "they'd be soaked." *Well, that makes testing my theory easier, no panties in the way.*

"Fuck, babe," Hudson moans, mimicking my thoughts exactly, but before we can take this further, the moment is interrupted when a commanding voice, bellows, "Reign Vanderbelt, you need to come with us for questioning in rela-tion to the murder of Thornton Vanderbelt."

HUDSON

ALANI and I stand here stunned as we watch one officer slap handcuffs on Reign, while the other reads him his rights and Reign being Reign, he refuses to cooperate, which is kinda fair. First Thatch was questioned and now Reign. Are they going to work their way through all the brothers before they realize that none of them did it? Sure, they hated their father —and rightly so—but none of them are killers.

Once he's restrained, they begin to cart him out of the lounge.

"Wait," Alani yells, chasing after them.

"Bitsy." My hand around her arm stops her. Her pained

look kills me, but she turns her attention back to Reign. He makes eye contact with us over his shoulder, and she reads the silent plea. It's enough to hold her back but she murmurs, "What the fuck just happened?"

And much like Reign, Alani being Alani, she pulls from my grip and chases after them. "Reign," Alani shouts again, but this time, he doesn't look back. She turns to me, grief all over her face. "Hudson, what's happening?" she asks, but she doesn't wait for my answer. She chases after Reign, calling out to him.

"Stop," she pleads with the officers when she catches up to them.

"Red. Stop, it's okay," Reign tells her. She crashes into his chest, throws her arms around his neck, and holds on to him as tightly as she can.

"You can't take him," she cries, "whatever you're accusing him of, he didn't do it. He's innocent."

Reaching them, I touch her shoulder, "Bitsy, come on, babe." I try to remove her from Reign, but she's clutching on to him tightly.

"No," she shouts.

The officer who read Reign his rights manages to pull Alani off Reign and he gives me a look that says control her.

By now, there's a group of students gathered outside the building, and everyone is murmuring the same question, 'What's going on' and 'Why is Reign in handcuffs?'

"The reason Mr. Vanderbelt is in handcuffs is no concern of yours. I suggest you all go back to your rooms immediately," the officer says, looking around at the small crowd, but no one moves. They all whisper amongst themselves and some even whip out their phones to take pictures. *Assholes.*

"He didn't do it," Alani shrieks, tears cover her cheeks as we stand by and watch them lead Reign away.

Pulling her into my arms, I wrap one arm around her

shoulders and one around her middle, plastering her to my chest.

"Hudson, he didn't do it. Whatever they're saying he did, he didn't do it," Alani whimpers.

"I know, Bitsy, I know," I say, kissing the top of her head, and I have no idea if I just lied to her. Reign hated his father, but did he hate him enough to murder him? All I know is whatever the fuck Reign has gotten himself into, we're going to help him out of it.

Two hours.

One hundred and twenty minutes, that's how long I've been pacing in my room, with no word about Reign. *Why the fuck isn't he back yet?*

"Hudson?" Alani whispers and I step over to her. Sliding one arm around her waist, I cup her face with my other hand and wipe her tears away, just as the door opens and Reign walks in chucking his keys onto my dresser.

"Reign," Alani shouts, pushing away from me. She races across the room and leaps into his arms before I've even taken a step toward them.

Reign holds her to him as she cries into his chest. Walking over to them, he grips the back of my neck and pulls me into him. My hand fists around his arm, holding him as tightly as I can.

"Y … you …" Alani hiccups, she's so filled with relief that she can't speak.

"I'm okay, Red," he murmurs, kissing her on the head.

"Are you?" I ask.

He nods and grips my neck harder. Then he pulls me to him and kisses me deeply. He lets me go and does the same to

Alani. Sliding his arms down to her ass, he lifts her into his arms, and she wraps her legs around his waist. Stepping behind her, we hold on to her in between us. They kiss and I stand here and watch from behind as he devours her lips.

"Reign," she whispers against his lips, holding his face between her hands. "You're here." She kisses him again. She rests her forehead against his. "Are you okay?"

"I'm okay, Red, I promise. I just need you, both of you."

Alani slides down between us and wraps one arm around us. She lifts onto her tippy-toes and kisses along Reign's jaw. Then she spins around to me and does the same.

The air in the room simmers with lust and relief.

"I need you both," she pants.

Without uttering a word, I take both their hands and lead them over to my bed.

Alani climbs on, shuffles to the middle, and watches us. Reign lifts his arm and removes his shirt with one hand, ripping it over his head before throwing it to the floor.

Following him, I do the same and I don't miss the way the side of his mouth lifts when I do. *Cocky asshole.*

We both look at Alani.

"Bitsy," I growl. She smirks at me seductively and then ever so slowly unbuttons her blouse. One by one the pearl buttons pop open and she slides the material down her arms. She holds it between her fingers and pauses before letting it drop to the floor.

"Fuck, Red." Reign groans as he takes her in. Reaching for her, he grips her bra and then pulls it down, freeing her gorgeous tits and revealing her pebbled nipples. Leaning down, he takes one into his mouth and sucks. Our girl whimpers as he bites down. He smirks up at her doing it again, this time a little harder.

Throwing her head back in delight, she reaches for me. Sliding her hand around the back of my neck, she pulls me to her, and I cover her mouth with mine. Her moans filter throughout the room as my tongue twists with hers. Sliding my hand down her body, I slip it under the edge of her skirt, skimming my fingertips along the skin of her thigh. I push her panties to the side and thrust two fingers inside her. Her back arches and whimpers fall from her lips. Reign continues his assault on her nipple, while I play with her cunt.

He turns his attention to her other breast but instead of freeing it, he sucks and bites her nipple through the material of her bra.

Watching him make our girl feel good is one of the hottest things to witness. That is until I see his cock straining within his pants. Reaching for him and his cock, I pull his pants and boxers down enough to slide my hand inside and wrap my fist around him.

"Fuck," he mumbles over Alani's tit.

Shuffling around so I'm bent slightly over them, my fingers push deeper into Alani as my other hand wraps tighter around Reign.

Reign groans and moves his hips in sync with the hand on his cock. Contorting myself around, I take a taste of Alani's sweet, sweet nectar. Swiping my tongue through her wetness, she whimpers.

"Oh, oh, Fuuuuuck," she hisses and then she growls when I remove my tongue from her folds but when she sees what I'm about to do, she grins down at me. Freeing Reign's cock completely, I open wide and take him into my mouth. Sucking hard before I hollow my cheeks and take him in deeper. I suck until he hits the back of my throat. My dick throbs in my pants but right now, this is about Reign. My pleasure can wait.

"Jesus fucking Christ," he growls, running his fingers through my hair, pulling on the strands. The sensation of his cock hitting the back of my throat and the pain from him pulling my hair is hedonistic. My cock is aching, and my balls are ready to explode, but all I can think about is getting each of them off. My release is second fiddle to theirs. I take turns between driving each of them wild with my mouth and hands.

"So not fucking fair," Reign murmurs before pulling me off his cock so he can kiss me hard. He then begins to strip my clothes from me. Reign stands up and removes the rest of his, just as Alani strips out of hers. She pushes me down to the mattress and climbs on, straddling me. She lowers herself down on me, forcing an audible sound from me.

Reign leans down, capturing my lips, then demands, "Turn over, on your knees, face the wall." *Fuck* me, is my immediate thought and then it turns to *holy fucking* hell when he adds, "I'm going to fuck you so hard tonight."

Alani's eyes light up at his words and she quickly climbs off, letting me get into position. Rolling to her back, she slides under me and takes my cock into her mouth. The head hits the back of her throat just as I hear Reign open the drawer beside us.

Looking over, I see him grab the lube and my cock hardens further in Alani's mouth.

He coats his fingers before bringing them to my ass, rubbing the cool liquid into my puckered hole.

Moaning beneath me, Alani works me in her mouth, taking me as far as she can before she pulls back, repeating again and again and again.

Reign inserts two of his fingers into my ass, making me almost come. "Fuck," I hiss, knowing I won't last long if they keep doing this to me.

"You need to come, baby," Reign whispers in my ear. Too afraid to speak again, I nod frantically. Closing my eyes, I focus on Alani beneath me. She closes her mouth around me again and I whimper. I'm on sensation overload right now. I need to come. I need to come so, so bad right now.

Reign pulls me upright, making my cock pop from Alani's mouth and I mourn the loss.

"Slide out from under him, Red," he orders, "spread your legs and fuck yourself with your fingers." She follows his request and lies across the bed, spreading her legs wide and sliding her fingers between her wet folds. Her arousal coats the inside of her thighs, glistening in the dim light of the room. Reign shuffles me around and I smile when I realize what he's doing. He moves me between her legs. Grabbing her hips, I pull her to me, she squeals, not expecting me to do that and her squeak turns into a guttural moan when I push inside her.

We both gasp loudly, and I give her a few moments before I lean over her, fucking her harder and giving Reign complete access to take my ass.

He pushes his fingers inside me again and I moan at the intrusion. He leans down and whispers, "I'm going to fucking own this tonight."

Kissing my shoulder blade, he removes his finger and I feel the head of his cock circling me. Then he pushes inside, slowly. So fucking slowly. It's exquisite torture. My mouth drops open at the sensation of his dick sliding into me and I almost come.

"Fuck me," Alani growls when I realize that I stopped moving. With a flick of my hips, I begin to thrust again. Alani moves with me and the three of us fall into sync, fucking in time with each of our thrusts. Our moans, whirring into one.

Alani's hands move across my body, gripping me the best she can. She straightens her legs and cries out in ecstasy from the new position. Her pussy grips me like a vise and I can't hold back. I come and I come hard, growling as I fill her with my cum. My hips move fast, giving her everything I can. Reign grunts from behind me and shoves me forward with one final hard thrust, his fingers grip my hips, and he explodes.

"Fuck, fuck, fuck," he chants, panting loudly as he empties himself in my ass.

Falling on top of Alani, I lie exhausted, sweaty, satisfied, and completely full. Rolling off her, I stare up at the ceiling, rapidly breathing.

Turning my head, I say the only thing that seems right for this moment. "I love you. Both of you. This is it for me."

REIGN

YESTERDAY WAS the day from hell until it wasn't, and it's all because of the two people I'm currently in bed with. Alani is snuggled up next to me, sound asleep. She's breathing heavily and after the pounding her body took last night, I'm not surprised.

My eyes roam over her tiny frame and I smile when I realize her body fits perfectly next to mine. And then there's Hudson, he fits perfectly next to her as well. It's as if the three of us were cast from the same mold. Our bodies fitting together to make one perfect whole.

Hudson softly snores next to her, his arm draped over his

face. The blanket slipped down at some point during the night, so I get an uninterrupted, spectacular view of his chest rising and falling as he breathes.

I know my brothers wanted an update on what went down yesterday and just like with Thatcher the other month, they tried to pin my father's death on me too.

Yes, I hated the asshole but I'm not a murderer. I didn't do it, and if I'm being honest, I don't fucking care who did. In actual fact, I want to shake the fucker's hand and thank them for giving my mother her life back, she's way happier with him gone, hell, we all are. We are all better off without Thornton Vanderbelt in this world.

My arm rests behind my head while I think over everything that transpired these last few months. My brothers and I have been hit hard, but we have pulled through it all because we have one another.

I slam my eyes shut, forcing my brain to forget it all but no such luck, my mind is racing.

"You're thinking awfully loud over there," Hudson mumbles.

Peering over at him, his arm is now resting on his stomach, his other arm behind his head as he watches me.

"Just a lot on my mind," I mutter, glancing at Alani still asleep between us.

"It's okay to not have all the answers, Reign, we can, and will, figure them out together," he says, shifting onto his side so he's facing me.

"Do you think it's wrong?" I murmur.

"Do I think what's wrong?" Hudson asks, confusion marring his beautiful sleep-addled face.

"That I don't feel sad he's gone."

"Reign," he breathes. Leaning over Alani, he grabs my hand, intertwining our fingers together. His thumb brushes over my hand and just having him here now feels safe.

"I'm glad he's gone, I don't ever have to be scared again,

you know?" I swallow. "Mom's happier too, now," I mutter mostly to myself. I let out a sigh because I know how this sounds but I don't care.

"Reign," Hudson growls, causing Alani to wake up.

"Are you okay?" Alani whispers, moving her finger across my arm.

"Never been better, Red," I say, smiling down at her.

"Reign, if you need to talk," Hudson begins but I silence him with my hand and shake my head.

"I'm fine, Hudson, I promise. I'm just overwhelmed, you know?" He nods but I can tell he's worried. I'm already tainted and there's no going back.

Rolling to my side, I climb out of bed while both Hudson and Alani watch me get dressed. At this point, I'm throwing on whatever my hand lands on and I'm positive I'm wearing Hudson's briefs but when your cock has been in each other's asses, I don't think it really matters when it comes to underwear.

Once I'm dressed, I look at them still in bed, wishing I could climb back in and join them. "I need to meet up with my brothers," I tell them but before I go, I lean down and plant a kiss on each of their lips.

"Be careful," Alani murmurs before snuggling into Hudson's side. I walk toward the door and before I open it, I look back at them and know that this is it for me. They are perfect and I will fight till the death for them.

Closing the door behind me, I make my way to Thatcher's room to wake his ass up. I know he'll still be sleeping next to Remy, no doubt naked, and I don't feel like getting punched by my brother for seeing his girl naked, again, so I stop outside his door and lift my hand to knock. Just before my knuckles wrap on the door, I hear something and I stop myself from knocking. Leaning my ear to the door, I shake my head when the sound of my brother grunting filters into my ears. "Fuck, Peach. Ride that fucking cock, baby."

His words have me stumbling back, almost going backward over the banister. My brothers and I are close and after the last time walking in unannounced, I do not want to hear, or see him railing Remy again.

Choosing to give each of my brothers more time, I decide to take a walk. I don't intentionally walk toward the library, but when the door shuts behind me, I shake my head, I always seem to find myself gravitating here.

It's basically empty at this time of the morning, everyone choosing to sleep in rather than study, so I move toward the back where it's more private.

Something hits the ground with a thud, and it sparks my intrigue. Clearly, I'm not alone here this morning.

Moving toward the sound, I almost chuckle out loud because isn't this like Horror Movie 101, never go toward the noise. It's how you get yourself killed. Coming to a stop near the back stacks, I see someone hunched over yanking on the bottom of the shelf. They are so engrossed in what they're doing that they don't notice me and then they pull something covered in a cloth out, which I definitely notice. They unwrap it and as soon as I see a gun, my mouth drops open in shock, but it's when I see a gold medallion sitting at their feet that I mumble, "What the fuck!" Giving myself away. At the sound of my voice, their head snaps up, revealing the last person I ever expected to see.

"Arlen?" I question, my voice laced with shock.

"Reign," he mutters, tossing the cloth in his back pocket and pushing the gun into the back of his pants. "We need to talk," he demands.

No fucking shit, I think to myself. "Talk?" I scoff. "You want to talk? Well, how about we start with why the fuck you have a gun? And who's medallion that is?"

He shakes his head and stands up, facing me. "It's nothing."

"Nothing," I repeat, and he nods. "Arlen, you, you have a

gun, why?" I'm so stunned at what I've just discovered, I can hardly find words to voice what I'm thinking.

"You don't need to concern yourself with these things just know, you, you'll be safe. I won't hurt you."

"Hurt me? What? Why?" I'm so confused right now, but there's a niggling low in my stomach that Arlen isn't who I think he is.

"You wouldn't understand," he pleads, clenching his jaw. I watch as it flexes back and forth while he stares at the ground between us.

"Make me understand then?"

"Fuck, Reign, you weren't supposed to get involved," he says, running his fingers through his hair. "It's why I did what I did."

"Arlen, what did you do?" I plead with him again.

"No, I can't tell you," he huffs. "Fuck. Fuck. Fuck," he repeats as he begins to pace back and forth. He starts muttering to himself again, all while I've managed to move closer without him noticing. Again, Horror Movie 101, you do not go toward the guy with the gun. He finally notices me coming toward him and raises his hand to halt me. "Reign, stop please," he pleads, his voice cracking.

"Arlen, what's going on?" My voice breaks as the panic that he's done something really bad reaches fever pitch.

"You can't fix it. Just leave," he tells me. "Forget you saw me." He looks straight into my eyes. "Please, Reign."

"Arl, I'm scared you've done something you can't get out of, but I want to help you. Let me help you."

"Fuck no, Reign," he groans, shaking his head. He begins to pace again, this time muttering to himself about doing what's right and they deserve to know.

"Arlen, just tell me," I bellow, forcing his pacing to stop. "What did you do?" I ask again, my tone alluding to him that I'm not leaving until I get answers.

He stares at me, and then he utters three words that shock the shit out of me. "I killed him."

"Killed who, Arl? What the fuck are you talking about?"

"Your father."

Everything stops.

My entire body feels like it stepped outside of itself and for the life of me I'm too stunned to speak.

No fucking way he killed my father. What reason would Arlen have to kill him?

Staring at the man I used to love, I process his words. My chest begins to tighten. This is too much, fuck. I can't breathe. Bending down, I fall to my knees and force air back inside my lungs as Arlen stands there watching me.

Arlen killed my father.

My father's dead because Arlen killed him.

I know I said I'd thank and protect whoever did kill the asshole but when I'm faced with it, my inner self can't not tell.

I can't protect him.

I just can't.

Fuck!

ALANI

IT'S BEEN hours since Reign walked out to talk to his brothers. I expected him to be back by now and I'm starting to worry. Hudson suggests we head over to Thatcher's room when we call and it just rings out. Hand in hand, we walk over to his room to meet up with our man and the rest of the gang. *Our man,* I love that.

Raising my hand, I knock as soon as I stop in front of his door, eager to see Reign. It swings open revealing a shirtless Thatcher. My eyes rake over him, his hair is a disheveled mess, so there's no question as to what he's been up to all morning.

Dropping my gaze, I murmur, "Ummm," shuffling on my feet before him.

Thatcher chuckles, causing me to lift my gaze again. "Huddy Boy, you might wanna wipe your girl's drool there off her chin."

"Screw you, Vanderbelt," Hudson snaps, peeking into his room. "Where's Reign?"

"Uh, not here," Thatcher replies.

That feeling of unease begins to fester again. We all silently stare at one another, processing the fact Reign isn't here. I finally say, "He came to see you a few hours ago."

"No, he didn't. We've, ummm, ahhh, been busy all morning. No one has come by." Hudson and I share a wide-eyed look.

"Hey, what's up?" Remy singsongs as she comes up behind Thatcher, sliding her arms around his waist, and resting her palms on his abs.

"They're looking for Reign," he tells her. "He said he was coming to see me."

"We haven't seen him," Remy confirms what Thatch just said.

"I'm going to text the others an SOS," Thatcher says, "see if they've seen him." Stepping back into his room, he grabs his phone. His fingers fly over the screen shooting off an SOS message for Reign's whereabouts.

Worrying my lip between my teeth, a strange feeling runs over me. Sensing my unease, Remy places her hand on my arm. "Hey, he's around here somewhere. I'm sure he's okay." She smiles, trying to reassure me but her words don't have the desired effect.

"Hendrix and Saint haven't seen him, and neither's Rian," Thatcher says, looking down at his phone.

"Where the fuck is he?" Hudson growls.

"Are you sure he's not just out to clear his head? I mean, a lot has happened lately," Remy says as Thatcher throws his arm over her shoulder pulling her into him. He begins to suck her neck like they haven't seen each other for hours.

Remy giggles pushing him away, glaring at him to calm down.

"Have you tried calling him?" Thatcher says.

Hudson pulls his phone out, calling him again and it goes straight to voicemail.

He tries again and again. By the fourth time, I can see he's ready to give up, but the call must connect. He puts it on speaker phone so we can all hear. "Reign?" Hudson says, but there's no reply. Just soft breathing and it's really creeping me out.

"Reign?" I try again, just as Hudson says, "Where are you?"

The line is silent then he speaks, "I … I …" Reign's voice fades out and then the call disconnects.

Shaking my head, I spin on my heel and run away from them, where too, I don't know. I hear Thatcher mumble, "Shit."

An arm reaches out, grabbing me and I'm pulled back into a solid chest. Wriggling, I try to get free. "Alani," Hudson snaps my name and I stop struggling. He spins me to face him and my eyes well with tears.

"He sounded so broken, Hudson. Why?" Tears slide down my cheeks, I know he only said I … I but I heard the undertone to it, he's broken. But why? What happened when he left us? "Where is he?" I cry as he pulls me into his arms, holding me tightly.

Once I've calmed down, he grips my face in his hands and kisses me on the forehead before telling me, "We'll find him, Bitsy, okay? We'll find him."

Nodding, I stare at him and then we hear footsteps behind us as Saint and Hendrix join Thatcher, Remy, Hudson, and me.

"Okay, game plan. You two check the cliffs." He points at

Hudson and me. "You two check the cemetery." He points to Saint and Hendrix and then looks to Remy. "We'll check the library. First person to find him lets the rest of us know."

We all nod and head off in different directions searching for Reign.

Hudson and I race to the cliffs. "Wait, what if …" I voice, but Hudson shakes his head.

"No," he forcefully refutes before taking my hand and squeezing, but I pull my hand free and take off up the path when I see Reign sitting by himself on the bench at the top of the cliffs.

"Reign," I scream as I race toward him. I can feel Hudson behind me. As soon as I reach Reign, I sink to my knees in front of him, gripping his hands tightly in mine. "Reign, babe, talk to us. Please," I plead with him, but he just morosely stares straight ahead, unmoving. It's like he doesn't even know we are here. "Reign?" I whisper, lifting myself up, I run my hand over the back of his neck. He moves slightly but doesn't utter a word, he just goes back to staring ahead.

"Baby, please," I cry again. "Please just talk to us?"

"He did it," he finally mutters softly, so softly we almost don't hear him over the sound of the waves and wind.

"What are you talking about?" I ask him. Taking a seat next to him and resting my head on his shoulder, covering his hand with mine, I let him know I'm here.

"Arlen, he …" He stops then swallows. "He killed my father."

Pulling my hand from his, I cover my mouth and gasp in shock, just as we hear from behind us, "No, no I don't believe you!"

We all turn around to find Thatcher holding Remy as she sinks to the ground sobbing. Thatcher and I share a look because if what Reign says is true, even more secrets are about to be exposed at Crestwood and I have a feeling, this time, not all of us will recover.

REIGN

MY BROTHERS all sit around me, each one of us in shock after I tell them everything I discovered earlier.

Thatcher glares off into the distance, unmoving. Not uttering a word, if it wasn't for the rise and fall of his chest, you'd think he was a statue.

"Fuck," Saint breathes, shaking his head, and Hendrix clicks his jaw, running his fingers through his hair.

"Okay," Hendrix finally says. "So, I don't care, he deserved it," Hendrix mutters, standing up and clenching his jaw.

"Thatch," I murmur, I need to hear from him. He always

knows what to do, and the only reason I know he heard me is because his jaw moves slightly before his face becomes stoic again.

"I thought it was Mom," Saint voices. My and Hendrix's eyes widen at his words, but I think we all thought the same thing. We all thought our mother had finally snapped and done it. Ended him, saving us, and herself, from his tyranny.

"Thatch," Hendrix tries and this time, Thatcher finally makes eye contact. His gaze flicks around us before dropping to the floor in front of him. Suddenly, he stands up and throws the chair he's been sitting on into the wall.

We all jump up and out of harm's way, no one wants to get in Thatch's way when he's like this. Thatcher's breathing becomes rapid and we all watch on as he tries to regain control of his temper.

And we all watch on as he fails.

Without a word he storms from the room, leaving Hendrix, Saint, and I staring after him. Chasing after him, we follow him out into the hall. People move from his path rather quickly as he storms through the school. Students sense his anger and the path clears as if he's Moses parting the Red Sea. He reaches the cafeteria; the doors bang against the walls as he throws them open.

Just as we reach him, I see him make a beeline for Grayson who's consoling an upset Remy. Ever since we rescued the Hearst siblings from Brennan and their psycho mother, Grayson has become an honorary member of our group. He's always here visiting his sister, they have a bond like I do with my brothers. And he's a pretty cool guy, seems we were wrong about all of the Hearsts, well, not Rochelle, she's a cunt.

Argh, fuck.

He yanks the oldest Hearst up by the collar and throws him across the table before getting in his face. "Where the fuck is he, huh?" Thatcher screams at Grayson.

Grayson squirms beneath him, trying to get out of his hold. Grayson manages to shove him, causing Thatcher to move from on top of him and allowing him to stand up.

"What the fuck are you talking about?" Grayson seethes in anger at our brother.

"Your brother," Thatcher snarls, "reveals he's a goddamn murderer then what, flees? He's not man enough to face us, huh?" Thatcher snaps, holding his arms out wide.

"I got questioned about the death of my father, and it turns out your supposedly dead brother was the one to pull the trigger. He deserves what's coming for him," Thatcher spits at Grayson.

The two of them stand facing one another. No one in the room makes a move. It's so quiet you'd hear a pin drop.

"Thatcher." The sound of Remy's voice floats through the room and normally when he sees or hears her, he calms down, but right now, I don't think he's even registered she's here. His gaze is locked on Grayson and Grayson only. "Where. The. Fuck. Is. He?" Thatcher enunciates each word through clenched teeth.

"Fucked if I know, man," Grayson tells him.

"Bullshit. You're hiding him, aren't you?" Thatcher screams, spittle flying from his mouth.

"Dude, calm the fuck down," I say, trying to ease the situation.

His gaze falls to the floor. His shoulders rise rapidly with each hurried breath he sucks in. Standing up, he looks around and stops his perusal of the room when he sees Remy standing here with Alani and Hudson. His eyes widen when he finally notices his girlfriend. He marches over to her like a bull in a china shop. "What about you, Peach?" he sneers at her. "Do you fucking know where your cunt of a brother is?"

His eyes are full of rage, he's completely lost to the anger over the situation and as I watch, I don't know what to do to calm him down.

"What are you asking me, Thatcher?" she murmurs, tears building in her eyes over his unspoken accusation.

"I'm asking if you're covering for him because it seems like something you'd do."

"Thatch, man, calm down," I say, squeezing his shoulder, trying to get control of this before it explodes even more. Before he says some dumb shit he can't take back.

"Wow," Remy hisses, shaking her head. She's trying to hold back her tears right now and I'm impressed with how she's handling herself, proving why she's good for him. "I guess I know where I stand." Hurt laces her voice as she stares at the man she loves.

"For the record, in case it's not clear, I stand with *my* brothers," Thatcher says. "Who do you stand with?"

Fuck, Thatcher just shut up.

The entire cafeteria is silent. They all watch the scene unfold before them. Remy stands with an open mouth and shakes her head again.

"You need to decide, Peach, me or them." He's putting her in a very difficult position, no matter what she chooses, someone loses.

"Thatcher," Hendrix exclaims, glaring at him in disbelief. We all know he's royally fucking this up. He's saying all this in the heat of the moment and come tomorrow, when the anger and surprise and hurt has eased, he's going to regret pushing Remy away.

Alani looks over at me, her own tears falling as she watches her best friend's heart get destroyed by my brother. After everything they've been through, I never thought this would happen.

What is Thatcher doing?

Remy surprises us all when she stands her ground and instead of giving Thatcher an answer, she turns her back on him and walks away. She strides out of the cafeteria with Alani right behind her.

Hudson shakes his head and when Thatcher catches his gaze, he doesn't hold back. "If I were you, Vanderbelt, I'd go after her because I don't think she'll still be there tomorrow." But Thatcher, the stubborn fucker, doesn't move. He stares off in the direction Remy and Alani just went.

Grayson glares at him and then follows the path Remy and Alani took, shoulder-barging Thatch on his way past.

Turning away from my brother, I follow after them. I'm so pissed at my brother right now. Exiting the cafeteria, I catch up to the others. Remy is slumped over crying into her knees while Alani rubs her back. Grayson squats in front of her, holding her in his arms. Every sob that comes from her, tears through me. It rips me apart because I know Thatcher will see through his anger soon and realize what's happened, I just hope he's not too late.

Removing my phone, I pull up my texts with Arlen.

REIGN

You need to come back to Crestwood.

He finally replies.

ARLEN

I'm around. I just need some time.

Things here aren't great, Arl, you need to fix this.

Sorry. I can't, not yet.

Shaking my head, I pocket my phone just as Alani helps Remy up. There's a commotion behind them and I see Thatcher's finally pulled his head out of his ass. "Remy, babe, please," he begs.

Alani glares at him and goes into protective momma-bear mode, reminding me I always want her on my side.

"Not right now, Thatcher," Alani snaps at him, shielding Remy from him.

"Peach, please. I'm an asshole," he pleads, "please don't shut me out."

Remy stops but doesn't turn around. She glances over her shoulder and even from where I'm standing, I can see she's broken and hurt. Don't blame her really, and then with a single shake of her head, she lets Alani lead her away.

"Fuck," Thatcher yells before his fist flies straight into the locker beside him. His emotions have finally gotten the better of him and he begins to slam his fist over and over into the locker until Hendrix drags him back, holding his arms down by his side.

Hendrix leads Thatcher in the opposite direction to the girls and Grayson. Turning away from my stupid brother, I stare after the girls. I know that I need to fix this because I'm the one who opened this can of worms.

The only way this is going to sort itself out is if Arlen confesses and is held accountable for his actions.

We need to know why. Why did he kill my father? And why the fuck did he fake his own death?

As I stand here, it hits me and I know exactly what I have to do … I just hope I'm not too late.

ARLEN

... one week later

HE WASN'T SUPPOSED to find out yet, and he certainly wasn't supposed to find out like that.

Fuck!

The vibration of my phone sounds again, but like the other million times over the past week, I ignore it because I already know who it is and I'm not ready to talk to her. My tenacious sister has called nonstop since she found out the news from Reign. In all fairness, she deserves to know the truth, they all do, but I'm not ready to confess all my sins.

Thornton wasn't the man I fell for, and neither was his son. Sure, hooking up with Reign in hopes of getting closer to his father was a shitty thing to do and when the guilt of being with him became too much, I came up with my exit plan. I thought faking my death so Thornton and I could run away and be together was the perfect plan, I just never expected my own fucking mother would seduce him. I thought Thornton was better than that.

I don't regret killing him. Thornton deserved it. I loved him but it turns out he was a cunt, just like Mother. If she hadn't offed herself in jail, I would have killed her too. Not just for fucking with my original plan but she is, well was, a despicable human being. She and Thornton deserve to suffer in hell for what they did to all those young kids.

For what they did to Thornton's niece and nephew.

I'm pacing back and forth in my hidden room. Nobody knows this room is here, it's my safe haven away from my place at Crestwood Central Apartments. I stumbled upon it when I was planning my death and I'm glad to have it now. This place isn't tainted by anyone, it's just for me.

Here in the walls, I come to think. I come here to fight the voices in my head, but since killing Thornton, that doesn't work anymore. They are getting louder and louder. The only time they are quiet is when I'm with *him,* but I pushed him away and now, that invisible fucker in my head is louder than ever.

Pressing my thumbs to my temple, I rub the aching spot on the side of my head. It's been throbbing since he found me in the library and I confessed. I knew by telling Reign I'd open up a whole can of fucking worms, but I had no choice. I was caught red-handed.

Forcing myself to sit still, I try to drown out the fucking voice but it's echoing around my brain. Dropping my butt to the mattress I have in here, I close my eyes, but the voice won't go away. Lying down on the mattress, it's old, battered, and someone most likely died on it, but it's enough to get me by. It's all I deserve. I stare up at the ceiling, listening to the footsteps of passing students and their voices. I sit up when I hear "he's here," but the fear dissipates when I realize they aren't talking about me.

I'm still safe.

Nobody knows I'm here.

Knowing I'm still hidden, for now, I drift off to sleep but I suddenly snap awake, jumping up into a sitting position.

Stumbling to my feet, I groan loudly feeling the kink in my neck, leaning my arms against the wall, my head still pounds.

Grabbing the pill container I keep in here, I shake a couple of pills out, swallowing them dry. Closing my eyes, I try to ease the tension but it's getting worse. Everything is getting worse.

Girls giggling pulls me from my focus. *Why isn't it the weekend? This place is so quiet on the weekends. I like the quiet. It's why I like the library so much. Even when there are students everywhere, it's still quiet.*

Staring at the direction from where it's coming, they continue and eventually, it passes and they take their giggling fest somewhere else.

Closing my eyes again, they pop wide open when I hear crying. *Crying is worse than giggling*, the voice sneers at me. I need to get out of here. Walking to the hidden door, I press my ear to it and listen for a moment. Once I know the coast is clear, I slowly open it. Lifting my head, my eyes widen when I see a girl. She stands a few feet away, wiping at her face. Clenching my jaw, I watch her, she doesn't know I'm here, so I creep farther out from my hiding place, softly shutting the door like it was never there, but the soft click echoes down the corridor. The girl turns, gasping out loud when she spots me. Her eyes widen. "I ... I know you," she whispers, stepping away from me. Her gaze looks around and I know she's going to make a run for it.

"Don't worry yourself, Lauren, I don't hurt innocent people," I tell her.

"Hhh ... how do you know my name?" she stammers, fear radiating off her. Just like last time, but last time, I was misinformed. My attack on her was a case of mistaken identity, oops. I don't need to play with her anymore so without a word, I begin to walk away. I need to get out of here before someone spots me.

"Wait," she calls out before I can get away.

Stopping in the middle of the hall, I turn to face her. Quickly, I check my surroundings to make sure I won't be caught, I'm not going to let this bitch be the reason they take me down. "Yyy ... you're Arlen, right?"

Nodding, I stare at her and pull my hood up when her eyes widen and she gasps. *Shit, she remembers.*

Marching over to her, I push her into the wall and growl, "You didn't see me, okay? And whatever you think, you're wrong. It wasn't me, it was *him.* Just visit with the family and go back to New York. Forget you saw me."

She nods and before she utters a word, I stalk away from her.

I'm almost to the exit when she cries out, "They're all looking for you, but I won't tell."

A smile graces my lips knowing I have her silence. Waving over my shoulder in acknowledgment, I sigh in relief. I know that eventually I'll have to face them but not today.

Pushing down on the door handle, I step out into the sunlight. Nearing the edge of the building, the sound of Reign's voice stops me in my tracks. Pressing myself against the wall, I peek around and see him talking to Hudson.

Closing my eyes, I breathe in deeply and when I open them again, I see red. Reign is kissing Hudson deeply.

"He's *ours,*" the voice sneers.

Hudson reaches out and holds his hand, their fingers intertwine, and he smiles at him like some lovesick fool.

"*Are you going to let that happen? You're a fucking pussy,*" the voice berates me. "*You're a fucking pussy,*" it repeats.

Standing here, I listen as the voice continues taunting me.

Reign leans in and kisses Hudson's lips again, and I wish he was kissing me. We used to kiss like that … in secret, but Reign is kissing Hudson out in the open.

"*You weren't good enough,*" the voice taunts.

I know I told him we were done and that I was over him, but seeing what Hudson does to him brings back everything we hid for so long, and I want that.

I want Reign again.

The voice inside my head isn't helping right now. My emotions are warring against each other. Seeing Reign passionately kissing him sparks something inside of me and I snap, like I did that night with Thornton.

Finally, they stop kissing and Reign walks away. He looks over his shoulder and smiles at Hudson, he used to smile at me like that. My dick thickens in my pants at the memory. Closing my eyes, I slip my hand into my pants and pull my dick out. Gripping my cock in my hand, I fist the shaft and tug myself to memories of Reign's hand around my dick. With a grunt, I come all over my hand and the garden bed.

Putting my dick away, I step out from my hiding place and smack right into Hudson. He falls slightly before catching himself and his eyes widen when he sees it's me.

"Aaaaa … Arlen?" he stammers.

Staring down at him, I grin. This is a sign, and listening to the voice in my head, I take the opportunity before me. The voice is encouraging me to do this and for the first time in a few weeks, I gladly want to listen to my invisible friend.

Gripping his shirt in my fist, I yank him toward me and slam him into the wall, his head bounces off the brickwork, making a grunt escape him. He holds his hands up in surrender. *Pussy.*

"I … I don't want any trouble. I won't say a word. Just let me go." I watch his throat as he swallows. Leaning down so my face is inches from his, I rest my forehead against his, our breaths mingling together.

Ignoring his whimpers, I bark, "What is it about you, huh?"

"I don't know what you mean?" He furrows his brows in confusion. What Reign sees in this guy is beyond me.

A dark chuckle escapes me and the urge to shut him up is like a drug shooting through my veins, I can't get enough of this feeling.

"Let's go for a little walk, shall we?" I singsong, gripping his arm tightly in my fist. His face drops when he realizes I'm not letting him go.

Pulling him along, he drops his backpack as I drag him behind me. He goes to yell out, but I shove him against a tree, smacking my hand over his mouth. Pulling out my knife, I place it across his throat. "Make a sound, I dare you."

Hudson nods in understanding and without another sound, he follows me, not that he has any choice in the matter.

Reign is going to see Hudson isn't worthy of him. That it's supposed to be him and me. I'm determined to make him mine again, no matter what it takes.

HUDSON

ARLEN'S BEEN PACING back and forth from one side of the room to the other for a while now. When we got to his apartment, he tied me to a chair, and began talking to himself. Answering his questions as if there's another person here with us.

He's completely lost it and although I never thought he was dangerous, I'm beginning to think that theory is wrong. I mean, after all he did murder someone in cold blood.

Trying to speak around the gag he put in my mouth proves difficult so I give up, saving my energy and trying to work out how the fuck I'm going to get out of here. My wrists are killing me and the more I listen to Arlen and his crazy one-sided conversation, the more I begin to fear that I won't be walking out of here. I think I'm about to die.

He's behind me, ruffling around in the bag he brought in with him, when from the corner of my eye, I see him pull his hunting knife out again. My eyes widen at the shiny sharp blade. He twists the knife in his hand, around and around and then he starts to pace the room again.

"Yes, yes yes," he says, breaking the silence in the room. He stops pacing and he turns to face me, a sinister look on his face. Stepping toward me, he yanks down the gag and I take a deep breath of air, gulping in fresh, well as fresh as this dingy room air allows.

"What?" he sneers, shaking his head before he screws his face up and begins to mutter again. "No, I—"

"Arlen," I utter, trying to get his attention.

"Shut the fuck up," he snaps, "you speak when spoken to." Not wanting to enrage him, I nod and do as he says.

After a few more paces, he walks over to me and straddles my thighs. "Why?" he hisses. "Why did he come out now?" He pauses. "With you and that slut you share."

Staring at him, I swallow but don't answer. I'm too afraid to speak just in case his question is rhetorical, so I keep quiet. And I'm glad I did because he's clearly not wanting answers from me.

"I loved him, you know? I loved them both," he states, a wistful look on his face and then it disappears, and he shakes his head. "But *he* didn't want me and wanted to hide me." Closing his eyes, he throws his head back and lets out a high-pitched scream. Shuffling off my lap, he sinks to his knees and utters over and over, "Why? Why? Why?"

He screams out before standing up before me. Leering down at me, his breathing has escalated. Leaning down and getting into my face, he holds the knife to my throat and smiles. "Taking you away would solve everything, you know? Without you, he'll be miserable."

Shaking my head, I swallow, feeling the pressure of the blade against my skin.

"It won't get him back," I say. "It will only upset him."

"You don't know him like I know him. I get rid of you, then I get rid of that slut, and then he'll have no choice but to turn to me for comfort."

"You leave her alone," I shout at him. Rage simmers within as I think about him hurting Alani. "She's innocent." For a moment, his face drops and he looks almost remorseful but then I fuck up, when I growl, "You leave them both a-fucking-lone."

That last statement triggers something and he lifts the blade to my neck and pushes it into my skin. Blood trickles down my neck. "Please," I beg. I'm not sure if I'm begging for him to stop cutting me or if I'm begging for him to leave Alani and Reign alone.

"No," he sneers, "hurting you and her will make me feel better, and then he will see that he needs me. That he only needs me."

"You're delusional," I tell him.

"That may be so, but I'm not tied to a chair." He taps my cheek with the blade. "It's time for part two to commence."

He shoves the rag back into my mouth and backhands me across the face with the handle of the knife. My vision dots and the last thing I hear before I black out is the lock of the door engaging.

ALANI

"CALL me when you get this Hudson. Love you." I hang up after leaving another message for him. Reign hasn't seen him either but he's currently with Thatcher, trying to keep his brother from making things worse with Remy.

That feeling of unease like the other day with Reign festers inside of me with each message I leave.

"Why do you look like your goldfish just died?" Remy asks, plopping onto my bed next to me. This is the most I've seen of her recently and it's only because she's still pissed at Thatcher, rightfully so, but seeing them on the outs is making me sad.

"I can't get hold of Hudson," I tell her.

"You've got it bad for that boy," she states, popping a Skittle into her mouth.

"I've got it bad for two boys." I waggle my eyebrows at her.

"I can't believe you're with both of them. You are the envy of most girls on this floor … and a few guys as well. Probably. Maybe."

"What can I say, I love dick and two dicks are better than one."

Remy chuckles softly, shaking her head with a grin because it IS surreal that I'm with both of them.

Remy's phone begins to ring, and she stares at it for a few seconds before answering. I get my hopes up that it's Thatch calling to apologize for being a douchehole but when she whispers, "Arlen," I sit up straighter, cocking an eyebrow at Remy as I listen to her chat with the other asshole male who is causing issues in her life.

"W-w-w-w … where are you, Arl?" she cries into the phone. Ever since the revelation that he's the one to have shot Daddy Vanderbelt, everyone's been looking for him. There are so many questions because no one knows why he did it.

"I'm with Alani, Arlen." He says something to her, she looks over at me, growling slightly but then says, "Okay, fine. I'll be there soon." Hanging up the phone, she lets it slip into her lap when she looks at me sadly. I hate seeing my bright and bubbly bestie not so bright and bubbly. "Arlen wants to see me."

"He does?" I ask.

Nodding, she licks her lips and shuffles to the edge of the bed. Reaching down for her shoes, she slips them on. "Hurry up," she says to me, "we have to go."

"Huh? What? I'm coming."

She nods. "Yep, he told me to bring you."

He did. Why?

Slipping my own shoes on, Remy takes my hand and walks us out of my room. We hurry along the corridor. Her head darts around as we go, no doubt searching for Thatch. "We can't let the boys see us," she whispers as we race down the stairs.

The exit is in sight, we're almost to the door when we hear. "Rem, Alani, where are you ladies sneaking off to?" Theon chuckles, staring and eyeing us suspiciously. Damn the Vanderbelt guard dogs.

"For a walk, Theon, you know that thing you do on two legs," Remy snaps, placing her hand on her hip.

"Whoa, didn't mean to upset you, just asked a question," he says, raising his hands up in surrender.

"Well, you can tell Thatcher to back the fuck off," she barks at him before grabbing my arm again and pulling me behind her.

Theon doesn't follow us and for the sake of his life, or possibly keeping his testicles intact, it's probably a good idea because pissed-off Remy is a little scary and intimidating.

"So where is he?" I ask her.

"Cemetery," and she says this as if we are meeting him at Starbucks. Meeting in the cemetery is creepy, yeah, he's her brother and all that, but he's also just confessed to a crime that's currently unsolved.

We walk for a bit before she stops, turns, and looks back at Crestwood. It's as if she feels the weirdness I do so I just go for it. "Rem, you know he murdered someone right?" As I speak those words, that strange gut feeling intensifies. My Spidey senses are telling me to turn back. I haven't officially spent any time with Arlen, but my gut is telling me something is wrong, I just can't work out what.

Closing her eyes for a second, she turns her attention from school to me. "Alani, I know my brother, he wouldn't have done that for no reason, something made him kill Mr. Vanderbelt. I just know it."

"Okay if you trust him, I trust him."

"Thanks," she murmurs and then bites her lip. She nods and sadly smiles before grabbing my hand and we continue to walk toward the cemetery.

Together we walk in silence. Darkness is creeping in and the closer we get to our destination, the more intense that eerie feeling becomes. I want to tell my bestie that I think she's wrong about her brother, but how do you do that without pissing someone off?

We walk between some gravestones when a shadow comes out from behind a tombstone. We both pause mid-step but when the person comes into the light, we both let out the breath that we were holding.

"Arl," Remy sings out, running and jumping at her brother.

"Hey, Jellybean," he says, kissing the top of her head. They hold on to each other tightly and when I see the love radiating between them, I begin to think maybe Rem is right. Arlen is a good guy.

"I've been so worried about you. Where have you been? Everyone is searching for you," she cries, holding Arlen's hands in front of her.

"I know, I know, Rem, I just need more time, but I promise to come home soon." He looks over her shoulder, finally noticing me and when my eyes meet his, instant fear simmers in my blood. His cold gaze cuts through me like a knife.

"So, you're the one?" he says, looking me over like he's somehow disgusted by my presence.

"Arl, what's going on?" Remy asks him, taking a step back and coming to my side.

"I just want to know what he sees in her. In them."

My eyes widen at his statement, and I realize this was a trap to get me here. He doesn't want to see his sister, this is all about Reign and me.

"I didn't bring her here for you to be an asshole, Arl,"

Remy snaps at her brother. She grabs my arm and pushes me behind her as we begin to slowly walk backward and away from her brother.

He just stands there and watches us go. Remy and I spin around and slowly walk away from him, but I can't help it and I look over my shoulder back at Arlen. He smiles a sinister smile, then salutes me before slinking back into the darkness like some creepy psycho in a scary movie.

"I'm so sorry, babe. I don't know what's up with him," Remy says, shaking her head.

"It's fine," I tell her but deep down it's not.

By the time we get back to Crestwood, it's dark out. Thatcher is leaning against the wall staring off into the distance, it's as if he was waiting for us to return. His arms are crossed across his chest and one leg is bent resting against the brickwork, he looks like the proverbial sexy bad boy.

Theon no doubt blabbed about our departure.

Looking at my friend, I feel sad for her. She loves the asshole, but he really hurt her with his actions. She sighs and looks over at me, giving me a weak smile. "I guess I have to face him at some point," she mutters and at the sound of her voice, he straightens up and when he looks at her, he looks just as broken and hurt as she does.

"You do," I nod in agreement, "just don't let him off too easily. Make the asshole work for it." Pulling her in for a hug, I whisper, "Call me later."

She nods and I leave her staring at her boyfriend. Walking past him, I glare at the douchehole. "Might want to grovel," I hiss as I walk past, "and grovel like you've never groveled before."

He frowns at my statement but doesn't take his eyes off Remy, giving me hope they'll be okay.

Once inside, I try Hudson again while I walk up to my room, but like the other million times today, I get his voice-mail again. "Where are you?" I groan.

Fishing my keys out, I unlock my door and chuck everything on my bed before I begin my nightly routine.

By the time I finish my shower, I'm exhausted. As much as I want my boys here to cuddle with, I'm happy to be crawling into bed right now. I can barely keep my eyes open but before I let sleep overtake me, I try Hudson again. Hitting his name, I once more listen to his voice telling me to leave a message. "Call me please, Huddy. I'm starting to worry."

Reign and I text for a little bit but when I can no longer keep my eyes open, I tell him goodnight and then place my phone onto my bedside table. Pulling my blankets up, I snuggle in and drift off to sleep.

Something touching me pulls me from my sleep. Glancing around my room, I don't see anything but then I feel a hand on my ankle. Looking to the end of my bed, I see a shadow sitting there.

Watching me.

I'm frozen in fear because without saying a word, I know who it is because that feeling from earlier today is back.

"It's our time to play," he says before grabbing my ankle and pulling me toward him. A scream falls from my lips but it's too late, he backhands me across my face and the last thing I see, before everything goes black, is his sinister face smirking at me.

REIGN

WHERE THE FUCK are Hudson and Alani?

I've been calling them both nonstop since I woke up this morning and neither of them is answering.

For the hundredth time, I get Hudson's voicemail and in frustration, I growl at the device in my hand.

"Still can't reach them?" Saint asks.

Shaking my head, I lean back frustrated with myself for being caught up in Arlen's revelation and Thatcher's reaction to Remy. Trying Alani, I once again get her voicemail, her sweet voice doing nothing to calm my nerves.

"Fuck," I hiss and throw my phone across the room.

"Not the smartest move," Saint smirks, picking up my phone and handing it back to me. Looking it over, there's no damage so I look at my brother in the 'ha ha, fucker, you were wrong' kind of way. "I don't need this right now, Saint."

"What do you mean?" he asks incredulously.

Pointing my finger at him, I glare. "This … this big brother crap, okay? I don't need you to be a smartass, I need you to help find my boyfriend and girlfriend because something isn't right."

Sinking back into the chair, Saint knocks my knee and I look over at him. "Hey, it's okay, we'll find them, they have to be somewhere."

Hendrix and Thatcher nod at me in greeting and then they look toward Saint and without uttering a word, he answers their unspoken question, "Still nothing."

Picking up my phone, I throw it again in frustration when I see a blank screen. "Where the fuck are they?"

Thatcher bends down and picks up my phone, scrunching his face when he looks at it and pushes the button on the side. "Screen's cracked but it still works."

"Thanks," I mutter while Saint sits there with a grin on his face that says 'told ya.'

It lights up with a text and excitement builds but then it deflates when I realize it's not from Alani or Hudson.

ARLEN

I need to see you.

Staring down at my phone, I read the sentence over and over. Hendrix knocks my leg. "What's up?"

"Nothing," I whisper. "Just some spam text," I lie, needing them to not suspect I'm speaking to Arlen.

"Have you heard from him?" Thatcher asks just as my screen lights up again.

"Reign?" Hendrix demands and when I look up, I know

my face isn't hiding it anymore. Tears fill my eyes and Thatcher snatches my phone from me.

"Jesus fuck," he snaps, shoving it at Hendrix before he does the same tossing it to Saint.

"What the fuck, Reign?" Saint growls. "You've been talking to the fucker?"

Another text comes through, and his eyes widen at the screen. He throws my phone in my lap and I catch sight of the photo. It's of Hudson and Alani tied up together. Hudson's eye is swollen shut and Alani's face is tear-stained and etched with fear. Another text comes through and it's the one sentence I feared the most.

ARLEN

Come alone or I'm going to have some more fun.

I can't breathe as I stare at the image on the screen. He's had them this whole time. Why?

"I need to go to them, I need to." I go to get up, but Thatcher's hand on my shoulder stops me.

"Reign, you need to go into this with a level head. Arlen is dangerous."

"H-h-h-h-he won't hurt me," I tell him, but even as the words pass through my lips, I don't even believe me.

"Bullshit," Saint barks, "he's a fucking psycho killer and kidnapper. No fucking way are you going alone. No. Fucking. Way."

"I'm going," I growl.

"That's a bad fucking idea," Hendrix sneers, digging his finger into my chest.

"Please, I need to go. Alone. I need to save them. I won't survive if they get hurt because of me." Tears fall down my cheeks and I can't stop them because I know Arlen will hurt them to get to me. I just know it.

"Fine," Thatcher barks, "but before you go, we are going

to come up with a plan. I'm not sending you to your fucking death, Reign."

"Fine," I murmur.

We discuss our options and when we have our plan, I head off to meet him. I just hope I'm not too fucking late.

QUINN

THIS PLACE IS GETTING MORE and more fucked up by the day. Just when I think it can't get any crazier, it does. After my attack earlier this year, I should have left. I should have gone to that school in Paris like Mom wanted me to, but no, I was fooled by a boy. A boy who I was falling for, but it turns out, he just wanted me for a good time and fuck, did we have a good time. The things he can do with his tongue are everything.

Those memories evaporate when I bump into someone coming out of the elevator. They reach out and grab me and a feeling of déjà-vu washes over me. Leaving me rattled. When

I look up and see the dark hood covering their face, I'm transported back to that night. "It's you," I blubber, "you … you attacked me."

"Like fuck I did," they growl. Their voice sounds different but maybe I've distorted it in my mind over time. "I don't even fucking know you."

"It was you. I swear it was. You … you raped me in that house."

He pushes his hood back and I come face-to-face with Arlen Hearst. "I didn't fucking touch you, it was that fucker, Brennan. I was trapped in the room next door, I heard it all go down."

My eyes well with tears as I remember the feeling of him rutting into me. The smell of his breath against my cheek. A lump forms in the back of my throat and I race over to the trash can and vomit. I seem to be doing a lot of that lately, the memories of that night causing me to physically be sick. My therapist said with time, it will ease but if anything, it's getting worse. *I really should have gone to Paris.* I shake my head and wipe at my mouth when a noise from inside one of the apartments garners my attention.

"You hear that?" I ask Arlen.

He shakes his head. "Hear what?" Then I hear it again and this time, Arlen looks panicked. "I'm glad I could clear up the rape thing for you, but I have to run." Before I can say anything, he unlocks the door across from me and my eyes widen when I see Alani Thomas tied up on the bed. Her face is red from crying, her hair matted. She looks scared.

"What the fuck?" I mumble but I should have kept quiet. Arlen spins on his heel and marches over to me. He grabs me around the neck and begins to choke me. I love a good choking, in the sexual kind of way, but this is anything but sexual and I fear for my safety and life. My vision begins to dot as I scratch at his hands, but he's too strong. He drags me toward the fire escape and opens the door, the sound of the elevator dinging surprises him. He stares into my eyes, and I see the moment he decides to end my life, he pushes me backward and I begin to tumble down the stairs, coming to a stop on the landing below.

Blinking, I stare up at a smirking Arlen and his smirking face is the last thing I see before darkness envelops me.

"Ouch," I hiss, rubbing the back of my head. Opening my eyes, it's dark and I don't know where I am. Taking a deep breath, my neck and throat hurt as the oxygen filters into my lungs.

Pushing myself up into a sitting position, I realize my wrist is broken when I push pressure onto it. "Fuck me," I complain and then I remember what I saw.

Pulling my phone out of my pocket, I click on *his* name. It rings and the asshole sends my call to voicemail. Ending the call, I try again. It rings and rings until I get his voicemail again. "Fucking answer, asshole," I hiss as I call again and like the first time, he sends the call to voicemail. I try again and this time he picks up.

"I don't have time for this shit, Quinn," he sneers through the line.

"Fuck you, asshole," I snap at him. "Maybe I shouldn't tell you what I know."

"Just tell me and then fuck off."

It hurts the way he's speaking to me right now. He and I could be something amazing, but he's running scared.

"Quinn," he growls, "you have three seconds and then I'm hanging up."

"I know where Arlen is."

"So do we," he snaps at me. "He's about to meet with Reign in the cemetery."

"He's not at the cemetery. He's at the Crestwood Central Apartments on the fifth floor and he has Alani."

"The fuck you just say?"

"Arlen, he's here at the apartments and he has Alani."

"Is Hudson there too?"

"I didn't see him."

"Fuck," he hisses. "What the fuck are you doing at Crestwood Central Apartments?"

"I was … it doesn't matter why I'm here," *and if you cared for me like you say you do, did, whatever, you'd know that Mom and Dad moved here a few weeks ago,* I grumble in my head. I hate that I care so much about him when he doesn't care about me in the same way. I should cut him out of my life but I can't, Hendrix Vanderbelt has sucked me in and I'm addicted. "But I bumped into him in the hallway an—"

"Stay the fuck away from him, he's a fucking psycho."

"I know, he pushed me down a flight of stairs when I saw Alani in his room."

"He hurt you?" The softness in his voice is a complete one-eighty from only seconds ago, reminding me of the soft and loving Hendrix. "Are you okay?"

"I think my wrist is broken and he choked me—"

"Bet you liked that," he teases.

"No, I did not. I only like it when broody assholes choke me while their dick is in my ass."

"Fuck, babe, the visions I have right now."

"Focus, dickhead," I snap at him. "The time for that is over and it's never happening again, you made that perfectly clear, but you need to get here now. I'm going to call the police."

"No," he shouts down the line. "Let us handle it, we need to talk to the fucker before he's taken away."

"Why do I get the feeling there's more to this than just him taking Alani?"

"Because there is." He pauses. "Just for once in your fucking life, Quinn, listen to me."

"Fine," I snap, "but can you at least call me an ambulance?"

"No," he snaps and I'm ready to give him a piece of my mind when he tacks on, "I'll come get you."

Before I can reply, he hangs up. "Thanks," I mutter to myself, once again, wishing I'd gone to Paris.

ALANI

"WHAT DID YOU DO TO QUINN?" I scream at Arlen when he returns. He's muttering incoherently to himself, he's completely lost it. If I thought I was scared before, I'm freaked the fuck out now.

"Shut your fucking mouth, whore. This is all your fault. If you had of kept your skanky mitts off Reign, none of this would have happened."

"Well, if you'd just stayed dead, none of this would have happened," Hudson throws back at him. His statement makes Arlen angrier. He storms over to Hudson in the chair, pulls him up by the front of his shirt, and punches him in the stomach. Hudson bends forward, grunting in pain. Arlen then hits him over the back of the head and kicks the chair Hudson is tied to over. His head connects with the corner of the wall, and he lands with a thud on the carpet. Arlen kicks him repeatedly and I scream for him to stop but he doesn't. He just continues to kick Hudson ranting "he's mine," over and over and over.

Finally, he stops kicking Hudson, but he doesn't move. "Hudson," I cry out, "are you okay?" I'm met with silence. "Hudson, please," I beg, "answer me."

Arlen looks over at me, snickering and laughing. He kicks Hudson one more time and then turns toward me. He now has a glazed over, far off look in his eyes and it's terrifying. He makes his way over to me and roughly grabs me by the throat. Gripping tightly, he pulls me up and drags me into him. His fingers twist and squeeze tighter. He's crushing my windpipe and I struggle to breathe. Clawing at his hands, he begins to breathe heavily as his face screws up, sneering. "Just fucking go, you bitch."

Gasping for air, I scratch at his hands but it's hard when they are tied together. My air supply is slowly slipping away. Blood rushes in my head as my lungs scream for oxygen. My fingers dig into his flesh, one of my fake nails breaks off as I struggle to keep conscious. White dots flicker before my eyes, and everything starts to go black.

Just before the darkness envelops me, I'm saved when there's a knock at the door. Arlen drops his hands from my neck and pushes me back onto the bed.

He turns and focuses on the door. "Saved by the knock," he sneers as I cough and splutter, trying to get air into my lungs.

Shuffling backward on the bed, I move as far away from him as I can. Panting heavily, I fall off the end of the bed with a thud, he looks over his shoulder at me and glares. "Don't say a fucking word," he growls as he slowly reaches for the door handle.

Pushing myself up into a sitting position, I peer over the end of the mattress and pray it's someone here to help. My prayers are answered because before he can open it, the door is kicked in. Arlen flies backward and lands on the floor next to me. My gaze flicks from him to the door and I smile in relief when I see Reign standing there with his brothers behind him.

"Red?" he says, seeing me peering over the end of the bed. Looking around, he spots Hudson on the ground, still unconscious. "What the fuck did you do, Arlen?" Reign bellows, anger all over his face. His tone is unlike anything I've heard before and I don't think Arlen appreciates it either.

Arlen pushes himself upright and stands, pulling his knife from his pocket. "They don't deserve you," he cries and then he tugs at his hair. Shaking his head side to side, he hits himself over and over, mumbling, "Shut up. Shut up. Shut up. Just shut up. Shut up. Shut up. Shut up." He keeps repeating it over and over. He covers his head, spinning around in circles but then he stops and turns his attention to me. He glares menacingly at me, pointing the knife toward me. "You should have just done what I asked. You should have walked away and none of this would have happened. This is all your fault, whore. It's all your fault."

"Arlen, Alani has nothing to do with this," Reign pleads but his words have no effect on Arlen, he's lost to the demons in his head.

"Yes, she does," he shouts. "They stole you from me, you were mine," he barks and takes a step toward me, but the sound of Reign's voice stops him.

"Arlen, please," he begs. His gaze catches mine and he mouths, "It's going to be okay."

Arlen walks over to me and towers above me. His presence is frightening me, I've never felt fear like this before.

Tears cascade down my face in streams as he looks down at me with utter disgust on his face. The hand holding the knife twitches by his side and that fear I just felt intensifies.

"I love them, please don't hurt them," Reign begs and takes a step forward when groaning in the corner catches all our attention. Hudson tries to sit up, but falls face forward again, groaning in pain. Saint races over to him and helps him up. Pulling him into a standing position, Hudson holds on to Saint's arm for support. He sees me behind Arlen, and he sees red. "You fucker," he growls and tries to launch himself at Arlen but Thatcher and Saint both stop him.

"Bitsy," Hudson croaks, struggling against the guys' hold on him but in his weakened state, he gives up and stares sadly at me.

Arlen now has his back to me and I expect Reign to try to negotiate with him, but it's Thatcher who speaks first. "Arlen, you know you won't get out of here alive if you hurt them any more than you have. What will Remy think of you?" At the mention of his sister, even with his back to me, I can tell that his features soften but in the blink of an eye, his shoulders stiffen and any compassion he has evaporates. He spins around to face me and lunges forward. He grabs onto my hair and pulls me up by it. Spinning me around so my back is to his front, he holds the knife to my throat and presses the blade to my skin. "Don't," he sneers when they all move to circle around him. He backs up and when his back hits the wall, his grip on me tightens.

"Please," I whimper but this only enrages him further and he presses the knife harder into my neck. He hasn't cut me yet, but it's only a matter of time.

"Why are you doing this?" Reign asks.

"Everything is wrong. He isn't supposed to be with her, he's supposed to be with ..." Arlen quickly stops himself. His grip on the knife loosens slightly but I don't move, fear ripples through me the longer he holds me. "He deserved it, he lied. He knew how I felt but he still did it anyway."

"Who did?" I ask, my brain not computing what he's mumbling.

"Their father," he sneers, pointing the knife at the Vanderbelt brothers before returning it to my neck.

"Arlen, your mother is to blame as much as our father. What they did is unforgivable," Reign says.

"No," Arlen yells. "No! No! No! He … she took advantage of him. He wasn't supposed to love her," he croaks, "it was supposed to be me."

My eyes widen when I realize what he just confessed, and I see the moment his confession registers in Reign's eyes too. He holds his hands up. "We know, Arl, we know, but please this isn't you. This person isn't you," Reign pleads with him. "He wouldn't want that for you either."

I feel the moment Reign's words register because his grip on me loosens. "I just want it to stop," Arlen cries and when he says this, he drops his arms from around me but I'm too scared to move. Worried that any movement I make will set him off again. It almost feels as if now his sins have been voiced, he can move on. He crumbles to the floor murmuring, "He was mine, not hers." Covering his face with his hand as his repeated cries echo around the room.

"Red," Reign whispers and when I hear his voice, I look up at him. He opens his arms wide, and I step around Arlen and run straight into his outstretched arms. Hudson comes up behind me, engulfing us both. Reign holds on to us as tightly as he can and I break down in relief. His lips land on mine and then the three of us trade kisses before resting our foreheads together. We stand here wrapped in each other's arms, holding on for dear life.

Reign is the first to pull back when a guttural wail comes from Arlen behind us. He cups our cheeks. "Go with Hendrix now, both of you. I need to deal with Arlen."

"No," I cry, while Hudson pleads, "We're not leaving you, not with him."

Reign runs his thumb across Hudson's cheek. "Please just do this, for me. I'll be safe, I—"

"I'm not leaving him alone with him," Thatcher interrupts.

Not wanting to be here a second longer, I cup Reign's cheeks in my hands and kiss him with everything I have. "I love you, Vanderbelt, you better come home to us."

Taking Hudson's hand, I tug him toward the door.

"Give it five and call the police," Reign tells us.

Hendrix nods and ushers us toward the elevators.

Stepping into the metal car, I lean into Hudson's side, relief coursing through me that we're finally safe.

Who knew Arlen was so messed up? But I know one thing, there's only one place he belongs and I hope they never let him out. I know he's my best friend's brother, but he's a fucking psycho. None of us knew he was in love with Mr. Vanderbelt. Hudson and I are lucky to be alive. He killed Mr. Vanderbelt in a jealous rage that could have easily resulted with him killing us too.

The elevator reaches the lobby and heading toward the security desk, the woman behind the counter's eyes widen when she takes in our state.

"I need you to call the police and an ambulance please," I ask her, my tone oddly calm considering what just went down.

I think I might be in shock.

Nodding, she does as I ask and within ten minutes I can hear sirens. A sob escapes me when I hear them because it means we're safe.

"Hold on, Bitsy, they're coming," Hudson murmurs before we slide down the wall and wait for the authorities. Tears begin to flow down my cheeks because it's over.

It's finally over.

REIGN

STARING at the man I thought I once loved as he breaks down tears everything inside me apart. Arlen may have threatened Alani and Hudson and killed my dad, but looking at him now, I can't bring myself to hurt him. Or hate him. Even with the revelation of him being in love with Dad, there's a part of me that still loves him and it's the part that wants to protect him.

Thatcher goes to step forward, but I hold my arm out and stop him. Looking over at my brother, I shake my head. "Don't, it's not worth it."

"Reign, he killed our father in cold blood," Thatcher growls.

"You know as well as I do that eventually the old man would have met his maker, are you really that broken up that he's gone?" I ask him truthfully.

Thatcher groans then storms over to the wall and lifts his arm to punch it, but I stop him. "Don't." He eyes me and nods. "Besides, he has to live with the fact he killed a man who didn't love him in the way he loved him."

Saint watches him then his gaze flickers back to mine and he nods. "Say your goodbyes and then let the authorities deal with him. I have a feeling there's more to it than just Dad not loving him," he tells me.

Nodding at him, I crouch down next to Arlen. He looks up at me and my heart breaks further. This isn't the face of the man I once loved unconditionally, this is the face of a broken man.

Reaching out, I take his face in my hands and wipe at his tear-stained cheeks as he looks up at me broken, distraught, and defeated. "Arl," I whisper.

"I'm sorry," he mutters.

"I know," I murmur, kissing the top of his head. "I hope you find peace," I tell him and without waiting for his reply, I stand up, turn around, and walk away, knowing that this is the last time I'll see Arlen Hearst.

By the time we step out of the elevator downstairs, the sound of sirens echoes across the empty space and a few moments later, police swarm the lobby and sidewalk.

My eyes search them out and I become frantic when I can't find them, I begin to run in circles as panic floats through my system and then in amongst the chaos, I hear it. My name is softly shouted by a voice that is like angels singing. "Reign," she shouts again and when I spin around this time, I see them. Hudson is being loaded into the back of an ambulance, while Alani holds his hand.

"Red," I shout and I take off toward them. Colliding with Alani, I break down into her neck, my sobs catch in my throat as I pull back, taking her face in my palms. "I'm so sorry, I'm so fucking sorry," I murmur. "Are you okay? Please tell me you're okay?"

"I'm fine," she mumbles through her tears.

Covering her mouth with mine, I kiss her. Needing to know she is in fact okay and when she kisses me back, I know she is. Resting my forehead against hers, I breathe her in. She's okay.

She's o-fucking-kay.

"I'm fine," Hudson teases from beside us, "thanks for asking." Turning toward him, I smile at the fucker grinning at me. Leaning down, I kiss him, just like I kissed Alani only moments ago.

"I will never get sick of seeing you two make out like that," Alani says, causing Hudson and me to laugh. Pulling away from him, I pull Alani into my arms and hug her from behind. "It's so hot watching you two like that."

"I agree," the male paramedic says before adding, "but we need to go."

Alani turns in my arms and places a quick kiss on my lips before she jumps into the back of the ambulance. Hudson grips my hand and kisses my knuckles. "I love you," he murmurs.

Leaning down, I kiss him again. Both Alani and the paramedic moan and when I look up, they both have dreamy expressions on their faces.

"I love you both," I tell them, "and I'm so sorry." My eyes fill with tears, feeling guilty for what they went through.

"Hey, we love you too," Hudson says, squeezing my hand and I know he means it, we will be okay. "And you have nothing to apologize for."

"You're stuck with us, Vanderbelt. You better get used to the idea 'cause three is my new favorite number," Alani mutters, kissing the side of Hudson's head and blowing me a kiss.

"I think it's mine too," the paramedic says.

"See you soon, hot stuff," Hudson says and then the paramedic closes the ambulance doors.

Standing here, I watch the ambulance pull away and I realize, this is it for me, I'm home. Wherever they are is where I belong and just like Alani, three is my new favorite number.

HENDRIX

THATCHER, Saint, Remy, Grayson, and I are in the waiting room, waiting to hear if Hudson is okay. Remy is beating herself up that her brother isn't who she thought he was, and no matter how many times we tell her none of us knew, it doesn't sink in.

"Hey, how's Quinn?" Saint asks.

"Fuck," I hiss, "I totally forgot about her. The revelation that Arlen was in love with Dad kinda has been at the forefront of my mind." Pushing up from my seat, I walk over to the reception desk. Putting on my most flirtatious smile, I look at the woman behind the desk. "Darlene, such a pretty name," I tell her.

"What do you want?" she says, ignoring my flirting. I try smiling again and she raises her hand. "Look, kid, I'm old enough to be your grandma, just tell me what you want and if I can do it, I will."

A laugh escapes me. "I fucking wish you were my grandma, you're awesome."

"Tell me something I don't know. Now, what can I do for you, sweet cheeks?"

"There's a girl—"

"It's always a girl," she teases.

"Well, this girl, I care for her very much and I'd like to see if she's okay."

"Name?"

"Quinn Ellis," I tell her.

"Room seven, I'll buzz you through."

"Thanks, Darl." I blow her a kiss and walk to the door, waiting to be buzzed in.

The door buzzes and I go in. Walking around, I find room seven easily but stop outside the curtain when I hear someone chatting with Quinn and when I hear what I hear, my eyes widen. "… we will schedule you an ultrasound later today and you can see your baby."

Pushing the curtain back, I step into the room. "You're pregnant?"

Both the doctor and Quinn snap their heads toward me. Quinn's eyes are wide and I'm not sure if it's in shock because I'm here, because she's pregnant, or both.

"Is it mine?" I ask.

Her mouth opens and closes. She doesn't utter a word, but then she utters three that shock the fuck out of me, "I don't know."

Quinn is pregnant and there's a chance it might be mine.

Fuck.

REIGN

... three weeks later

FEELING a pair of lips around my cock first thing in the morning never gets old. It's my favorite way to wake up. A groan escapes me when they take me deeper into their mouth, the head of my dick hitting the back of their throat. "Fuck," I moan as they increase their speed.

The bathroom door opens and when I turn my head, I see Hudson step out freshly showered. His towel sits low on his hips, his torso still slightly bruised from Arlen's attack a few weeks ago.

He nods toward Alani under the covers. "I see you guys started without me."

"Hey, I woke up and our girl's delectable lips were around my cock. I'm innocent in all of this."

Alani lifts her head from under the covers. "Did you want me to stop, Vanderbelt?"

"Fuck no. Get back down there," I look to Hudson, "and you, get your ass into this bed now."

"Yes, sir." He mock salutes, drops his towel, and runs and jumps onto the bed, lying next to us. Alani stares up at us and as much as I love her lips around my cock, I need to kiss her. Sliding my hands down her body, she giggles as I move my hands under her arms and pull her up my body so she's now straddling me. Gripping her cheeks, I yank her down so I can capture her lips, kissing her senseless. She begins to grind over my cock. "Fuck," I growl against her lips before I flip her so she's beneath me.

Staring down at her, I take in the gorgeous woman beneath me. "Just where and how I like you, Red."

"And how's that?" she seductively whispers, grinding her cunt against my hard shaft.

"Naked, wet, and ready to be fucked." And proving once again that she is perfect for me, for us, she lifts her hips, slides her hand between us, and guides my dick toward her waiting cunt.

Hudson leans over and takes her lips in a searing hot kiss. I groan at the sight before me.

"I want you both," Alani breathlessly whispers. "Fuck my ass, Hudson, while Reign fucks my pussy."

Hudson looks at me and I nod. "What our girl wants, our girl gets."

While Hudson shuffles down the bed, I roll so Alani is now on top. He climbs behind Alani and palms her ass cheek, squeezing gently causing our girl to moan as she continues to ride me.

"Hand me the lube," he asks, nodding to the side table. Handing him the tube, our fingers graze and an electrical current jolts between us, he feels it too because his gaze turns molten. He flicks the cap open and squeezes a glob onto her ass crack. He slides his hand over her cheek, and I can tell the moment he presses his finger into her ass.

"You love that, don't you, Red? Your cunt just hugged my dick when he put his finger in. You'll choke it when it's his cock in there." Looking at Hudson, over her shoulder, I stare intently at him. "Fuck her ass, Huddy Boy, fuck her ass good."

"Yes," Alani pants and Hudson practically drools as he positions himself between her cheeks.

"Oh, fuck," he groans as he sinks his cock into her ass. I don't know what's better, fucking Alani's cunt, her ass, or Hudson's ass. Fucking these two in general is a dream come fucking—pun intended—true.

Alani moans as Hudson presses into her ass. I can feel his shaft through the walls of her pussy.

"Fuck, baby," I hiss, "I can feel his dick against mine."

"Me too," she pants, "me too." I kiss her neck, sucking hard as I thrust back into her.

Contorting myself around, I hold on to Hudson's ass cheeks, sandwiching Red between us. Hudson and I fall into a rutting, fucking rhythm. Slipping my finger into his ass, he groans from above us.

"I love when you do that to my ass," he breathlessly says, his eyes closing as he gives himself over to the pleasure of fucking our girl and my finger in his ass.

"I do too but right now, it's all about our girl's ass so shut up, Huddy Boy, and fuck it harder."

Hudson groans. Alani screams and I grunt as we head toward nirvana. My orgasm sneaks up and detonates without warning. My release sets them off and the three of us explode as we each ride through the orgasmic bliss. Hudson pulls out and collapses onto the bed next to us. Alani collapses onto my chest, breathing deeply, and me? I'm pretty sure I become one with the mattress, completely sated and worn out from our morning cardio workout.

Turning my head toward Hudson, I place my hand behind his head and pull his lips to mine, kissing him until he moans. Alani lifts her head from my chest and then I lift up and do the same with Alani, she smiles against my lips and then kisses Hudson.

She lays her head back on my chest and Hudson leans his on my shoulder.

It's only been three weeks since everything happened, but I know without a doubt, Hudson and Alani are my endgame. I just hope they realize how obsessed I am with them but regardless of that, I'm never letting them go.

The End!

That's the end of Reign, Alani, and Hudson. We hope you enjoyed their story and the surprise twist of who the killer was and why, but now I'm guessing you want to know more about Quinn, Hendrix, and the baby. You'll get their tumultuous story in the next Lords of Crestwood book, coming out next month.

SPOTIFY PLAYLIST

When You Love Someone - James TW
I Don't Want To Love You - Taylor Mathews
Secret Love Song - Little Mix feat. Jason Derulo
Here Tonight - Oh, Weatherly
A Little Too Much - Shawn Mendes
Wasted - MKTO
Boys Like You - Anna Clendening
Make You Mine - PUBLIC
Youth - Troye Sivan
Adore You - Miley Cyrus
I Can't Fall In Love Without You - Zara Larsson
Complicated - Olivia O'Brien
Just Friends - Ally Barron
This Is My Version - Conor Maynard
If This Is Love - Ruth B
All I Ever Need - Austin Malone
Its Gotta Be You - Isaiah FireBrace
Lights Down Low - MAX
Rewrite The Stars - Zac Efron and Zendaya
All Around Me - Corvyx
Give Me A Kiss - Crash Adams
What A Man Gotta Do - Jonas Brothers
I Like Me Better - Lauv
You Set My World On Fire - Loving Caliber feat. Selestine
Secret - The Pierces
Butterflies - Zendaya
Afterlife - Hailee Steinfeld
They Don't Know About Us - One Direction
What Am I - Why Don't We
Ruin My Life - Zara Larsson
It's You - HENRY

This playlist can be found on Spotify.

Want to find out what happens next? Well, you can in Hendrix, book 3 in the Lords of Crestwood Prep series.

HENDRIX

This is our school, our kingdom.
My brother's and I rule, we are The Lords.
Secrets run riot through the halls and I thought I was immune.
And I was, until her—Quinn Ellis.
A positive test changed everything but I manned up and stood by her side, even when I didn't have to.
Little did either of us know, we were in for another surprise.
Nothing is as it seems and when all is revealed, our lives will change forever.

ABOUT TARA LEE

Tara Lee is an Australian author who writes spicy romance, and men to swoon over. She comes from Hobart, Tasmania where she lives with her husband and two children.

When she's not a stay at home mum wrangling her two small children or fighting the voices in her head to be quiet she's getting up before the sun rises as a quali-fied baker.

Tara is a Pisces who survives on energy drinks, chocolate frappes and busting moves at Jazzicise for some me time.

ALSO BY TARA LEE

PLEASANT GROVE SERIES

Taking chances

Second chances

New beginnings

THE BEAUTIFUL SERIES

Beautifully Broken

Beautifully Mine

Beautifully Damaged

STANDALONES

Chance Encounter

HARLING HILL DUET

We All Fall Down

We End With Us

All of these books are available on Amazon.

ABOUT DL GALLIE

DL Gallie is from Queensland, Australia, but she's lived in many different places all over the world, including the UK and Canada. She currently resides in Central Queensland with her husband and two munchkins. She and her husband have been together since she was sixteen, and although they drive each other crazy at times, she couldn't imagine her life without him.

Shortly after her son was born, DL began reading again. With encouragement from her husband, she picked up the pen and started writing, and now the voices in her head won't shut up.

DL enjoys listening to music, drinking white wine in the summer, red wine in the winter, and beer all year round. She's also never been known to turn down a cocktail, especially a margarita.

ALSO BY DL GALLIE

STAND ALONES

Antecedent

Doc Steel

Oops

Off the Books

Fractured:A driven world novel

Deck…the Balls

Secrets and Sunrises

Always in the Cards

Out of Nowhere

After the Ashes

Love Me Like You Do

Never Let Me Go

Seven Nights

Seven Kisses

PUCKING NOVELS

I Pucking Hate That I Love You

A Pucking Good Christmas

…and a few pucking more

FALLING NOVELS

These men make it hard not to fall for them

Falling for Dr. Kelly

Falling for Dr. Knight

Falling for Agent Cox

Falling for Agent Cruz

Falling:The Complete Collection

THE UNEXPECTED SERIES

When it comes to love, expect the unexpected

The Unexpected Gift

The Unexpected Letter

The Unexpected Package

The Unexpected Connection

The Unexpected series: The Complete Collection

THE CASTAWAY GROVE COLLECTION

Love has arrived in the Grove

Oasis

Unequivocal Love

Five Words

Broken Rules

…and a few more to come.

The Castaway Grove Collection, Vol 1

THE LIQUOR CABINET SERIES

Liquor has never been so disturbingly saucy

Malt Me (Book 1)

Tequila Healing (Book 2)

Wine Not (Book 3)

The Final Shot (Book 4)

The Liquor Cabinet: Series boxset

All of these books are available on Amazon.